PAINT CAN KILL

BOOK #9 IN THE CARA MIA DELGATTO MYSTERY
SERIES

JOANNA CAMPBELL SLAN

To Katrina Gracan, and to the memory of my friend, Eddie Drake.

The Treasure Coast of Florida comprises the state's Atlantic coast, including Indian River, St. Lucie, and Martin counties. A multitude of murals adorn the exteriors of buildings, adding color and beauty to the urban landscape.

CONTENTS

CHAPTER 1

Florida only has two seasons: rainy and not rainy. Today, it was pouring both outside and inside my store, The Treasure Chest. Two of my three employees were crying buckets as we watched the parade of movers carrying bulky wooden crates covered with waterproof tarps out of my establishment.

My downtown Stuart shop is known for recycling, upcycling, and repurposing. That's a fancy way of saying we turn trash into treasure. We're also the premiere showroom and sales hub for Highwaymen art, because we specialize in showing and selling the work of the 26 original African-American painters of iconic Florida landscapes.

At least, we *used* to be the premiere sellers of Highwaymen art.

Bang! Bang! Bang! All morning long, hammers rang out. Movers in bright yellow tee shirts sealed the last of our Highwaymen paintings into wooden crates. The rain dripped off of their hair and soaked their garments, but they kept working. By my rough calculations, they were hauling away half of a million dollars' worth of art. They were also yanking MJ Austin Slatkin's career out from under her and taking away a major portion of my revenue. My store gets a commission for each of the paintings we sell. That dollar amount has not been insignificant.

MJ is considered the world's foremost expert on Highwaymen art. As the yellow-and-black moving van drove off, the beefy workmen took her reputation with them.

Both MJ and Skye Blue Murray were crying but for very different reasons. Their distress left me at a loss. These women are my friends, as well as my employees. Skye, although she looks sweet and fluffy, is strong as a piece of rebar and always optimistic—until now. We've been through a lot together. But a recent miscalculation on her part was going to cause me a significant financial loss. During the doldrums of summer, every bit of income is important, making her mistake a major blow to my bottom line. MJ can be as prickly as a porcupine; she never gets weepy. Except for today, when her eyes were red, and she dabbed them repeatedly with tissues. At this rate, we'd need to do a grocery store run to replenish our Kleenex supply. But that was trivial compared to the task of turning back the current tsunami of emotional distress. Admittedly we were facing problems, but it was up to me to deal with them. My late father's words came back to me, "Bosses make the big bucks because they have to solve the big problems, the ones that get dumped in their laps." He'd taught me this as he helped me learn the finer points of owning a restaurant. I had worked in our family business since I was strong enough to carry dirty plates to the dishwasher. Dad added more responsibilities along the way, always seasoning my chores with lessons in management. Over the years, I've seen ample testimony that Dad was right about everything. At this moment, there were a gracious plenty of problems taking up space in my lap. Yes, I'd figure out a way to deal with these disasters, but I need more time. The problems had come from out of nowhere. Sort of.

There'd been a sense of unease growing for months. I should have nipped it in the bud, but it seemed ethereal. If forced to describe the discontent, I would admit that Skye and MJ had been acting weird. They spoke to each other with their heads close together, breaking apart when I came near. Given that this was one of the hottest summers on record, it was reasonable to assume that the endless heat was getting to them. It was certainly taking its toll on me. Daily I fought my tendency to be short tempered.

But if I was honest with myself, I blamed the soaring temperatures for my crew's behavior because I hated to imagine the alternatives. I'd considered, and rejected, the idea there'd been a return of MJ's breast cancer. I'd brushed aside worries that Skye and her husband, Detective Lou Murray of the Stuart Police Department, were having marital difficulties because they were new parents. I was good at ignoring both possibilities because I couldn't face my true concern, the possibility all of this rested on my shoulders, not theirs. Maybe I was to blame.

I'd been grief stricken, and my loss had made me ineffective as an entrepreneur. Unable to sleep at night, I couldn't plan. Prone to bouts of sadness during the day, I used my meager crumbs of energy to keep shuffling forward, one step at a time. Was it possible that my misery had been infectious, like Covid? Perhaps there was a parallel truth at play. Maybe Skye and MJ were sick of me. I had to admit, I was sick of myself and my moping around.

It almost came as a relief early this morning when Skye burst into my office and threw herself into a chair while she sobbed. Between her desperate gulps of air, she confessed that she'd broken a store rule. A month ago, she'd neglected to collect a deposit for a large order of customized party gifts. It shouldn't have been a problem, most people are honest, but this particular customer wasn't. She had decided not to pay our bill.

We were out $800 in supplies, which meant we'd actually lost twice that amount. The bad news hit me like an angry fist to the stomach. And it wasn't even nine o'clock! What a lousy start to the day!

"If it's any consolation, you're not alone. This customer also owes Rocky $800 for food she ordered from Pumpernickel's," said Skye.

Pumpernickel's Deli was across the street. It had been recently purchased by Rocky Wilson. He'd purchased it shortly after Covid forced the old owner to throw in the dish towel.

I didn't take comfort in knowing I wasn't alone. In fact, I almost burst into sobs. In my head, Dad warned me, "Steady, steady."

"How did this happen?" I asked Skye. As I had guessed, there was a story behind the loss.

"Mrs. Morrison told me she lives in Hobe Sound," Skye said, "which she does, and she said the party was for the Jupiter Island Garden Club. They'd secured the Jupiter Island Country Club for the meeting, but not the food. This being off-season, the country club's kitchen is short-staffed. I kept asking for the deposit. She kept deferring it, saying the garden club's treasurer was on vacation. Then she told me the check was in her other purse. She used that excuse three times. Things got away from me, Cara. I am so, so sorry. I hate to put this burden on you."

Until this horrible, no good, rotten morning, I'd been slowly recovering from the ache of loss. Grief isn't something that's over in a couple of weeks or even months. Each day you feel the bite of it, the way its sharp teeth take a hunk of your flesh. At first, grief touches every surface of your life with deep-seated, soul-searing misery. After a time, an occasional hint of sunlight pops through, although mostly you spend your days wallowing in sorrow. Eventually, the pain releases its grip, but only for a moment, and you are able to breathe again. But like the tide, you can count on grief to rush back in and overtake you. Today, with Independence Day less than a month away, I knew I had to buck up. This was the one holiday of the season that promised a chance to make good money. I concentrated on pushing aside the darkness with positive affirmations and a healthy dose of John Phillip Sousa marches. For a corresponding visual, I imagined the fun our youngest customers would have making fake firecrackers. Now my sparkling mental preview of our celebration melted in my mind. It felt as if life had paused for a rain delay, of sorts.

Skye burst into noisy sobs. Maybe I could comfort her. After all, I was the boss, the solver of big problems. My father had said as much.

Leaning back in my black office chair, I tried to think of a bright side to this. A customer refusing to pay her bill? Well, she'd refused to pay Skye, but maybe I could wheedle the money from her. And if I couldn't collect it from Mrs. Morrison, maybe I could get it from the garden club.

I smiled at Skye and said, "We'll deal with it. I'll call the customer and—"

But I never finished the sentence. A loud banging at the front door forced me to open the store early. I stood face-to-face with a short man. He had a face that only another bulldog could love. On a pooch, it might be adorable, but on a human, his smashed-in nose, bug eyes and permanent snuffling was unattractive. He bounced on his toes, the up-and-down motion causing the stripes of his gray suit to jump around. His cheap polyester tie flapped as if waving goodbye to me.

"Mrs. Delgatto?" he asked.

"Ms. Delgatto," I corrected him. Behind the visitor stood a quartet of bulky guys in egg-yolk yellow tee shirts and black pants. Their colorful attire stood out against an ominous gray sky. "May I help you? We don't open for another half hour."

"I am Mr. Grassley, attorney-at-law. This is for you. It's from Irving Feldman. Mr. Feldman is serving you notice that he wishes to withdraw all of his property from your premises. These gentlemen will pack up the paintings." Mr. Grassley looked immensely proud of himself, as if he'd handed me an Oscar. His fat cheeks reminded me of a hamster I once owned. Or a chipmunk. Maybe more like a chipmunk, given how short he was.

I opened the envelope. My eyes refused to focus. The words swam in front of me, but I managed to parse Irving's name and signature. The embossed seal of a notary was rough beneath my fingertips. Slow down, I warned myself. In response, I read the letter one word at a time. In sum, Irving had decided that he no longer wanted me or my employees to represent his mother's vast collection of Highwaymen art. Furthermore, the pieces he'd loaned me on commission were to be removed immediately. There was no mention of compensating me for the loss of potential revenue. Nor did he offer to pay me back for building a state-of-the-art storage vault. That alone had been a huge expense, and that safe had been constructed expressly to house the Feldman collection of paintings.

How on earth would I replace MJ's income from sales of the landscapes? What would she do now? Go and work in a gallery? If so, how would I replace her? She was essential for evaluating all sorts of Old Florida décor items.

Did this mean we'd have to take down the website we'd created? The one that garnered thousands of hits every day, promoting Highwaymen art and explaining why these oils had such cultural importance? Would Irving pay me back for Sid Heckman's time in creating the website? Apparently, Irving didn't care about the financial problems his snap decision caused me.

In fact, he hadn't even done me the courtesy of calling to

discuss the matter in advance. He'd simply instructed his minion to oversee the removal. I asked Mr. Grassley to explain Irving's reasoning. When the squat little attorney stuttered around instead of answering, I asked him if Irving planned to compensate me for the expenses incurred and revenue lost.

Mr. Grassley drew himself up to his full height of five feet nothing and said, "You'll need to speak to my client."

"Believe me," I said, "I intend to talk to Irving. In fact, I'm going to call him right now."

But the number in my cellphone had been disconnected.

"I need Irving's new number," I said, trying not to sound as angry as I felt. My temper is my worst fault. This was one of those situations when I needed to keep it under control.

Mr. Grassley tittered. "You don't have it? Well, well."

That burned my biscuits. "Listen up, buster. Give me his new number now!"

"I'll have to speak with Mr. Feldman and get permission to share his number with you." Mr. Grassley's face beamed with a smug satisfaction. His fat cheeks bunched up. Did he store food in them?

I was close to exploding. My grip on my feelings was coming loose. After counting to ten, I said, "You, sir, need to remove yourself from my premises."

"When the movers are done."

"No way, José. You need to get out of my shop right now!"

"Where would I go? It's raining," said the little man with a plaintive cry.

"So I noticed. Good luck and good riddance, now scoot!"

"I can't believe that Irving Feldman did this to me. To us." MJ shook her head as we went back to staring at the rain. The sidewalk in front of the store was dark, and the grassy verge was waterlogged. A miserable-looking Mr. Grassley tried to take shelter under the store's awning, but that spot put him in the path of the movers. Consequently, he had to move often, stepping out in the rain frequently. I got a mean little thrill about that.

MJ continued, "After all this time, Irving suddenly decides I'm not trustworthy?"

"We don't know what he's thinking," I said. "Don't jump to conclusions."

"What other reason could he have?" MJ fairly shouted. "Give me a break!"

I've known Irving since we were both kids. He was always a nerdy little twerp. His mother rightfully lamented that he was not—and would never be—a *mensch*, the Jewish word for a real man. She had been right. Today his behavior was bush league, immature and unfair.

It was also unbelievably cruel.

Had Skye and MJ known this was coming? Was that why they'd spoken in hushed huddles? Why they'd broken apart whenever I came near? Why neither had much to say to me? I'd never felt so alone, and I tried to chalk it up to the grief of my personal losses. Even so, I could have weathered my misery much better with my two besties at my side. Usually, we were like the three musketeers, but lately I was a third wheel, rotating on the outside of their friendship. What was going on with them?

Skye shuffled her feet and stared at a wall display of reused drawers. She'd taken lately to wearing knit harem pants and loose tops in jewel tones. These washed better than her gauzy skirts and linen blouses, an essential perk when you have a toddler. Her face looked bleak, even though she should have been proud of turning a bunch of junk into cool wall décor. By adding paint stirrers, we chopped the drawers into small compartments, making the drawers from discarded dressers into fake printers' boxes. These were perfect for displaying tiny treasures. Usually, Skye smiles like a proud mother when she looks at her handiwork, but today her mouth flat lined. I had a hunch there was more bothering her than her customer's unpaid bill. Maybe her husband was working on a tough case?

"Could Lou help us?" I asked her as I watched the movers brave the rain. "With the money your customer owes us?" Although I doubted non-payment of a bill was part of a detective's remit—it couldn't hurt to ask. That's my philosophy. Ask, ask, ask. You never know what you might get.

Skye shook her head. "It's not his patch. Even though you and Rocky are both local vendors, Lou would leave this to the Jupiter Island Department of Public Safety."

I moaned. I'd been on good terms with Chief George Fernandez, the former Director of the Department of Public Safety. But George had done such a stellar job that he'd been promoted. A new guy took George's place, and we hadn't met.

Skye continued, "Mrs. Morrison is your neighbor, Cara. She lives on Jupiter Island."

"I didn't realize Mrs. Morrison is my neighbor."

"I didn't know that either!" Skye's voice rose an octave. "She made it sound like they lived off of Bridge Road in Hobe Sound."

Hobe Sound is the postal address for the island. While Hobe Sound is lovely, the little town has an economically diverse population. By comparison, you can't buy a house on the island for less than $10 million. Those of us who are residents have grown accustomed to the "Jupiter Island tax," which is the upcharge vendors add to prices when they see where we live. Hence, we learn to say, "I live in Hobe Sound." That must have been what Mrs. Morrison had done.

"Yes, well, Mrs. Morrison pulled a fast one on you," said MJ, shaking her head. MJ walked toward the back, talking over her shoulder. Her tight pink jeans picked up the fuchsia color of her patterned, low-cut blouse. "I plan on staying in the bathroom until the movers leave. Somebody text me, okay? Be sure to do it several times so I can hear the sound over my sobbing."

"Will do," I said to MJ's retreating back. "Where exactly does Mrs. Morrison live?"

"I don't know her street address," said Skye. "I delivered everything to the Jupiter Island Country Club. She gave me the club's address for my estimate."

"We'll be going now, ma'am," said the guy who appeared to be in charge of the movers. Water ran down his face and dripped on his broad shoulders. I'd offered the movers towels, but they decided these would slow them down. "Here's a receipt for everything we crated and loaded. Mr. Grassley seems to think we got it all."

I took the inventory and nodded. The word "thanks" stuck in my throat. Instead, I said, "Drive carefully."

"Yes, ma'am."

I texted MJ three times, and she rejoined us. She'd touched up her makeup. Makeup remover pads and cotton tips are stored in the bathroom for emergencies like this. While Skye and I are minimalists when it comes to painting our faces, MJ slathers on the equivalent of an entire cosmetics counter. She's an artist when it comes to displaying her best assets.

A wail from upstairs turned our attention to the Murrays' apartment. The noise was slightly distorted by the baby monitor. Skye and Lou rent one of the two second-floor apartments where they live with their two-year-old son, Nickolas Davos Murray. The other apartment is occupied by Lou's mother, Bippy, a woman we used to call five feet of Greek fury before Skye tamed that particular shrew.

"Bippy's shopping for groceries," explained Skye. Little

Nick's cry gained volume. "That's my cue," said Skye as she raced upstairs to see to her little man.

"How's it going?" said Eddie Drake, loping in through the front door. "Looks like we're getting a break in the rain."

Two steps behind him came his partner, Katrina Gracan. "We brought the sketch for the mural. Mind if we spread it out on that table in your back room?"

I'd totally forgotten they were coming. "Help yourselves. There's coffee back there, too."

Eddie and Katrina are professional painters. They'll not only spruce up the exterior and interior of your house, they'll also do decorative work to your specifications. Want a faux lattice motif on your wall? Or a view of the sea where there is none? Or a woodgrain instead of your plaster? Eddie and Katrina are magicians with paint. Today, they planned to show me a drawing that would be the basis for a mural covering the west-facing outside wall of The Treasure Chest.

"MJ? Can you watch the floor?" I asked. "I need to see what Eddie and Katrina have done."

"Of course. After all, it's not like I'll be selling Highwaymen paintings!"

I sighed and followed the painters into the backroom.

———

The mural outside had been Skye's brainchild. Two months ago, she pointed out cars idling at the stoplight. "Why not give them a memorable scene and point them toward the store? That way drivers can see your logo and something uplifting? In fact, why not have Eddie and Katrina copy an iconic Highwaymen painting? "Not exactly, of course, but close enough to be a reminder of what we sell."

"Otherwise, that huge wall is a waste of space, a blank unused canvas," Skye had said.

She made a good point. Skye followed up by giving me a list of their murals, images that dotted the Treasure Coast. When I called the next day, the two painters were totally booked.

"We can't get to it until July. Will that work for you?" asked Katrina.

Of course it would.

Two months had passed quickly. Eddie unrolled the line-drawing. "Without the color, this looks a little bland. You have to remember the photos you showed us."

I heartily approved of the landscape and The Treasure Chest logo. He said, "If it's okay with you, Cara, we'll come back tomorrow and start work right away, even though it's a Sunday. If we get going early, we can get a lot done before the heat of the day."

"That makes sense," I agreed, doing my best to seem happy. It was nearly impossible to ignore the voice inside my head that screamed, *I might not be to afford that mural! Not with the High-waymen art gone!* But I wrestled those worries to the ground. The money had already been set aside for this project. It came out of my marketing budget. Somehow, I'd figure out what was happening with Irving. Maybe a face-to-face talk with Mrs. Morrison would convince her to produce a check. Yes, having the money she owed me in hand would be nice since I didn't know when I'd get the paintings back from Irving.

I tried not to chew on a fingernail as Eddie and Katrina unrolled a long sheet of butcher paper. Our back room is cramped and overflowing with business supplies. MJ slipped past everyone to grab a cup of coffee, making the back even more crowded. Eddie bumped into a stack of marketing materials and a brochure fluttered to the floor. From the vibrant colors, I knew from eight feet away that the flier was a sales brochure for the Highwaymen paintings. That vivid red-orange cover picture could only be a blooming poinciana tree. The distinctive blossoms and the umbrella shape of the tree's canopy were easily recognizable.

Katrina picked the brochure off the floor. She studied it gravely before running a thumb over the picture of the poinciana tree. "I've seen this painting before. At the Landaus' house. They are very proud of it."

Holding her coffee mug in one hand, MJ made a dismissive snort. "I didn't sell it to the Landaus. I sold that to the Todds."

I cringed. MJ could be rude, and I didn't like that. Normally, I would have called her on her bad behavior. Today, I didn't. As long as Katrina could shrug off MJ's nasty tone of voice, it didn't matter.

Eddie took the brochure and stared at it. "Katrina is right. This is the painting the Landaus have. I remember because the white shape in the foreground isn't very clear. It could be a duck or a small sailboat. I asked Phil Landau about it, and he said he wasn't sure either. Weird."

Eddie handed the sales piece to me. I tried to look interested, but I wasn't. The Highwaymen often painted poinciana trees. I love Highwaymen art, and I appreciate the way these paintings capture old Florida, but I've grown blasé about their subject matter. The 26 original painters took their inspiration from the local scenery. Consequently, many of their canvases look alike. It can take an expert like MJ to tell who painted what. The Landaus' landscape probably included a copy of the white sailboat. Big deal.

"Phil Landau?" asked Skye as she returned with Nick on her hip. The baby had her blond curls and his father's serious expression. "I remember you working with Phil Landau, MJ. He made you angry, didn't he? You spent all that time, educating him about the Highwaymen and then he didn't buy from you. Or did he?"

"No," MJ said flatly. She turned away to dump the spent coffee grounds into the trash.

"Maybe you sold that picture to the Todds and they sold it to the Landaus?" Skye asked MJ. MJ seemed to freeze in place.

I stiffened. Although Skye was merely curious, MJ could be a firecracker and go off like a Roman candle. I hoped Skye wasn't courting an explosion.

"There's no way that Mrs. Todd would have turned around and sold the painting after all the time I spent with her," said MJ curtly. "None. She wanted a specific painting for her husband's office. She was adamant about the colors and dimensions, as well as the subject matter. Took me forever to find exactly what she wanted. Why would she turn around and sell something that she gave her husband as a gift?" MJ ended on a shrill note. "After that painting was sold, I intended to put a different one on the brochure. I never got around to it."

Katrina and Eddie gave each other puzzled looks. Katrina is a little more than five feet tall and a size zero. Her sun-streaked hair often escapes from a ponytail to frame a face that's honest and direct. Eddie is taller than six feet with long fingers and capable hands. His hair is thinning, but you never notice that because he wears a white painter's cap. However, no one can avoid seeing and feeling the kind light in his eyes. He is such a gentle soul. Eddie said, "Maybe Katrina and I are mistaken about the painting. Okay, see you tomorrow."

My employees went back to various projects. I wondered how I'd make it through the rest of the day. *I would not cry, I would not cry, I would not cry*. This was my new mantra. Skye, MJ, and Honora had faith in me. If I broke down, they might wonder whether the store would survive—and it would. It had to.

I could sob at home once this crisis was over.

Because it would be over.

But when?

CHAPTER 2

At heart, I'm a fixer, a peacemaker, a smoother-over. The misery on my friends' faces was enough to make me crazy. Their expressions of gloom seemed etched in my mind. The unkindness of Mrs. Morrison and Irving Feldman bothered me the most. Both Skye and MJ work hard. They are honest, good people. They didn't deserve to be treated unfairly. How dare Mrs. Morrison skip out on her bill? How could Irving have removed all of his late mother's Highwaymen paintings?

The rest of the day proved as gloomy as the dark clouds overhead. The down mood sapped every smidgeon of my energy. After my work day was finished, I didn't feel like cooking. Instead, I walked across the street to Pumpernickel's Deli. A waitress I'd never seen before asked if she could help me. Her puffy red eyes and chapped lips suggested she'd been crying. There was a lot of that going around.

"May I speak to Rocky, please?" I asked as I scooted onto the vinyl-covered bench. I hate vinyl seats. They stick to your skin on hot days, and that is every day in Florida.

"Sure thing. Let me get him." She walked away, leaving the smell of frying onions trailing behind.

Minutes later, a heavy hand patted my shoulder. "Cara? What's up?"

Rocky looked like his namesake, the character in the Sly Stallone movie. A lock of dark hair fell onto Rocky's forehead. His face had been battered by repeated punches, and his lips were uneven. Yet his eyes were kind and soft, especially when they turned to me.

"New server?" I asked with a nod toward the young woman who'd seated me.

Rocky gave me a wonky smile. "Just started. I am always on the lookout for servers. What can I do for you, Cara?"

"I know you're busy, Rocky, so I'll make this fast. Did Mrs. Morrison refuse to pay you for her food? The stuff she ordered for her party last month?"

He ran that large hand through his salt-and-pepper hair. Rocky's given name is Robert. "Yeah, Mrs. Morrison told me the bill was my tough luck. Laughed in my face about paying it. Why?"

"She did the same to me. Skye took the order, actually. To the tune of $800."

He let his head droop and inhaled deeply. "I should have gotten a deposit. In fact, I tried and she kept saying the money was in her other purse. I'd heard rumors from other food service people that Mrs. Morrison was trouble. Unfortunately for me, I tend to give everyone the benefit of the doubt. All I wanted was to do our job and walk away, you know? It seemed like an easy enough gig at the time. Cater a luncheon for thirty women. Along the way, Mrs. Morrison kept adding to the menu. She'd call and talk to my second-in-command. Slip the changes past me, you know?"

I nodded sadly. When we offered catering at our restaurant,

my father warned me about this common tactic. The customer would sign an invoice for one amount and a specified menu. Then he or she would make changes and slowly up the ante. If you didn't catch it early, you wound up with a heck of a problem and no legal recourse.

Rocky interrupted my thoughts. He rolled his hands palms up. "What you're going to do? Huh, Cara? Are you going to let this ride?"

"I don't want to give up on the money. If word gets around that folks don't need to pay me, how will I keep our doors open at The Treasure Chest?" I swallowed the lump in my throat. Without the income from the Highwaymen paintings, staying in business was going to get harder and harder. I continued, "I need to think about this. Weigh all my options. Is it worth having Mrs. Morrison bad-mouth me? Or should I write off the debt?"

"She definitely will bad-mouth you. No matter what you do." Rocky's expression was hangdog. "She's the type who's always complaining about something and someone."

"Honest, Rocky, I hate problems like this. Letting this woman get away with ripping us off stinks."

"I hear you. The money she owes me is coming straight out of my pocket. Yours too, I bet." Rocky sighed. He was buying the deli on contract. After Covid, the old owner decided that he wanted out, forever. I could sympathize. Although state-wide politicians bragged about that nothing shut down in Florida, the ugly corollary was that we had one of the country's highest death rates. Thank goodness for The Treasure Chest's online business. Otherwise, we wouldn't have eked by.

The new waitress led a couple to the booth next to mine. More people waited to be seated.

"You're getting busy. I better go. Thanks, Rocky" I said, getting to my feet.

Calling after me, Rocky said, "If you come up with a good way to pursue this, let me know." He gave me a thumbs-up.

I returned the gesture and headed for my car.

The journey through Hobe Sound to Jupiter Island might be one of the most photographed images in Martin County. Fifty years ago, one of the Jupiter Island matrons got the bright idea to line the Bridge Road going onto the island with ficus trees. Today, these stately trees curve in a graceful arch, forming a green and gray tunnel that promises the grandeur that lies ahead. The trip beneath the intertwined limbs never fails to sooth me, and this evening was no exception.

At my driveway, I put the car in park. In addition to collecting my mail, I also jogged next door and picked up the mail for my friend and neighbor Aurora Hamilton. She and her husband Bill were out of the country on a combination cruise and golf trip. I didn't have much in the way of mail, but the Hamiltons had plenty. I would add Aurora's post to the growing stack on my dining table. Turning into my gravel drive, I saw Seaspray, my little cottage on the beach. Once upon a time, the sight of this sweet cottage caused my heart to sing. These days, grief stabbed me in the heart when I came home. My sweet little dog, Jack, the rescue Chihuahua, had died recently. He'd been going downhill for months, eating less and less while sleeping more, but I couldn't bring myself to have him euthanized. Not when he still wagged his tail at me and licked my hand. One night while he rested in my lap, his entire body convulsed. When his muscles relaxed, he was gone.

That pup and I had been through a lot, and I missed him terribly. Jack's death was a precursor to another loss, the death of Dan Pateman, the gorgeous man who lived with me. I met Dan when he was moonlighting as a pizza delivery guy. I still blush when admitting that I felt uncomfortable dating a pizza delivery guy. Honest labor is honest money, but I'm an ambitious woman. For weeks, I struggled with my snobbery. Gosh but my face was red when I learned Dan had taken the delivery job to keep busy while waiting for the fall session to start at Jupiter High School. There he would take a position as a history teacher. In fact, I was doubly chagrinned when I found out that Dan was actually overly employed. By that I mean, he was also on-call with the US government. As a former member of the Special Ops, Dan's unique training and experience as an Army Ranger made him an important resource for our government. The phone could ring any time and Dan would be on a plane, flying to a trouble spot and participating in a mission.

Attractive, smart, worldly, and ambitious. Dan looked like a rockstar and acted like a gentleman. He was incredibly loving and generous. From my rearview mirror hung a silver and gold charm, a mariner's cross he'd given me. "This will protect you when you travel," he'd said. "My mother gave it to me, and I want you to have it." In short, Dan was a hero straight out of a romance novel.

MJ had purred when she met Dan. Skye was more reserved but equally impressed. At first, I kept my heart under lock and key because my new beau hadn't cut ties with his ex-wife, Sonya. Each time she rang him, I felt physically ill. I was sure she wanted him back. Yes, Dan was cool to Sonya, but I wondered why he even bothered to pick up the phone. Why not simply ignore her? I told myself not to ruin a good relationship by pushing for more information. However, my resentment grew.

I must not have hidden my feelings very well. A couple of months after we started dating, Dan announced, "We need to talk. We need to clear the air."

Over glasses of a California red wine, while watching the

sun set over the ocean, Dan explained that his only tie to Sonya was his enduring love for Gavin, his stepson. "Gavin is my son," Dan said. "I raised him. I couldn't love a biological child more than I do Gavin."

Sonya used Dan's attachment to her son as a way to hang on to her ex. Meanwhile, I fought my growing attachment to Dan. I was sick with worry. I became more and more certain that he would tell me it was over. I just knew I was going to get hurt. I began to pull away. Everything changed when he told me that he and Sonya were through.

For nearly two years, Dan and I lived together blissfully. I'd never been so happy. And now he was gone.

Getting out of my car took an enormous act of will. The house wasn't the same without Jack and Dan. Not just one loss, but two.

It pained me to realize that Jack would never bark again when someone came to my door. Dan's truck would never be parked here, waiting for me. I left his belongings in the ocean-side bedroom and moved into the street-side bedroom. I tried to pretend that Dan had never happened, never existed. The thought of boxing up his things made me want to puke. Besides, where would I send them? His stepson had moved to Miami. His ex-wife lived nearby, but we weren't on speaking terms and mailing Dan's things to her seemed pointless. I knew he had two sisters, but I had no way to reach them.

I wrestled with grief every day. I'd once been house proud, but lately I couldn't find the energy to do the simplest tasks. Consequently, all my surfaces were dusty and my floors demanded to be mopped. My clean clothes were heaped in plastic baskets. My windows were streaked with dust. What I needed was a cleaning person, but I was too depressed to find one.

Even my Royal Bahamian Potcake pup moped around the

house. Gerard has always been a happy dog, but the loss of Dan and Jack depressed him, too. Usually, the moment I came home, the yellow hound greeted me as if I'd been gone for days rather than hours. Lately, he'd taken to licking my hand and staring up as if to ask, "Where are Dan and Jack?"

These were questions I couldn't answer.

Sinking onto the sofa, I gave Gerard copious amounts of belly rubs and attention. As is her wont, my gray rescue cat, Luna, came slinking down from the studio upstairs where she likes to hide out. A cloud of cat hair followed in her wake. My housecleaning efforts were pitiful these days. The fur babies had gathered for dinnertime. They were hungry, but I wasn't. Since Dan and Jack have gone, I've lost twenty pounds. My clothes hang on me. It is not a good look, and it worries my grandfather Dick Potter, aka Poppy, and my crew. My general practitioner was alarmed enough to shake a finger in my face and threaten me with hospitalization. I think she was exaggerating, but since she and Poppy were in cahoots, I vowed to eat three times a day, no matter whether I am hungry or not.

I fed the pets, heated a slice of lasagna, toasted a piece of garlic bread, and sat down to pick at my meal.

Resting my elbows on the table, it was my turn to cry. MJ's tears had been ladylike and reserved. Skye had whimpered as she sobbed. Me? I dissolved into ugly crying, salting my food with my tears.

SUNDAY

I've had trouble sleeping since Dan's been gone. This being a Sunday, I stayed in bed until ten-thirty. The weather report called for rain ending around one, only to be replaced by miserable heat. The sun would come out, and it would bake southern Florida, with temps soaring into the high 90s. After eating, dressing, and putting on makeup, I climbed into my Camry, Black Beauty. She's way past her expiration date, but she runs like a pinto pony thanks to the careful attention of my grandfather. I've considered passing Black Beauty along to my son Tommy and getting a newer car. A model with back-up cameras would be especially useful. Something other than black, a color totally unsuited for life in Florida. Cranked up full volume, the car's air conditioner barely keeps pace with the summer heat. But this morning, it wasn't so bad. A few splats of water speckled the windshield. I turned on my headlights, as the law requires when you use your wipers. The drops changed to a fine mist. At least the rain would cool things off. Meanwhile, I needed to be cautious as I drove.

Each time my thoughts flashed to Irving and his stunt with the paintings, my jaw clenched. He had a lot of nerve, withdrawing his mother's collection like that. Financially, we'd bailed him out, providing income he could have never generated without my store's help. The fact he hadn't even talked to me before repossessing his artwork made me literally see red, as if a piece of ruby-colored cellophane covered my world.

Those thoughts led me to thoughts about Mrs. Morrison. Another spike of anger bubbled up. How dare she treat Rocky that way! He had worked hard to prepare a menu according to Mrs. Morrison's specifications and putting in long hours to meet her shifting demands. His reward? The client had stiffed him. I bet she hadn't tipped his servers, either.

And yes, she'd stiffed me, too. Mrs. Morrison had basically stolen from my store. In the aftermath of Covid, business was mostly good, thanks to pent-up demand, but losing a lump sum like that would dramatically hurt my bottom-line.

Who the heck did this woman think she was? As if my car read my mind, the Camry didn't turn west onto Bridge Road, which was the way to Stuart and my store. Instead, Black Beauty drove straight, cruising south toward the more populated part of Jupiter Island. I took the cosmic hint. My car wanted me to do a little reconnaissance, checking out the Morrison home. No big deal. That wouldn't take me much out of my way. If I kept driving south, my meanderings would land me at Bagel Bistro in Tequesta, a place that serves the best bagels I've ever had. Given my dramatic weight loss, eating an entire bag of bagels might be a good idea.

I poked along Beach Road. Keeping to the 35-mph speed limit wasn't hard as I was in no hurry. In fact, I waved to one of the white Jupiter Island police cars as I passed him. The cop gave me a nod of approval. The JI police know most of residents by sight. The law enforcement officers (LEOs) keep a record of the cars we drive, as well as noting the makes and models of our regular visitors.

It didn't take me long to figure out which house belonged to the Morrisons because Eddie's white Ford truck was parked at the curb. A tall hedge of Clusia, bordered the property, affording privacy. The island's property code states you must maintain foliage that shields your home from your neighbor's. You can't rip down the plants that shield one piece of land from another. A code enforcement officer regularly makes the rounds to inspect properties. He can fine you if you don't adhere to the island's rules. True, from the street, you could clock the comings and goings of Mrs. Morrison, but once on her property, the Clusia formed a nearly opaque barrier. Falling rain forced the silver-green leaves to dance a constrained jig. Would this rain ever stop?

A sign that said "service" directed workers to use the far end of a circular driveway, but Eddie had parked at the curb. But why hadn't he simply loaded up his ladder and left? Why was his truck sitting there? More importantly, where was Eddie? It's hard to hide when you're carrying an extra-tall ladder.

I pulled up behind his truck and got out of my car. Shielding my face with cupped hand, I peeped inside the vehicle's window. The painter wasn't there. The truck was unlocked. Standing next to it, I put one palm on the hood. *Warm.* Eddie had driven it recently. He must have arrived shortly before I did.

In the distance, I could hear the church bells from the Christ Memorial Chapel, the only church on the island proper. They chimed ten times.

The Morrisons' driveway was hogged by a white Bentley convertible, parked in front of an upraised garage door. A soft rain ran down the sleek shape and onto the concrete drive. Like most residences on the island, the garage was unattached from the domicile. The reason is simple: A lot of Jupiter Island garages have guest quarters, and most have bathroom facilities for workers. At first, a bathroom in the garage seemed like a needless luxury to me, but that toilet is used nearly every day by various workers. You can't underestimate the structural and horticultural damage that salt water does. Not a month goes by that I'm not hiring someone to replace a decaying board, pressure-wash my walkways, or trim my sea grapes. The list seems endless. With the garage door open, the laborers are free to relieve themselves even if I am not home.

On the other hand, the presence of the Bentley suggested that someone was home at the Morrisons'. Someone besides Eddie.

Good.

My meanderings allowed me to get a good look at the stainless-steel racks filled with clear plastic bins inside the garage. Everything was neatly labeled. The orderliness reminded me of a TV show that featured two energetic hostesses who organized by dumping everything into clear plastic containers and making handwritten labels. The only discordant note was a battered bike that rested against an inside wall. The dark green paint flaked off its bumper and struts, and the tires looked balding on the battered Schwinn. The two-wheeler had seen a lot of miles. Further evidence of the bike's busy past included a pair of dusty canvas panniers, a wicker basket, and a crate strapped to the back. Another sign that someone besides Eddie was here.

I paused to consider my options. Did Mrs. Morrison have company? Probably not. The hour was early. Only the Bentley sat in the driveway. I couldn't imagine a Jupiter Island resident riding a beaten-up old bike. But Eddie was here.

Like me, the painter must have decided that confronting Mrs. Morrison couldn't wait. If she wasn't going to pay Eddie and Katrina, at least she could return their tall ladder.

"Eddie?" I called out, thinking he wouldn't stray far from his unlocked truck. But as I scanned the property, I didn't see him. I moved closer to the house. A sidewalk marked the preferred pathway.

"Hello?" I said. Beyond the garage, the sidewalk split, pointing me toward the front entrance or the back. I paused to look at the house. The exterior was pale yellow stucco with hurricane shutters in a deep blue. The lawn was immaculate. Emerald grass met a tall border of Clusia. Terracotta pots of pink-and-white vinca broke up the solid silver-green of the hedge.

"Hello?" I called out again. Hearing no answer, I walked into the backyard. A stunning pool was set like a precious gem. A few raindrops splashed the water's surface. The blue-green serenity of the scene was enhanced by tiles that had been hand-painted in matching watery shades of blue. Blue, green, and white cushions rested on a matched set of white wicker seats. The grouping sat under a retractable navy-blue awning. This picture of serenity made me chuckle. This setting was totally at odds with what I'd been told about Mrs. Morrison. Serene people don't go around honking off their neighbors and cheating vendors. Or do they?

Teak lawn chairs were placed at intervals along one side of the pool, allowing the occupants—when there were any—to chat easily. Between the seats were low tables. A man's tee shirt was draped over a lounge chair. Two empty champagne glasses collected condensation as they sat on a table.

But there were no people. The setting was deserted. The sunbathers had probably left when the rain started.

"Hello?" I tried again. "Eddie?"

No answer.

I was growing increasingly damp between the drizzle and the humidity, but my determination was fired up. Eddie had to be here to ask for money and their extension ladder. Someone must have let Eddie inside. Either Mrs. Morrison or a housekeeper had to be home.

Turning in a tight circle, I called, "Anybody here? Hello?"

Woof! The bark was lonely and half-hearted. It came from the yard on the far side of the house. Judging by the volume, the pet was a small canine, definitely not a guard dog. *Woof! Woof! Woof!* The pooch had either scented me or heard my approach. The barks were not warning signals. They were plaintive. I moved closer to the source.

I found a metal enclosure, a doggy playpen. Inside, a small white-and-tan dog with curly hair bounced up and down, hurling itself against the wire walls. The nearer I got, the more the puppy wiggled with excitement. When I offered him my outstretched hand with my palm down, the dog's pink tongue licked my skin with total dedication. I scratched behind his ears. He panted with joy. A quick survey told me, the dog didn't have any water. No dish and no dispenser. That was odd.

According to the weather report, as the day progressed, the rain would stop and the temperature would climb. This playpen would be in direct sunlight. The poor pooch had no shelter. The fact his fur was light-colored meant he could get a sunburn. Being without water was not good. If it got as hot as predicted, the dog could get heat stroke.

Perhaps someone had gone to refill the bowl of water?

I scanned my surroundings while the dog licked my fingers.

"Hello? Anybody home?" I called out. A prickling at the back of my neck urged me to run. But why? No one was around but me. The place looked like a deserted movie scene. I wiped my forehead with my sleeve. The day was warming up.

The dog panted.

This was ridiculous. Why wasn't anyone answering when I cried out? I marched along the flagstone path leading to French doors. One was slightly ajar.

"Hell-ooo? Mrs. Morrison? Eddie?"

Still no answer. In a flash of anger, I gave the door a push. Okay, it was fine to ignore me, but what about the dog? The door flew open to reveal a small mud room. Black and white tiles marked its boundaries. Even though I hadn't been outside all that long, water dripped off my clothes. Should I step deeper into the house? Seemed silly to turn around and leave now. On the other hand, I didn't want to create a trail of wetness. I yelled, "Anybody? Hey?"

No one answered. *Okie-dokie.* Decision time.

Eddie might be on the other side of the house. Or behind the garage. He might even have left already, passing me by, but I would not take off until the dog had water. Now I was a woman on a mission. I would find a bowl and fill it for the fur-baby. Mrs. Morrison could like it or lump it, tough luck. Even as I stiffened my spine, hairs stood up on the back of my neck. A tingle zigzagged through my body. Something was wrong. Something I couldn't put my finger on. I decided to enter the house boldly.

Rather than be quiet, I made plenty of noise and kept repeating, "You-who?"

The kitchen was styled after a French chateau. Blue-white-and taupe tiles created an expensive-looking backsplash behind a copper sink. Marble countertops, copper hardware, a huge Sub-Zero fridge, a wine rack with glasses, copper pots hanging from a wrought iron rack, and a deep sink. This space belonged to a gourmand. Except on closer inspection, the pots had never been used. They were hung there purely for decoration.

An archway opened from the kitchen into a sitting room, a lounge. The molding was exquisite and thicker than any I'd ever seen. Every piece of furniture was decorated with gold trim. Framed paintings aped Old Masters, but on closer inspection, they had to be copies. I'd seen these famous works before in the St. Louis Art Museum. This was a curious juxtaposition of wealthy and cheap decorating. Very odd.

"Hello?" I continued to announce my arrival as I moved deeper into the house. The marble floors amplified my greetings. Even the scattered rugs couldn't quell the acoustic clatter. Wandering around, I made my way through a second archway. This one opened onto an office. The built-in walnut shelves were filled with books on a variety of topics. Many seemed well-worn, as if someone in the Morrison household was a keen reader. The desk was perfectly sized for the space, a simple piece made luxurious by the gleaming wood grain. A squat crystal canister on a desk blotter was the only decoration. The variety of jellybeans inside offered a delicious jolt of rainbow colors. Underneath the desk was a rug with brightly colored stripes, making what would have been a staid and starchy room zing with energy. Gosh but Skye would love this particular room. She's really into decorating.

"Hello?" My curiosity kept me moving. Another archway beckoned. This one was narrow, almost like a frame. The opening allowed a glimpse of a room decorated in peaceful colors of blue, green, and aqua. The ambiance was soothing. Facing the entry was a large painting of the Loxahatchee River. Immediately this landscape was recognizable as an example of Highwaymen art. The dimensions were surprisingly large, making the painting in front of me one of the biggest Highwaymen pieces I'd ever seen. To get closer to the picture, I skirted a cream-colored sofa with its back to the narrow archway. The couch was tall, but the tops of a few throw pillows peeked over the back. These decorative accessories matched the colors of the Loxahatchee scene.

Then it hit me. A peculiar smell. One I'll never forget. Inwardly, I groaned.

"Eddie? Mrs. Morrison? Anyone?" I was almost parallel to the sofa when I froze. My senses shouted in alarm as I inhaled the tang of copper and body fluids. I knew that odor. It was the sweet perfume of death.

Oh, crap.

CHAPTER 3

A movement near my left jolted me into action. I jumped and made a tiny, "Eeek!" of surprise. I wasn't alone. Kneeling on the carpet was Eddie. His face was pale as mashed potatoes and his expression was the human equivalent of a vacancy sign.

"Eddie? Are you all right?" I went over and touched him on the shoulder.

His eyes stared off into space. His palms were spread wide over his knees. His shins were tucked under his thighs, a position that Yoga practitioners call Child's Pose. His white chinos and matching tee shirt were dotted with various shades of paint. But his expression was what I focused on. His face had gone slack like a balloon that's lost all of its air.

"Eddie? What's up?"

He didn't answer. Instead, he gazed straight-ahead.

I spoke in a gentle tone. "Eddie? What are you doing here? I've been walking through the house and yell—"

A muscle twitched near his eye. This was such a strange tic that I stopped talking. His expression and his pallor scared me.

"Eddie?" I shook him gently. Now I was really worried. What

had gotten into him? Slowly, my eyes followed his downcast stare. I gasped.

In front of the cream sofa sprawled a figure. I assumed I was looking at Mrs. Morrison. She was dressed like the mannequin in a fancy department store window. She wore cork-sole platform espadrilles and a crocheted cover-up that was lacey enough to reveal a black one-piece bathing suit. Against her tan and crepe-like skin, she sported an entire jewelry box of gold accessories: bracelets, multiple necklaces, rings, and earrings. Her dark brown eyes stared straight up at the ceiling without blinking. Heavy makeup had been artfully applied. A halo of brown hair formed the backdrop for expensive gold streaks. Her pink tipped nails had been freshly painted. Her ruby-red lips were parted in an astonished, "Oh!"

Had she fainted?

No.

Was she unconscious?

Maybe.

But doubtful.

She looked dead.

I took two steps to my left. From my new vantage, I had an unobstructed view. A large pool of crimson had gathered under the crown of her head. The crimson liquid connected her to a marble bust, representing a man in a military jacket. An odd stray thought occurred to me. The military man and Mrs. Morrison were wearing identical skullcaps of dark red. But the blood wasn't all that fresh. I squatted down for a better look. A skin had formed on top of the red liquid. Splatters were drying on the carpet. Where the blood was a thin layer, it had turned brownish.

"Is that Mrs. Morrison?" I asked the painter. As if on cue, my stomach lurched. I swallowed down the bile.

Eddie nodded.

The two of us were riveted by the body.

"Did you call 911?"

Eddie didn't answer. His Adam's apple bobbed repeatedly. Like me, he was doing his best not to puke.

I leaned out over the body. The dispatcher would need to know if the victim was dead. Was there anything I could do to help her? I didn't think so. Could she be in a coma? I craned my neck to get a better look at her skull. It had been bashed in. Bone and brains and blood mixed together in the disgusting slop that poured from her head.

That bust had been the killer's weapon of choice. Heavy and deadly accurate.

I whispered to Eddie, "I think she's beyond help."

Eddie said, "Right."

"Have you called 911?" I asked Eddie again.

"No. I, um, no. I saw her car in the driveway. I rang the door-bell. When no one answered, I went to my truck and grabbed my phone. I called Mrs. Morrison's cell. I got out of the truck and walked closer to the house. The ringing was loud. I could hear it. I looked through the window," he said with a gesture to the parted curtains behind us. "Her...well, her legs... I could see them, so I walked around to the back. The door was open."

"Yeah, that's how I got inside, too." Beads of perspiration sprouted on my upper lip. My damp clothing now chafed my skin. The AC kicked on. Cold air blasted from a vent overhead. A chill seized me. After it swept through me, I shivered. The only way to stay sane was to focus on the facts. I asked Eddie, "Her phone is here somewhere?"

"Under her body, I think."

"Eddie, are you going to faint?" I asked.

"Maybe."

"Go sit over there on the sofa and tuck your head between your knees," I said, but he ignored my suggestion.

Rolling to my feet, I reached into a pocket of my Lilly Pulitzer skirt. By now, I was thoroughly chilled. My fingers shook so badly that it took three tries for me to dial 911.

"Is she breathing? Conscious?" the dispatcher asked.

"Uh, no."

"Address?"

I didn't have the exact house number.

Over the phone came the warning, "Ma'am? You need to focus. Stay with me a little longer. I need you to remain on the scene. Ma'am? Did you hear me? What's the address?"

I turned to the painter. "Eddie? *Pssst!* Eddie? Do you know the street address?"

He didn't respond. His eyes had gotten wider and his skin was even more pale.

I spoke more sharply to him, hoping to offer a distraction and get the information I needed. "Eddie, do you know the address here?"

No sound.

I told the dispatcher, "I think my friend is going into shock. There are two of us here with the body, and I don't know the exact house number. This is the Morrison residence on Seabreeze on Jupiter Island. The home is cream with blue trim. There's a white Bentley sportscar in the drive. My black Camry and a white truck are parked out at the curb. We're north of the public park at the end of Bridge Road."

"Stay on the line, please. It's important," said the dispatcher. Her voice was hard-edged with authority. "Don't leave the scene."

As if responding to her demand, Eddie jumped up and ran out of the room.

"Hey!" I yelled. "Eddie! Come back! Eddie? Don't leave me alone!"

His footsteps echoed on the marble tile. What on earth?

Why had he deserted me? I considered following him but the voice on the phone warned me not to leave. The dispatcher asked, "Are you safe? Miss?"

My stomach plummeted. I shivered. Raindrops had begun again. The moisture coalesced and ran down the glass of the window. Outside a gentle patter was becoming more insistent. *Was I safe? Oh, lord. What if the killer was still here? What if Eddie had left me to chase the assailant?* Now that he was gone, I was all alone.

"Are you in any danger?" the dispatcher repeated.

In the distance, sirens wailed, screaming their way to Mrs. Morrison's body.

"I think I'm safe. I mean, I can't tell! How would I know?"

From the hallway came a squeaking sound. I knew what it was. This was the sound of tennis shoes on tile. Their wet rubber soles protested each step. Eddie must have come back. "Eddie? You still here?"

The squeaking stopped.

What if it wasn't Eddie? My heart skipped several beats. I'd been wrong: I wasn't alone in this house. Had Eddie come back? Could it be the killer? Was the murderer coming to get me?

Stay calm, I told myself. Think! You have to save yourself!

"The police are on the way!" I yelled, hoping the intruder would hot-foot it and leave. The pitch of squeaky footsteps changed, indicating they were moving away from me. A door slammed shut. Outside came the faint sound of that poor dog, yipping at the person who was running away.

Was it the killer? Had the murderer been coming for me? Was I safe?

When would the police get here?

CHAPTER 4

Sirens grew louder and louder.

Soon, I thought. They'll arrive soon.

Suddenly, the pitch changed. The emergency vehicles were heading away from me!

I said to the dispatcher. "Make them turn around! They're going the wrong way!"

Once again, she asked me to describe the location of the Morrisons' house. Her calm tone became more strident. "No, no, it's on the north side of the island," she said, "not the south side."

What if they didn't get here before the killer came back? Saliva flooded my mouth. I swallowed hard, repeatedly. Any minute, I would puke. Ignoring the instructions from the dispatcher to "stay put," I stuffed my phone in my skirt pocket and hurried to find a bathroom.

That proved harder than I'd expected. I opened one door after another. I discovered a coat closet, a butler's pantry, and a room crammed with AC equipment. Each second of delay made me more desperate. My body kept warning me that I was going to throw up.

Finally, one door revealed a powder room with black wall-paper and gold fixtures. I dropped to my knees and worshipped the porcelain god. Over and over again, I heaved. It felt like I was sick forever. Once my tummy was empty, I rinsed out my mouth in the sink. Cold water splashed on my face did wonders for my stomach and my mood. In the distance, a muffled siren wailed again. I slumped against the powder room wall, letting the cool tile surface help me regain control. My clothes were nearly dry. They felt stiff on me. A glimpse in the mirror confirmed that I looked awful.

Suddenly, I couldn't hear sirens. Had the emergency vehicles turned around? Or gone to another scene? Should I step outside and try to wave them down? But I decided to give myself a few more minutes to recuperate. I didn't want to walk out and start puking again. What a totally crappy day!

But it occurred to me, I had nothing to complain about, because I wasn't dead in the other room.

The dispatcher said, "Sorry, miss. The emergency vehicles are stuck waiting for the bridge to come back down. They'll be there soon."

Drawbridges mark both the north and south ends of Jupiter Island. No vehicles can come onto the island without crossing over a bridge. These are raised by a bridge keeper to allow tall boats to sail by. In the summer months, the metal structures can be up in the air for ten minutes or more if several vessels go by. The police must have gotten thoroughly turned around if they wound up on the west side of the bridges.

One more time, I splashed my face with cold water and rinsed my mouth. Feeling better, I slowly retraced my steps. The smell of the body seemed even more acute. If I was going to stay here in the Morrisons' house, I needed a distraction. A way to keep from thinking about the carnage. I opened my iPhone and started to play a game. But my avatar died after a few moves. Not what I needed, for sure. What else could I do? Text a friend? At ten on a Sunday morning? And say what? Hi, I'm standing here with a woman who's had her skull bashed in?

Um, no.

I decided to take pictures of the decor. Skye would enjoy seeing it. Using my phone, I photographed the remarkable blue-white-and taupe tiles. I captured the ornately carved molding. Carefully framing the shot to exclude the dead body, I shot a photo of the Morrisons' Highwaymen painting. MJ would enjoy seeing it.

Standing there and staring at the Loxahatchee River, I tried to imagine myself in a boat on the way. I was miles away mentally when flashing lights sliced the walls into red ribbons. At last! The cavalry had arrived.

The back door flew open. Four people in uniforms surrounded me. Two looked to be medics and two were uniformed cops. I put my hands on my head as a precaution. I wasn't about to get shot for finding Alicia Morrison's body. No way.

Yip-yip-yip! Came a frantic barking from the side yard.

Well, drat. The poor dog still didn't have any water!

I gave my name to the officers. The younger of the two phoned the new director of the Department of Public Safety, otherwise known as the Jupiter Island police. I had only met Steve McHenry once at a social function. That was a shame because I knew his predecessor, Chief George Fernandez, and we'd gotten along well. I hoped my reputation preceded me, and the new guy would realize I was a law-abiding citizen. Typically, I wouldn't talk to the cops. My father had drummed it into me that I should always have a lawyer by my side before agreeing to speak to the police. But in this case, I was eager to go home and change my clothes. I was tired of smelling the increasingly pungent stink of the dead body, and I had a store to run.

The younger of the two policemen, Officer Scott Siegel according to his name badge, handed me his phone. "Chief wants to talk to you," he said.

I took the phone. "Cara Mia Delgatto here."

"Cara? What kind of trouble did you land in?" Chief McHenry asked. His voice boomed over the phone. "The dispatcher says you're there with a dead body. Did you murder Mrs. Morrison?"

"No, sir, I did not."

Meanwhile, the medics tended to the corpse. One of them phoned and asked for a medical examiner to pronounce the victim dead. The older cop started the process of securing the crime scene. He cordoned off the living room with bright yellow-and-black crime scene tape. The younger man stayed close to me with one hand resting on his taser. The gesture was a message. I was not free to leave. Not yet at least.

I took a deep breath and did my best to explain my situation to the chief. "When I got here, I found a woman dead on the floor. I'm assuming it's Mrs. Morrison? Someone bashed in her skull. Her dog is outside in a pen without any water. You know how dangerous that is for a pet. I was determined to get the animal something to drink. The back door was unlocked. A car was in the driveaway and a worker's truck was here, too. There were two champagne glasses on a table outside. Condensation dripped from them, so I could tell people had been out there recently. I kept calling out as I walked into the house. No one answered my shouts. My goal was to find a bowl and get water for the dog. Just so we're clear, I hate people who are cruel to animals. If I'd been Mrs. Morrison's killer, I would have given her a slow and painful death."

The chief's laugh was terse. It was the sort of laugh you make when something is not really funny. Because this wasn't funny, and it sure was awkward. For me at least. The chief continued, "We'll add your name to a list of suspects, but you're at the bottom of the rankings, Cara."

"Really? Why?"

"Let's just say Mrs. Morrison had a lot of conflicts in her life."

Officer Siegel could overhear what the chief said. The words "a lot of conflicts" must have hit a chord because he rolled his eyes. Clearly, the chief was not alone in his low opinion of Mrs. Morrison.

I needed particulars. I asked, "What sort of problems did she have? If Mrs. Morrison was attacked by someone randomly, do I need to be scared? Am I at risk? Is someone targeting women on the island?"

The chief sighed. "Not that I know of. I think this was probably linked to a personal problem. Mrs. Morrison had a talent for rubbing people the wrong way."

This time the young cop covered his mouth with one hand to hide a grimace. Scott Siegel was a young man of mixed race. His biceps bulged beneath his short sleeve shirt. His shaved head was as smooth as the inside of a clam shell. Startling amber eyes looked out on the world with a sense of calm.

"Is that so?" I said, asking a rhetorical question.

"Tell me again, Cara. Why were you there at the Morrisons' place? Besides offering aid and comfort to their dog?"

"I dropped by because she stiffed my store to the tune of $800. I figured I would have a better chance at collecting the money in person. I know that's wishful thinking."

"You still believe in the Tooth Fairy and write letters to Santa?" the chief chuckled at his own joke.

At least the new guy had a sense of humor. I found that comforting. "You've got me, sir. I figured an in-person visit couldn't hurt. I had to do something, Chief. I couldn't sit back and let this slide without trying to convince Mrs. Morrison to pay up. It's not the money so much as the principle of the thing."

"You realize, young lady, that you just gave me a motive for this crime?"

"No, sir, I beg to differ. I can't collect money from a dead woman."

"Good point. How about you make a statement? Hitch a ride with Officer Siegel to the department. Someone can drive you back to your car when you're done."

"Yes, sir. Will do." I handed the phone to the uniformed officer. He took it with a nod of gratitude. I waited patiently while he listened to his boss. Once the chief told the cop I was an island resident, the young policeman's whole persona relaxed. The island community is tight-knit, and the Department of Public Safety is like a concierge service. We have a high ratio of officers to residents. I've yet to call them and not have them appear quickly.

Until today.

After Officer Siegel ended his call with the chief, I explained that the Morrisons' dog still needed water. "Could I get some for him?" I asked.

Officer Siegel bobbed his head and nodded toward the kitchen cabinets. I opened one and rummaged around for a bowl. What I found was exquisite china, lavishly painted with scenes of pheasants and bordered in gold. I flipped a plate over and read the words Lenox on the back. Definitely not your everyday Melamine. The next cabinet also held fine china. In fact, every cabinet was stuffed with exquisite place settings. Finally, I gave up. I rummaged through the recycling and found a plastic bowl that once held salad fixings. The container needed to be rinsed out. As I ran water over it, I did my best to eavesdrop on the conversation between the older cop and an

EMT. While I'd had my head in the recycling bin, we'd been joined by a crime scene investigation unit.

In the living room, an investigator was snapping photos. My stomach was still queasy about the corpse, but I wasn't terribly worried about being blamed for the murder. The puddles of blood were congealed and the splatters were drying. Clearly, that woman had been killed long before I'd walked into the scene. My call to 911 could prove that. Sort of. Eddie could vouch for when I showed up. I'd purposefully not mentioned Eddie's name to the chief. It had been a snap decision. I didn't want to squeal on someone else, and the cops would know about Eddie's presence soon enough. I figured someone on this street had security cameras. These robotic sentries were positioned at the mouth of many driveways. They reminded me of something out of Star Wars.

I filled the clean plastic bowl with water for the dog.

The young policeman opened the French door for me. His blue nitrile gloves were in harmony with the patio décor. I hadn't noticed him pulling on the gloves. Officer Siegel watched as I set down the plastic bowl of water. His hands rested on top of his Sam Brown belt, and his eyes are glued to me. Resident or not, the policeman was taking no chances on me running away.

The pup immediately caught the scent of the water, raced over, and lapped up every drop.

"I hate people who are cruel to their pets. Whoever did this should be locked up," said the officer.

Yeah, well, good luck with that, I thought. Mrs. Morrison was way beyond the long arm the law. When the dog was finished, I picked up the bowl. "I'll take this back to the kitchen and refill it."

"I better call Animal Control. They'll come and pick the dog up," said Officer Siegel.

As he held open the door for me, I glanced around before

walking back into the house. The bicycle had disappeared. Eddie's truck was gone. The Bentley waited in the driveway and my Camry sat beside the curb.

I put the dish in the sink and turned on the tap. "What will Animal Control do with the pup?"

The officer shrugged. "Take it to a shelter."

"Can I take him home with me? He seems like a nice dog. I could foster him until a family member claims him."

"Ask the chief."

That's exactly what I did.

CHAPTER 5

Chief McHenry raised a thick eyebrow. A muscular man with a full head of hair, he looked to be in his fifties. There was a wariness in his eyes, and a tilt to his mouth that could look cruel when he didn't smile. "Mrs. Morrison stiffed Rocky Wilson, too? Rocky over at the deli?"

"Skye took the order from Mrs. Morrison and made the arrangements to deliver the party favors and decorations while Rocky agreed to supply the food. You could say Skye was the party planner." I sipped the cup of coffee that the chief had given me. Considering all the police procedurals I've read, I expected my drink to be swill, but this brew surprised me by being pretty good.

"Huh." He played with his ink pen. "You're telling me that Mrs. Morrison also cheated Skye Blue Murray?"

"Sort of. Skye works for me, so I'm the one who's out the money. Skye set up the event. Mrs. Morrison kept changing her mind. Skye felt like she was chasing her own tail, trying to pin the woman down. As you might guess, changes to any order like that are expensive. Rocky said he had the same problem with Mrs. Morrison. Her indecision drove up the cost of the food.

Making menu changes at the last minute can cause all sorts of problems."

"You know this how?"

"My family owned a restaurant in St. Louis. They named it after me. I grew up working at Cara Mia's. When I was thirteen, I bussed tables. I graduated to helping with the catering and eventually I took over all of our outside events."

"Why didn't you stick with it?"

"Almost five years ago, my mother was diagnosed with Stage Four cancer. After she died, my father lost all interest in life. I had no choice but to take over all the operations, and it was too much for one person. Plus, my son enrolled in University of Miami. My grandfather lives in Stuart. It made sense for me to sell the business and move here."

"You got thrown into the deep end of the swimming pool," said Chief McHenry.

"That's one way of putting it. Particularly in this situation. I was blissfully unaware of the missed payment until recently. I think Skye and Rocky wanted to keep it from me. I've been going through some, uh, personal problems."

The chief nodded his understanding.

"Chief? I got the distinct impression that the woman has done this before. I vaguely recall Rocky saying something similar. After all, Mrs. Morrison lives—lived—on Jupiter Island. She told Skye that no one would dare come after her. Doesn't that sound like someone who's had experience stiffing people?"

"You have a point."

"Now if it were me, I'd be worried about my reputation. This woman wasn't worried at all. She thought the situation was a laugh. That really stunned Skye. The idea that other people's problems weren't worth a moment's consideration."

The chief rocked back in his chair. His mouth settled into a flat line of disgust. "That's a shame."

I raised my palms to signal that I understood. "Since moving here, I've observed that some residents on this island are real stinkers. The men seem to understand how important it is to look past superficialities. A lot of the women act full of themselves."

Jupiter Island boasts the world's most expensive country club because you must be an island property holder to join. Homes here start around $3 million. If my cottage hadn't been sold to me at a steep discount by my grandfather, Dick Potter, I could never have afforded it. In season, there are fewer than 900 residents on this island. Off season, only 300-some. Wealthy residents appreciate the fact the island is intensely private. There are the two drawbridges on the north and south end. You have to drive over them or arrive by boat. Once you are on the island, your vehicle is tracked by numerous security cameras, monitored by the Department of Public Safety. They regularly run license plates.

No one has confirmed this to me, but I suspect the high level of security is why Jupiter Island is a haven for captains of industry, celebrities, and other individuals with a high net worth. I am clearly an odd duck, but the solitude of this place appeals to me.

The chief tilted his head and regarded me thoughtfully. He said, "Cara? You are too young to understand the mindset of the wives on this island. Most of them have never had to work. They're part of an older generation, a bygone era. Their status derives from their husbands' careers. Folks used to joke that behind each successful man was a woman, supporting him. The older women on this island are incredibly jealous of their lofty perches. And they're insecure. Most of them are scared to death. Without their husbands, they have nothing. No status. No money. No means of support. Women like you are mirrors, and they aren't keen about the reflection you cast."

The chief was right. My mother had said similar things for

years. Growing up, I'd watched our female customers treat Mom with unimaginable rudeness. Especially if they were dining out with their husbands. Mom had shrugged it off. Dad had explained the women were jealous of my mother. Admittedly, my mom was a head-turning beauty. I'd never stopped to wonder if their disdain was based on more than her looks.

Of course, it had been!

"Am I free to go?" I asked the chief.

"After you make a statement. My officers tell me you were there alone when they arrived."

I hesitated. I hated tattling on Eddie. He was such a sweet guy. Clearly, he'd been in shock. That must have been why he'd hightailed it out of the Morrisons' house. He'd simply freaked. But if I didn't tell the chief the truth, I'd be lying by omission. I'd ruin whatever goodwill I'd built with the chief and the Public Safety Department. I'd also make the entire situation more difficult when Eddie regained his composure. Surely, Eddie would tell the cops why he ran! He could have had any of a hundred reasons for scampering off.

Maybe he was guilty.

I didn't want to go there. I liked Eddie and Katrina too much. But I had to be honest. As I dithered, it occurred to me that I might get Eddie in *more* trouble if I didn't admit to seeing him. Somebody probably had Eddie's arrival and departure on a security camera.

"I wasn't alone, Chief. Eddie Drake was there when I arrived. His truck was parked out on the curb. I found him in the same room with the body. He seemed to be in shock. I asked him a question and he didn't answer. His color was bad and he looked shaky. He took off before your officers arrived."

Chief McHenry nodded. His ink pen did double-duty tapping his desk. "That's what we heard from a neighbor. There's a busybody who lives across the street from Mrs. Morrison. She came charging in here right after our officers arrived with blues and twos. Gave us a full report on the goings on."

I finished my coffee and cradled the empty cup in both hands. Time to change the subject. "May I foster Mrs. Morrison's dog? Can you believe someone would leave an animal like that? Out in the sun without water?"

"Hmmm," he said. "Yes, I can. That same busybody neighbor has complained several times about how Mrs. Morrison treated her dog. Galls me to no end. If she wasn't going to take care of it, why not give the dog away?"

"Beats me." I rose and looked around. "I guess I'd better write up my statement."

The chief craned his neck and stared at me. "Don't forget to explain why Skye Murray was there earlier."

"Excuse me?" I nearly dropped the empty coffee mug.

"Mrs. Murray left the scene shortly before you arrived."

"She what?" I asked. I could not have heard the chief right.

"You didn't know?"

Officer Scott Siegel drove me back to Mrs. Morrison's house so I could get my car and the dog. The young cop must have decided that I wasn't a danger or public nuisance because he seemed relaxed, almost affable. I wondered if the chief had told him I was okay. Or maybe Officer Siegel had surmised that if the chief didn't want me handcuffed or whatever; I wasn't worth worrying about. Before he put the cruiser in drive, Officer Siegel radioed ahead and asked another officer to search the house and find dog food for me. That was good thinking on my escort's part because switching an animal's food too quickly can lead to all sorts of gastric distress.

At first, I wasn't sure I should be talking to Officer Seigel. I probably shouldn't have spoken to the chief. Maybe I was in the clear. I hadn't touched Mrs. Morrison's body. My fingerprints wouldn't be on anything but doorknobs and the powder room, as I'd carefully avoided touching surfaces. But I had snapped photos. I decided not to share that. It did not reflect well on me.

I'd been the only person on the scene when the cops arrived. The busybody neighbor must have noticed my arrival time. Or had she? I wondered if Eddie would vouch for me? Or would he be angry that I'd told the police he'd been there when I arrived?

If my arrival time could be verified, I was sure I couldn't be blamed for the murder. The blood was already drying when I arrived. I didn't have a drop of it on me.

But Skye *had* visited the Morrisons' house before I'd arrived. How long had she left before I'd arrived? Did Skye confront Mrs. Morrison? Skye couldn't have bashed the woman in the head! That would be totally out of character. On the other hand, I'd known from the day we met that Skye's background was murky. She'd been honest with me, explaining she had been briefly incarcerated. The details didn't matter. Nothing could change my opinion of Skye. As far as I was concerned, she was my dear, dear pal. There wasn't a single vicious bone in her body.

Or was there?

She'd been very angry with Mrs. Morrison. After all, the woman not only cheated me but also stiffed Rocky, leaving Skye to feel doubly responsible. Had Skye snapped and hurt Mrs. Morrison? Was it possible that Mrs. Morrison had charged Skye, and Skye defended herself?

"You aren't going to take that dog directly to your house, are you? As I recall, you already have a dog. A big one," Officer Siegel asked, breaking into my thoughts. His eyebrows were raised in curiosity. His baritone voice was deep and melodious.

"I also have a cat, Luna," I said. "They are both rescues."

I wasn't surprised that Officer Siegel remembered seeing my

Royal Bahamian Potcake, Gerard. The Potcakes are named after the crusty leftovers in the bottom of a cooking pot. They began as a mixed breed, a throwaway group of animals who survived on the Bahamian islands against all odds. Short-coated, tall, and intelligent, they make excellent companions. Since Gerard loves going for walks, most of the JI police force have seen me with him. Gerard is a sweetheart, but surprising him with a new furry friend wouldn't be a good idea. Not for him and not for the newcomer. I said as much to Officer Siegel and added, "I'll take Mrs. Morrison's dog to my store. He can stay at work with me today. That way I can monitor the situation at home when I introduce him to my pets."

"Good thinking," said Officer Seigel. "Introducing a new animal can be tricky. I found this stray, a Springer Spaniel-beagle mix? I brought her to our house. After I went to work, my wife's cat totally flipped out. That tortoiseshell tabby climbed our curtains and stayed there for hours."

"What a mess," I said.

"Yeah. The wife called and begged me to get Primrose down. That's the cat's name, Primrose. Chief is good about letting us take off for family problems, and Primrose definitely counts as a family member. She's my wife's pet, but golly, Primrose was too freaked out to let Chantell grab her. Chantell was sobbing by the time I got home. Primrose was one unhappy kitty, I'll tell you. She fought me like I was the enemy. I still have scars on my forearms. Of course, now Primrose and Brody are best friends."

I chuckled as he told me about his disaster, and Officer Siegel laughed, too, despite the fact he had been wounded in action.

"Sounds like your new arrival made quite a scene," I said.

"She sure did!"

Officer Siegel seemed guileless. I decided to ask a few questions. "Speaking of scenes, the chief didn't sound surprised to hear Mrs. Morrison had come to harm. I got the impression that she kept the Department of Public Safety busy." I pitched this as an offhand remark.

"You mean calling up and complaining? For sure. She was on the phone every time she saw a black worker. Mrs. Morrison was openly hostile to folks like me. The county sent a crew to her street to mark underground electric cables. Mrs. Morrison called our dispatcher and screamed that the men outside threatened her. They all were rapists, according to her." He paused and snorted a laugh. "She was convinced that every man on God's green earth was interested in her, romantically."

I liked Scott Siegel, and I was glad that the chief had asked this young man to drive me to my car. When we arrived outside of Mrs. Morrison's home, another officer met us with a bag of dog kibble. "Yo, Scott? This what you needed?"

Officer Siegel took the dog food from the other cop. He and I walked over to the dog pen. I lifted the pup into my arms and headed to my car.

"If you think of anything else, Ms. Delgatto, give me a jingle. Any information you find out about Mrs. Morrison might help us solve this crime," said Officer Siegel as he loaded the bag of kibble into my back seat. Then he opened the front door for me and the dog. Gosh, a man with manners! I caught a whiff of his cologne and approved of the clean scent with its metallic edge. Rolling down my window, I thanked the officer. The puppy explored the passenger side seat.

But before I could drive away, the young policeman rested one hand on my doorframe. He lowered his face so we were staring at each other. Then he added, "I'd appreciate it if you don't phone your friend, Mr. Drake, or Mrs. Murray. Officers have been dispatched to interview both of them. It's best if you don't warn them in advance. Give us twenty-four hours at least. We don't want them to work on their stories, if you get my drift.

In my old department in Chicago, we would lock you up and hold you overnight to make sure you didn't get in contact."

A shiver swept through me. Officer Siegel noticed and added, "But I'm sure we can rely on you not to discuss this situation."

I bobbed my head in agreement despite the fact my fingers itched to phone Skye. I needed my best friend! I desperately wanted to share my horrible morning. But I couldn't. The cop stared at me, waiting for my promise. Of course, I understood why Officer Siegel was asking. It was important for the police to interview us separately. There was a chance one of us saw or heard some tidbit that might otherwise get lost or distorted if we shared information.

"Do I have your word?" Officer Siegel asked. "All we need is 24 hours."

"I won't talk to them," I promised. I could keep this under wraps at least until Monday. Skye was scheduled to work that morning, and I could avoid Eddie until then. Yes, Katrina had told me they would be at the store today, working on the mural, but I could still stay mum about what I'd walked into. If necessary, I'd explain I'd promised not to talk about it.

The dog decided he wanted to sit in my lap. Obviously, the puppy liked going for rides. I shifted into drive but didn't take my foot off the brake. A thought had struck me.

"Officer? If Mrs. Morrison stiffed my store and the deli, isn't it a good bet that she also owed money to other merchants? Maybe someone else decided she should pay up or else?"

His face creased into a thoughtful frown. "Good point. We'll ask around. Meanwhile, if you hear that another merchant was crossways with her, let me know."

"Will do and thanks for the ride."

A woof from my passenger prodded my memory. "He says thanks for the kibble!"

CHAPTER 6

"What's your name?" I asked the fluffy dog next to me.

The plume-like tail wagged in response, but that wasn't enough information to give me a clue.

"Hmmm. I guess you're not a big talker, huh? That's fine. You've probably had a rough day. You didn't happen to see who killed your owner, did you?"

No response.

"I guess I'd keep that information secret, too, if I were you." My blinker signaled a left turn, and we headed east toward downtown Stuart. "I wish you could talk, puppy. Otherwise, Skye and Eddie are in hot water. Me, too, maybe."

The fluffy pup was easy to tuck under my arm and carry into the store. The size of the dog made me think about Jack, the Chihuahua I'd adopted when I first moved to Florida. Tears welled in my eyes, but I brushed them away with the back of my hand. I missed Jack tremendously. I thought of him, a dull ache nearly crippled me. How is it that the loss of an animal can hurt so much? I guess it's because pets never falter in their love for us, never lob a cross word our way, and never fail to shower us with affection. Or maybe the real problem was my compounded grief. The loss of Jack multiplied the pain of Dan's absence. I had to pinch my upper thigh to distract myself from giving into depression.

Being at work would do me good, I decided. I needed activity to take my mind off the horrid scene at the Morrison house. That was my hope, at least.

But I didn't plan on being accosted by Pete Slatkin, MJ's husband, the minute I climbed out of my car. Pete must have been lying in wait, because he came sprinting across the alley. It was like he'd appeared out of nowhere.

"Hi, Pete. What's up?" I asked, holding the dog with one hand and shading my eyes from the sun with the other. Only then did I get a good look Pete, and his angry expression scared me. I've never seen him look so menacing.

"It's about time you got here," he growled. Glancing down at the dog in my arms, Pete did a double-take. "Why have you got Bailey Morrison?"

"Pardon. Bailey who?"

"That Havanese you're carrying. That's Bailey Morrison. He's one of my patients," Pete explained. I should have guessed that Pete would recognize this dog. He and his partner at the veterinary clinic take care of most of the Jupiter Island pets.

Pete took my keys out of my hand and opened the back door of The Treasure Chest for me and my new friend.

"Bailey? Is that this pup's name?" I carefully set the dog on the floor. The pup ran from one spot to the next, eagerly sniffing and exploring.

"Yes, it is. He's neutered and belongs to Alicia Morrison. Nice dog, actually. Bailey is part of a championship bloodline. Havanese were bred to be lap dogs. But Alicia has never really bonded with Bailey. That's a shame because Havanese desperately want to be companions, and Alicia could care less about

Bailey. She's about the only pet owner I've ever met who isn't in love with her baby." Pete squatted and patted his thigh, calling Bailey to his side. Bailey raced to the scrawny vet, stood on his hind legs and placed his paws prettily on Pete's leg. The little dog's tail wagged so hard that the whole pup shook with the motion.

"I have temporary custody of Bailey. Mrs. Morrison isn't able to care for the dog right now. I was asked to dog-sit." The words were hard to form, but once they were out, I decided my story was a keeper.

Pete nodded. "Got it. I'm surprised Mrs. Morrison needed your help. Usually, she delegates anything having to do with her dog to her maid. Look, I came by to talk with you. In private. Nobody's here yet, right?"

"Right," I said. "We don't open until noon. I've got five minutes. Let me start a pot of coffee." I bit my lip and got busy with the hot water and grounds. Pete banged a chair around and finally sat in it. I wished I could tell someone my personal tale of woe, but I couldn't, and Pete was acting upset enough for the two of us. I hoped that he would simmer down. This wasn't a good time for him to be snippy with me. My cup of woe overfloweth.

While the coffee steeped, I claimed a chair at the break table. I'd no sooner gotten comfortable than the vet came at me with both barrels blazing.

"Cara, you can't treat my wife like this. MJ is upset, and that makes me upset. I told her to stay home today. She's too emotional to work. Besides, what would she sell? Cara, you have to get Irving Feldman to return the Highwaymen art. You know how much it means to her. You should never have let them take those landscapes away! What were you thinking? My wife is suffering, and it's all because of you."

My goodness. What a passionate diatribe! I wouldn't have guessed that Pete had it in him. But he did.

Pete had used the words "my wife" with great pride. He'd been in love with MJ for years before she agreed to marry him. Now he was a proud husband, complete with major league protective instincts. Bully for him.

"Pete? Do you honestly think I'd let Irving load up his mother's prized collection of paintings if I had any other option? Yes, MJ is upset, and of course, I feel sorry for her, but this is my livelihood, too. Doesn't it occur to you that I'm upset?"

"That's why you need to call Irving and get this straightened out!" Pete's normally blotchy skin solidified into a bright red mask.

"Pete, I hear you. I've called Irving several times!" That wasn't entirely true. I hadn't called Irving while I was in the police station. To atone for my exaggeration, I added, "In fact, I would be phoning Irving right this minute if you weren't sitting here fussing at me."

"Then do it!" Pete yelled.

I retrieved my phone and put it on speaker. While Irving's number rang, I poured two cups of hazelnut coffee. A mechanized voice said, "The number you have dialed is no longer in service."

"Crud!" Pete jumped to his feet. He paced the short length of the back room while gnashing his teeth and literally wringing his hands. "You should have called him earlier!"

Of all my faults, and there are many, my temper is the worst. Given my morning so far, I was in no mood for Pete's tantrum. "Hello, Pete? Weren't you listening? I've phoned Irving repeatedly. You heard the message about the number no longer being in service. Do you really think I'm happy with this situation? Think about it. I had a special safe built into the wall, just so we could keep all of Irving's mother's pictures secure. Any idea what that cost me? It was a bundle. Five figures, pal. You've got a lot of nerve, coming in here and giving me a hard time about those Highwaymen paintings. You think that isn't impacting me? Of course, it is! In fact, every minute you yell at me is time that I could be tracking down Irving! You are literally wasting my time!"

"You'll never find him! He and his wife are long gone." Pete's derisive sniff punctuated his statement.

"How the heck would you know that?" I asked, feeling incredulous. If Pete had insider information about the Feldmans, why hadn't he told me straight-away?

"One of Irving Feldman's neighbors brings his dog to our clinic. After MJ told me what Irving had done, I called my client and asked if he'd seen Irving lately. At my urging, the client walked over to the Feldmans' house and looked through a window. The place was empty. Cleared out."

"Did the neighbor have any idea where they'd gone?"

"No," Pete mumbled, rubbing a hand over his mouth.

"Is the Feldmans' house for sale? Was there any sign that this move is permanent?"

"My client asked around. Another neighbor reported seeing a moving van. They didn't spot a 'for sale' sign. Not yet at least."

That reminded me. "Did you know Irving's wife has a chronic health condition? Last time we talked, Irving told me she had been accepted into an experimental program at the Mayo Clinic in Jacksonville. Maybe they moved to there to be closer to the treatment facility."

"Then that's obviously where they went! What are you going to do about this?" Pete snapped at me. I told myself to ignore his harsh tone.

"I'm going to track Irving down," I said.

"How?"

"First, I'm going to ask Sid Heckman for help. You know that Sid uploaded all of Irving's mother's collection onto our website, right? Every bit of it. Sid worked closely with Irving. Plus, Sid has all of the original photos, pictures I paid for. I hired a professional to take shots of the artwork. The way I see it, Irving isn't going to sit on those paintings. He needs money too badly. His wife's treatments are expensive. His best chance of selling the paintings without us would be through the internet. Sid might be able to trace Irving that way. In the meantime, I'll continue searching for the Feldmans. They can't have vanished into thin air. Did your client say whether anyone saw the Feldmans drive away?"

"No, but their car was gone," Pete said. He sipped his coffee. He didn't thank me for the drink, but I didn't much care. The brew had done its job by calming him down. Pete continued, "Irving drives a purple Kia. That's what I was told."

"Okay," I said, making a note on a desk pad. "Good to know. Again, I want to assure you that I'm as distressed about this as MJ is. Without the revenue from those landscapes, I might have to close my shop. Rest assured, finding Irving is a high priority with me."

My phone vibrated, signaling me it was time to open the store. "Hang on while I unlock the front door," I told Pete.

The instant I returned, Pete shoved back his chair with so much force that it nearly toppled over. "Cara? I'm holding you personally responsible for straightening this out. Don't forget, MJ is staying home." Pete stormed past me toward the front door. Bailey barked at Pete's retreating figure.

Terrific. How was I going to wait on customers and hunt down Irving Feldman?

I buried my face in my hands and sighed.

Pete's curt accusation and his nasty attitude wounded me deeply. To think that I'd considered him my friend! Funny how fast a friendship can fall apart. My dad always said, "Money changes everything." In this case, MJ's livelihood had been destroyed, and her husband blamed me. Yet, I was a victim, too. Plus, I was responsible for keeping open my store. MJ wasn't my only employee.

As if summoned by my thoughts, Honora came crashing through the back door. "Is that man out there waiting for you, Cara?"

"What man? No one that I know of is waiting for me." I said as I moved toward my oldest employee. The tiny octogenarian was loaded down with canvas shopping bags. Her daughter, EveLynn is a superb seamstress who makes soft goods for the store. Lately EveLynn has taken it upon herself to decide what the store needs, what will sell, and what she wants to create. She no longer consults with me. A little voice inside my head warns me that I should exercise more control over her. I should sit her down and give her orders for new merchandise, covering specific price points. But why monkey with success? EveLynn's soft goods get snapped up the minute we put them on the shelves.

Even more importantly, why fuss at EveLynn when she's bound to turn around and get snippy with her mother? Honora has enough trouble living under the same roof as her adult daughter without me riling up EveLynn.

Honora has become more and more unsteady on her feet. Racing to her side, I grabbed the bags and tried to wrestle them away. Honora gratefully relinquished her parcels. I was relieved to see her take a seat at the break table.

"I made fresh scones," I said as I put the bags aside. "You should have one, Honora."

Over time, my oldest employee has become thinner and more fragile. Her stride used to be sure and forceful. Now she shuffles along. I worry that she might take a tumble. That could be life-threatening for a woman her age.

Woof! Woof! Bailey raced over to Honora. My heart skipped a beat. Would Bailey be a good ambassador? Or would he bark all day at people?

Honora looked down and said, "Bailey? What are you doing here? Cara, darling, how are you? And why do you have Bailey Morrison?"

If anyone could keep a secret, it was Honora, and I badly needed to talk. I hastened to spill the beans about my rotten morning. I started with, "I decided to drop by Alicia Morrison's house on the way to work. A white Bentley was in the driveway so I figured she was home. I called out, and no one answered, but Bailey started barking. He was stuck in an outdoors pen without any water or shade. There wasn't even an empty bowl in sight. The least I could do was get him some water. When I got closer to the house, I saw that the back door was open. I wandered in."

"You let yourself into her house?" Honora's eyebrows lifted in surprise.

"Only to get the dog some water. I kept calling out, but no one answered. The house was wide open, Honora. It was crazy. I found Mrs. Morrison lying there in a puddle of blood. Her skull was bashed in, and she was obviously dead."

"Poor you! And poor Bailey!" Honora's sincere concern encouraged me to keep talking. I rationalized what I was doing. I promised Officer Siegel not to say anything to Skye or Eddie. Honora's name hadn't come up.

Still, I had to make sure I could trust my friend with this news. "Honora? You have to keep this quiet. You can't share this with anyone. Promise me that you won't talk about what I told you."

She pantomimed zipping her lips shut.

"Thanks," I said. "You don't know where Skye is, do you?"

"No." Honora got up and busied herself, making a pot of tea. "MJ's scheduled to come in any minute."

"She won't be here. Pete left right before you arrived. He jumped all over me for letting Irving remove his mother's collection, and then he announced he'd given MJ the day off."

"For goodness' sake! That man is nothing but a bird-brained boy. Pete has never moved out from under his mother's shadow, has he?"

This was surprise coming from Honora. Usually, she's very circumspect in her opinions about other people. Of course, I wasn't sure whether she was talking about Pete or Irving. I kept my mouth shut, hoping she'd go on and she did.

"Pete is tied to his mother's apron strings just like Irving Feldman," Honora continued. "Yelling at you must have made him feel very grown up. Honestly! As for Irving? If Essie hadn't died, Irving would have never married Evie. She would have been a fiancée for the rest of her life—or at least as long as she'd put up with Irving. Makes me glad I had a daughter. I can't stand a man who can't stick up for himself or the women in his life. Pete has no right to keep MJ from coming to work. Now about Mrs. Morrison. I must have misunderstood you. You aren't telling me she's dead, are you?"

Honora didn't have a bee in her bonnet; she had a bumblebee!

"She sure is," I said. "And she had been for a while. I had to go to the Jupiter Island Department of Public Safety and make a statement."

"All that before starting your day. Doesn't that butter your toast?" She fussed around, making herself a cup of tea.

After talking to Honora, the adrenaline left my body, and I was able to think about work. I picked up the bags she had been carrying and placed them inside my office. Since we weren't officially open yet, I'd log in the soft goods and write descriptions for each piece. Next I would take photos. I would send the images and verbiage to Sid. He would put the goods online, while I put them out on the sales floor. Over time, he and I had developed a system for working together that was easy and efficient.

"I'll open the store," said Honora. "I can see you're busy."

Working with the soft goods kept my mind off of Mrs. Morrison's dead body, but only for a short time. There were a lot of questions to be answered. When Honora walked past my office to reheat her tea, I did my best to sound casual as I said, "I expected Eddie and Katrina to be here by now."

Honora scrunched her face into a frown. "Oh, that's right! Eddie and Katrina are supposed to work on the mural, aren't they? Dear, dear, and it's past noon. I'll check the store voice mail. Maybe something came up. That reminds me. I bumped into Cooper Rivers yesterday. He asked about you."

"Oh?" That was the best I could muster under the circumstances. I stepped out of my office, trying to ignore how weak my knees felt. After all this time, Cooper could still cause my heart to race. Emotions swamped me, but I told myself, *This is not the time to get all dreamy and caught up in a fantasy that will never, ever happen.* I steered the conversation to safer territory by picking up the dog and stroking him. "I can't imagine leaving an animal outside without any water, can you?" I ran a hand over Bailey's silky ears.

"That's no surprise," said Honora. Her pleasant expression changed to revulsion. "Alicia Morrison thought it would look chic to own a small dog. An accessory she could carry under one arm and fit under the seat of a plane."

"You know Alicia Morrison?" I asked. "I mean, knew her?"

"Sadly, I plead guilty," said Honora. "Bailey most definitely will not fit under the seat of a plane."

I said, "He's too tall for that."

Honora laughed. "You're absolutely right. I remember the day Alicia told the garden club she had found a hobbyist breeder. She drove all the way to Tampa to get Bailey. As a pup, you couldn't tell that Bailey was destined to be the Godzilla of Havanese. But he already is larger than most of his breed. The joke was on Alicia since Bailey is too tall to fly as a carry-on pet. Not that it mattered. She absolutely hated Bailey, almost from the beginning. That little guy is full of love and affection, and Alicia wanted a dog that was more like a stuffed toy. Now her late husband, Prescott, would have been thrilled with Bailey. But he would have hated the way Alicia treats her pet. He should have known better than to marry her. Honestly, some men are absolutely blind to a woman's faults if she's pretty."

"You knew both Prescott and Alicia Morrison? Did you socialize with them?" I waited for a response. Honora knows almost everyone in town. The idea she had known the Morrisons as a couple shouldn't have surprised me.

"I knew them very well, but socialize with them? Of course I didn't." Honora bustled over to the counter to refill the electric kettle with water. She drinks endless cups of tea. I'd been drinking cold brew coffee to counteract the heat wave we were enduring. For Honora, hot tea was her drink of choice no matter what the temperature was outside. As her water heated, I poured a new tumbler of cold brew coffee for myself. I didn't worry about customers. The door minder would tell us if someone walked in. Instead, I settled into a chair and listened to Honora's story.

"I was a member of the Hobe Sound Garden Club when I met Prescott's first wife, Mary. She was an heiress. Her wealth funded Prescott's business ventures. In return, he was a devoted spouse."

"What are you skirting around?" I asked, feeling hung up on

her odd comment "in return." Honora had a habit of getting coy. Today, I needed the truth, the whole truth, and nothing but the truth. Her sly reference irked me. There was too much going on in my life for me to wade through social niceties.

"Mary was terribly unattractive, poor dear. Her features were out of proportion, and her forehead was huge. Such a shame. Also Mary didn't give two hoots about her wardrobe. If the occasion was important, Prescott would advise her on what to wear, but her every day clothes were often mismatched. Many people snubbed her because of her looks and her lack of sartorial style. When they learned she was an heiress, they'd try to cozy up to her. Mary was always gracious about it, but she never forgot who had originally been dismissive. I shall give him this: Prescott didn't care about her looks. He fell for her keen intellect and brought out the best in her. We all look prettier when someone loves us. Mary fairly glowed when he was near her."

"I bet you and Mary got along from the start," I said. A wry smile lifted the corners of my mouth.

"Ah, how well you know me. I saw past her exterior. Mary was ostracized by shallow people. Even before I knew about her wealth, I did my best to make her my friend. I continued after I realized that we came from different economic strata. Once I got to know her, I discovered that Mary had a rare inner beauty. She was a kind and considerate woman with a plethora of interests. We actually had a lot in common." Honora got up and stood beside the counter, waiting for the kettle to click off. When it did, she poured the water into a tea pot that already held a silver tea ball. The scent of bergamot and oranges filled the air.

"Prescott divorced her to marry the second Mrs. Morrison?" I wondered. "I only knew of him as Alicia's husband."

"Heavens, no! Prescott would never have divorced Mary. He absolutely adored his first wife. He was an attentive husband even when Mary lay dying of colon cancer. After she was gone, he mourned her terribly. He always attributed his success to her. He would tell anyone who would listen that without her backing, he could not have started his hedge fund business. He truly was a rich man by the time she died, and it was thanks to his own acumen. But he still credited her. Knowing he was self-sufficient, she only left him a little of her money when she passed. The rest went to charities they both supported. Of course, Prescott was still young when he became a widower. Only 47 and quite the catch. Naturally, women threw themselves at him, but he ignored them. At first, he was a lost soul. You see, he had nothing to distract him from his grief. He and Mary never had kids. His business ventures had matured. For all intents and purposes, he was semi-retired. As a favor to a friend, Prescott agreed to teach economics at Miami Dade College. Because there was a two-hour gap between his classes, he volunteered as an ESL teacher. That's how he met Alicia, who barely spoke English. Spanish was her native tongue. She was a freshman. From what I've heard, Prescott was captivated by her. She definitely was a beauty, and I suspect she set her cap for him as soon as she learned he was well-heeled. Alicia was as different from Mary as chalk from cheese, and no one was surprised when he decided to marry her. Prescott told everyone that she came from a wealthy, influential family."

I caught the shading of the words. Again, I searched for what Honora didn't say. "Are you suggesting that Alicia wasn't a beauty queen? Or that she wasn't from an influential family?"

"Ha!" Honora smirked. She took out the tea ball and poured herself a cup before joining me at the table. "Alicia is—was—too coarse to have come from good stock. Her conversations were peppered with crude comments. She had no table manners, and she was often both abrasive and rude. Of course, a person can pick up polish, if they so desire, and that's what Alicia did over the years. And she'd met Prescott when he was terribly lonely.

He was happy to overlook Alicia's unrefined qualities because of her nice figure and pretty face. The rest of us saw her for what she really was. Pretty is as pretty does. Alicia was trashy and low life, inside and out. Whereas Mary had a good heart, Alicia was a monster with a lovely face."

"Wow," I said, borrowing my friend Kiki Lowenstein's favorite adjective. Honora was on a real rampage. I'd rarely heard her speak poorly of anyone. Yet here she was, castigating a woman who'd been killed earlier this same day. I was flat-out astonished. It took me a few minutes to come to grips with what my friend was saying. Honora always tempers her insights with a healthy portion of kindness. Her generosity of spirit is amazing. But right now, Honora was thoroughly trashing the second Mrs. Morrison. This behavior was wildly out of character.

Then it dawned on me. There had to be more to this story!

Honora noticed I was nonplussed. She patted my arm. "As you know, I rarely hold a grudge. I try to be a good Christian. Being charitable toward others is important. But I can say without flinching that my better angels all go to heck when it comes to Alicia Morrison. That woman was undeserving of my elevated thoughts. She was a miserable excuse for a person."

"Honora, what happened? Why are you so negative about Mrs. Morrison? This isn't like you at all!"

The older woman fidgeted, ignoring her tea and toying with her white patent leather belt while avoiding my eyes.

"Come on, Honora. Whatever happened must have been pretty dramatic for you to be so angry. That's what I hear. Anger behind that negativity."

"Mrs. Morrison came to an arts festival event in downtown Hobe Sound. EveLynn and I had a booth. Alicia showed up with a group of her cronies. She took one look at EveLynn's work and proceeded to make fun of my daughter's sewing. That's fine. Arts and crafts are subjective. What one person loves another person hates. But Alicia wasn't content with telling her pals how trashy she thought EveLynn's soft goods were. She waved over another group of passers-by and made more rude remarks about EveLynn's pieces. Alicia was particularly dismissive of the appliqued pillows, the ones EveLynn specializes in. To this day, I shudder at how nasty Alicia was."

Honora added more sugar to her tea cup and stirred it vigorously. "In the course of making fun of my daughter's handiwork, Alicia must have realized that EveLynn is different. I could practically see the recognition in Alicia's eyes. And, sadly, Alicia latched onto that difference."

EveLynn is neurodivergent. She's what people used to call autistic because she lacks the ability to pick up on social cues. Her speech can sound robotic and childlike. She sees the world in black and white. When she's overly stimulated, she reacts with a meltdown.

"Alicia could see she was getting to EveLynn. I could, too, but there was nothing for it. This was a street fair, so we couldn't get away. We couldn't duck into a restroom, and I couldn't find a quiet spot where I could calm EveLynn down. All we could do was stand there and take the abuse. Sadly, it got worse. To taunt EveLynn, Alicia snatched up one of the pillows and threw it at another pal. Like it was a giant football! Unfortunately, the intended catcher didn't grab it. The pillow landed in the street, falling in the path of a passerby who stepped on it. The pillow got dirty. Too grimy to sell. You know how EveLynn is. She likes her things just so. Alicia smirked and said, 'Oops.' Her friends laughed nervously while EveLynn turned white with rage."

My friend paused her commentary. She got up, refilled the sugar bowl, sat back down, and dumped three heaping spoonsful of sugar into her tea. I fought the urge to gawp. Honora avoids sugar. This uncharacteristic move was a sure sign that our conversation was stressful for my friend—and that shocked me because Honora typically takes life in stride. Looking up from her cup, Honora gave me a sad smile. "Eve-Lynn lost it. She had a tantrum. Next thing I knew, she was smashing everything in our booth and screaming. The police were called. We were asked to leave the art festival. In fact, we've been banned from that art festival ever since. While all of this was happening, Alicia stood on the opposite side of the street, pointing and laughing at us."

"My word. That must have been horrible!"

"It was. The officers marched us away from the wreckage of our booth. I tried and tried to explain what had happened to EveLynn, and why she'd been so aggressive, but as you well know, my daughter looks perfectly fine. It's hard for people to recognize that EveLynn is different in a complicated way. Finally, we were joined by an officer whose brother is on the autism spectrum. He understood immediately what had happened, and bless his heart, he interceded. Of course, EveLynn was unwilling to return to our booth. Luckily for me, I was able to text a caregiver who immediately showed up and gave EveLynn a ride home. I went back to the booth and packed things up. The memory makes me physically ill. That was four years ago, and I'll never forget it."

CHAPTER 7

"That's awful," I said. I didn't envy Honora. It's hard enough to be a parent without trying to raise a child who is different. And yes, they're all different, but not in the extreme way that EveLynn is.

"It was a nightmare. To this day, people still talk about it. They aren't sure whether to pity me or think I'm a poor excuse for a mother. Alicia told everyone that EveLynn physically attacked her, and the police came in response to the commotion." Honora threw up her hands. "What a mess. And yet, despite how she acted toward my daughter and me, Alicia Morrison has people convinced that she's a saintly patron of the arts. Of course, Prescott was a great help with that. Bless his heart."

"I don't think I ever met him," I said.

"Regrettably, he died back in 2003. That poor man. His second marriage didn't turn out as he expected. Consequently, he traveled and played golf as much as he could. When he was in town, he did a lot of charity work. You might have seen his portrait at the hospital. He donated a lot of the money for the cancer wing."

I snapped my fingers. "That's right, and I remember seeing Alicia Morrison at the hospital charity ball. Someone pointed her out. She was up front in the expensive seats, and I was in the nosebleed section. My tablemates were going gaga over the huge diamond she was wearing. A person at our table said the stone had been a gift from her husband."

"Ha!" Honora laughed. "That was a huge bone of contention in their marriage. Shortly after they were wed, Alicia saw a lovely portrait of Mary, wearing her diamonds. Prescott had commissioned it. The gems figured prominently in that painting. I think it is on display now at the hospital, on the donors' wall. No matter. Well, Alicia got it into her head that Prescott should give that jewelry to her. She didn't like the idea she was second-fiddle, and she told him as much. He explained the pieces were not his to give. Mary had specified in her will that her family heirlooms would be sold and the money would go to various charities. Somehow Alicia found out they hadn't been sold. Not yet, at least. There'd been a hiccup in settling Mary's estate. It took a couple of years to get everything worked out. Alicia went bonkers. She spent every waking hour haranguing Prescott. She desperately wanted those gems. On occasion, someone would ask Alicia why she wasn't wearing Mary's six-carat emerald-cut diamond. Alicia would turn crimson with anger. She couldn't stand the fact she wasn't decked out in jewels like Mary had been."

"But she didn't get Mary's things?"

"No. She most certainly did not. As I said, they were being held until every bit of the red tape was cleared up. Then they were sold at auction with the money going to charity. Alicia was furious. She often complained about it in public. I heard her, as did many others."

"But when I saw her at the charity ball, she was covered in diamond jewelry!"

"She might well have been. Shortly before Prescott died, Alicia came into her inheritance, her own mother's gems. At least, that's what she told everyone. I think what you saw were the diamonds she eventually inherited."

"From what you've told me Prescott had plenty of money," I said, watching Honora's face. "Why didn't he buy something for Alicia? Something as nice as Mary had?"

"Like other enormously wealthy men, he put a good amount of his personal fortune in a trust that was pledged to various charities. Certainly, he kept enough to live on, and enough to make most of us delirious with joy, but the bulk of his money was promised to a variety of good causes. He made provisions for Alicia so she would have plenty to live on, but he refused to replace Mary's family jewels. He couldn't without breaking into the trust fund! Those diamonds were literally worth millions. But Alicia never got over being angry. I do believe that's another reason she was so very nasty to people. She felt cheated." Honora finished the entire pot of tea. She got up and added more water to the kettle. As the pot heated, her mouth worked from side to side. I'd seen this before. Honora was literally chewing something over.

She continued, "Things aren't always as they seem. The world is full of fakery. To my way of thinking, Prescott and Alicia sort of deserve—deserved—each other. They both got less than they bargained for. Instead of marrying for love the second time around, Prescott was fooled by Alicia's good looks. Meanwhile, she thought she'd hooked a big fish who would shower her with expensive baubles and leave her his fortune. They were both disappointed."

I had no doubt that Honora was right, as usual. I decided we needed to move on. "While Pete was here, I phoned Irving, for the one-millionth time. But all I got was a message that his number is no longer in service."

Honora carefully examined a spoonful of wet tea leaves. Slowly, she said, "It's not fair for Pete to take this out on you, Cara. I hope that MJ isn't following his lead."

"They have to blame somebody, Honora. I'm the safest bet. One of Pete's clients lives near the Feldmans' house. Pete convinced him to go over and see if he could find Irving, but the place was empty."

"Where do you mail the money after MJ sells a painting? Why not check that address? Surely Irving wants to collect his portion of the payments. He wouldn't have left money on the table." Honora tilted her head in that way she has, reminding me of a sparrow searching for a worm.

"Any money we collect is directly deposited into Irving's bank account minus the commission. He insisted we use an Automatic Clearing House. I think they call it an ACH."

"Hmmm." Honora got up and tossed the old tea leaves into the trash. "How about if you track down the movers? They must have taken the paintings somewhere. Some place with proper climate control and security. I bet Irving's moved them to another art dealer. That would solve the problem of storage. Irving couldn't possibly sell them himself. He doesn't have the contacts, and he isn't knowledgeable about their value."

Why hadn't I thought of that? A lump crowded my throat. A wave of dizziness swept over me. For the briefest of moments, I was certain I couldn't cope. I felt incredibly stupid, and that's a feeling I hate more than anything on this earth.

Honora put a gentle hand on my shoulder, and I had to fight the urge to bury my face in her shoulder. Times like this, I really missed my mother. Instead of succumbing to Honora's kindness, I pulled away slightly. I used both hands and scrubbed my face.

"Cara, darling, you've hit a rough patch. Take a deep breath. It'll be all right. I promise you this thing with Irving isn't as big of a problem as it seems right now. We'll get this sorted. We both know what an imbecile Irving can be. The question before us is, where did the paintings go? Follow them and you can track down Irving."

I swallowed hard. The loss of the paintings had hurt like a splinter jammed under a fingernail. Throughout the whole ugly mess, I'd done my best to stay calm. When the movers demanded that I unlock the safe and allow them access, I literally pinched my upper thigh to stay in control of my emotions. My father had drummed into me the wisdom of keeping an even keel in business situations. "No one wants to deal with a hysterical woman," he'd said. "I'm sorry if that sounds sexist, sweetheart. A ranting and raving man will get a pass, but a woman who comes unglued will be labeled a shrew or worse."

After he said that, I'd gone running to my mother to complain about Dad's unfairness. Mom listened intently, made a tiny huffing noise, and grabbed me by my elbows.

"Cara, are you really that naïve? Haven't you witnessed this already? Good lord, child. Have you been asleep on your feet? Your father is telling you the truth, and he's doing it for your own sake. He's right. Let me go one step further. No one likes dealing with anyone who is uncontrollable, male or female. It's a sign of weakness and lack of character. People don't trust others who go ballistic when a problem crops up."

The memory brought a prickling sensation behind my eyes. I pinched the bridge of my nose to keep the moisture in check.

"You've had a rough go of it, haven't you?" asked Honora in a soft voice. "With Dan and your little dog…"

Her kindness nearly pushed me over the edge. I choked out, "Too many losses." Honora went beyond her habit of patting my shoulder and hugged me. Throwing away my pride, I clung to her until I mastered my emotions. Then I stiffened, thanked her, and poured myself another large tumbler of cold brew coffee.

"Do you remember the name of the moving company? The

one that took away the paintings?" I asked, when I could manage to form the words.

Honora cocked her head again and tapped a finger against her lips. "Let me think."

She closed her eyes and thought.

With a jolt, I wondered where Bailey was. Turning around, I scanned the back room but I didn't see him. Finally I stuck my head under the table. The fluffy dog was at my feet. His tail was curled like a squirrel tucks his tail against his body. Bailey was such a sweet animal. How could anyone have treated him cruelly?

"That's it!" Honora nearly shouted. "Hercules Movers. You've seen their ads, right? Strong as Hercules? Those were the movers."

A jingle played in my head, and I groaned. For the rest of the day, I'd be hearing the stupid theme song from the Hercules commercials. No way around it, I would have to give them a call sooner rather than later.

Honora volunteered to check in her daughter's soft goods. That freed me to duck into my office and find the number for Hercules Movers. Of course, no one answered the phone. A machine-generated voice reminded me that today was not a normal working day, and the office would reopen on Monday.

Another dead-end. My door minder rang. I left the office and walked onto the salesfloor where I welcomed customers. Bailey proved to be a wonderful ambassador. Everyone who visited The Treasure Chest that day cooed over him. He was a terrific dog. The Jupiter Island Department of Public Safety would have no trouble finding the Havanese a new home.

After work that evening, I held my breath when I introduced Bailey to Gerard. I shouldn't have worried. The Potcake pup was thrilled to have a new play buddy, and Gerard had obviously missed Jack. Luna took several swipes at Bailey as he ran past, but for Luna, that passed as a friendly greeting. The gray cat didn't spit or hiss at the newcomer. I counted that as a win. It was too early to tell if all three fur babies could live together peacefully, but so far so good. Tomorrow while I was out and about, I would close Bailey up in my bedroom with plenty of water. My new petsitter, Joyce Gannon, would take him along when she walked Gerard.

I turned my television to a local channel. The news reports were brief. "A woman's body was found in her home on Jupiter Island," said the commentator.

Using the remote, I switched the TV off. As I did, I noticed a film of dust on the console. With a groan, I remembered when I was houseproud. Now I lacked the will and the energy to care. At least, not much.

Honora's stories had convinced me that Alicia Morrison had wanted admiration in the worst way. Too bad Alicia wasn't around anymore, because the next day her name was on the lips of every local reporter. Her murder was called gruesome, heinous, and aberrant. Interviews with neighbors produced bland remarks such as, "We're shocked. This is awful." No one stepped forward with expressions of grief. Most people seemed blasé, bored even. Typically, a gory death would send folks into a tizzy, demanding that the perpetrator be caught. The loud silence of Mrs. Morrison's Jupiter Island neighbors suggested they weren't particularly concerned that she had been killed. Perhaps they thought the killer had done a public service.

After ten minutes of blather, I turned off the radio. I drove the rest of the way to the store in blessed silence except for the comforting *swish-swish* of the mariner's cross as it swayed back and forth from my mirror.

At the store, MJ's pink Cadillac straddled two parking spaces. That was unusual. MJ gets cranky if we don't line up our cars properly. As for her early arrival, that was weird, too. She has a tendency to slide into work, barely on time. But today, the day after her husband had excoriated me for not tracking down the Highwaymen paintings, MJ was here at The Treasure Chest bright and early. It was an hour before we opened. Was she planning to pounce on me the way that her husband had when I walked inside the store? I cringed in anticipation.

"Pull up your big girl panties," I told myself.

I opened the door to find Skye patting MJ's back in a soothing manner. MJ isn't a warm and fuzzy person, but there she was, leaning against Skye. Their closeness stopped me in my tracks. MJ and Skye could have been mistaken for sisters, given their blond hair. But in every other way, the two are vastly different. MJ is a sex siren, a Floridian version of Marilyn Monroe, and Skye is a copy of Stevie Nicks. Personality-wise, they are opposite ends of the pole. MJ is a porcupine; she's hard to get close to. Skye is warm, welcoming, and loving.

When they heard me enter, the two women moved apart. Skye gave MJ one final pat, turned her back on us and hurried away. My heart winced as Skye's footsteps rang out on the stairway. She hadn't even said hello to me! That hurt a lot. Since the day I arrived in Stuart, Skye had been my best friend and my own personal guardian angel. Today she'd hurried off without a word. Was she avoiding me because of Mrs. Morrison's death? Was she embarrassed about visiting the Morrison home? Had she seen the dead body? Had the police warned her against talking to me? What had she seen? Something I hadn't?

I'd promised the chief to keep quiet for 24 hours. By my watch, I owed him three more hours before I shared my experience with Skye. Then I could approach her about Mrs. Morrison. Clamping my jaw shut, I shifted my focus to MJ.

"Mrs. Morrison is dead," MJ said. Her voice was flat. Her fingers dug into the silk of her blouse. "Good luck getting the money she owes you."

"Yeah," I agreed, "that might be tough."

MJ quivered, like a piano string after it's struck. I'd seen her like this before. She was holding herself together. Surely, she didn't care about Mrs. Morrison. There had to be something else bothering her.

"MJ? You okay?" I asked tentatively.

Her lower lip trembled, but she didn't respond.

"Look," I said. "I know you are upset about the paintings being taken by Irving. I am, too. I'll do everything I can to track him down. Honora made a good point. He has to have moved them to another dealer. They're too valuable to store anywhere that isn't a secure, climate-controlled facility. Honora also pointed out that Irving couldn't be the person selling them. He isn't knowledgeable enough. Nor does he have the contacts."

"That's only part of the problem."

My stomach took a rocket ship ride to the floor. "Has your cancer come back?"

"No, no, no."

I waited.

"I'm okay," she said, drawing the last word out. "At least, I think I am. But there's something else. I've been meaning to talk to you. But I didn't say anything earlier because I hoped I was wrong or confused. I kept waiting until I had proof one way or—"

The back door creaked and Honora bustled in. Loaded down with paper bags and grocery sacks stuffed to overflowing, she could barely make it through the back room. I hurried to take several bags and a small shoebox out of her hands. MJ grabbed Honora by the elbow to steady the older woman. After Honora plunked down in a chair, MJ ducked into the restroom. I imagined she was calming herself down. The intensity of her emotions had put a scare into me. Once upon a time, nothing bothered MJ. Nothing.

What had caused this seismic shift? This didn't seem like the MJ I'd known for more than three years. The last time I'd seen her so upset she'd been diagnosed with breast cancer. With sudden clarity, I recognized that the Highwaymen paintings, like her breasts, were integral to MJ's sense of self. All of us have internal images of who we are. When those are threatened, our world is at risk. MJ's core self was in danger. But was it only the missing paintings? Or was something else bothering her? I needed to find out, and I had to do it sooner rather than later.

"Cara?" Honora interrupted my thoughts. She gestured for me to open the shoebox. Inside were a handful of patriotic pieces in 1:12 scale and adorned in red-white-and blue. "I want to teach a class on making a fireworks stall," my favorite minia- turist explained. Honora loved showing others how to make the small-scale projects. When she first suggested classes, I worried they might cut into our profits. After all, if a customer learned Honora's secrets, they might duplicate her process. However, I've changed my mind. As it happens, the more comfortable a person feels with a craft, the more likely he or she is to stay engaged. Engagement equals a need for supplies. Supplies translate into revenue. As a bonus, once a person learns how time-consuming crafting can be, they understand why minia- tures are priced the way they are.

Honora plucked out a stall and set it on the table. The minia- ture building was constructed entirely of popsicle sticks. As I watched, she threaded a banner of patterned triangles under the eaves. Each shape was imprinted with a letter to spell out: July Fourth!

A shelving unit was attached to the front of the stall. On it sat packages of fireworks, tacked down with museum wax. From small hooks, Honora had hung tiny door wreaths in patriotic colors. The back wall of the structure featured more shelves, and these were packed with jars of red, white, and blue candies.

The pièce de résistance was a sign with Uncle Sam cunningly painted on a white background. This was held up by a stake. With deft fingers, Honora jammed the sign into a four-sided miniature flower box. Inside the box, she'd planted a crowd of red geraniums, blue delphiniums, and yellow marigolds all made with paper. The stall and the signage were stunning.

"Honora? You've really outdone yourself. This is fabulous."

Her smile lit up her face as she explained, "The flowers are part of a kit my students can do as homework. The class will take two sessions. They can buy extra flowers, if they so desire. They can also add a picnic bench, food, and accessories."

Immediately, I grasped the intelligence of her plan. Instead of merely hoping that students would come back to buy more, she was showing them add-ons that would complement the stall. Who could resist adding a picnic in progress?

"You're amazing," I said as I hugged her.

"Keep the faith," said Honora, whispering my ear. "Everything will turn out fine. The police are investigating Alicia Morrison's murder. They'll get this solved."

CHAPTER 8

MJ came out of the bathroom. She seemed to have control over her emotions.

"Come on, MJ. Let's take a walk," I said. "Honora? Will you hold down the fort? MJ and I need a little fresh air."

"Of course. You two run along." Honora swept past us and out onto the sales floor. Her blue-and-white striped seersucker dress had been heavily starched. It swayed with each step. Those sturdy white shoes of hers *slap-slap-slapped* as she moved with determined strides. I watched her go with thankfulness. Yes, she could be unsteady, but that seemed to happen only after she'd been sitting for a while. Despite her age, Honora was spry and healthy.

I motioned MJ to the front door. Together, we walked outside.

Thankfully, the sky was overcast. We'd both neglected our sunglasses. MJ wore a hashtag of a frown between her eyes. "Okay," I said. "Take a deep breath. Just calm down and tell me what's bothering you."

Her sigh was heartfelt. "Right," she said. "Give me a second to collect my thoughts."

We strolled over to the Riverwalk Park, where benches would afford us a view of the St. Lucie River. MJ sank down, as weary as I'd ever seen her. I waited, letting the silence gather. Finally, she said, "As you know, most of our customers discover us through our website."

MJ and Sid had spent months setting up our website. They'd worked with a professional to photograph Essie Feldman's entire collection. Once they had the images, MJ had labored over the descriptions of the landscapes, plus their dimensions and notes of interest. She linked biographies of the individual painters to their pieces. The job had taken a ton of time and effort. It had been a monstrous task.

"The process goes like this. A potential buyer calls, together we look at the website and discuss which paintings they like. Then we go over the pros and cons of their favorites. Eventually, they narrow their choices down to one or two. From there, I can usually close the sale. But lately, customers have turned me down. When I pressed for a reason, they explained they'd found a similar painting by the same artist at a better price."

"How often did this happen?" I asked.

"At least six times, and maybe more. Possibly as often as ten times. Of course, some people never did respond when I tried to follow up."

I did quick calculations in my head. Highwaymen paintings can run from five to six figures. Even if all of these landscapes were priced at the low end of the scale, MJ had lost a sizeable amount of revenue. That surprised me. She's a great salesperson, our inventory was top-notch, and she was talking about motivated buyers.

"What was going wrong?" I asked.

MJ sighed deeply. "At first, I thought I had set our prices too high. But when I lowered the cost, people still decided to buy the other picture. Each time the customer bailed out on me, I asked them to tell me more about their new purchase. I explained that would help me keep abreast of the market for Highwaymen paintings and stay knowledgeable. I'd spent a lot of time educating them, and in return, I hoped they would educate me."

I held my breath. People can get pretty stinky when you question why they aren't buying from you. MJ had taken a big risk by following up.

She must have read my mind. "I know that was a gutsy move on my part, but I had great rapport with these people. In each case, the picture they finally bought was very much like what they would have gotten from me. In fact, in most cases their purchase was nearly identical to what I'd offered them!"

That wasn't surprising. The Highwaymen painted the same Old Florida themes over and over again with surprisingly little variation. The main differences were size, tiny details, color palettes, and the skill of the painter.

"I've been losing sales steadily for several months now," MJ said. "I wanted to chalk it up to Covid, but that didn't make sense. After the shots came out and people felt free to mingle, there was a pent-up demand."

Covid had changed the world, and many of our buying patterns. I had seen the dip in Highwaymen sales, but I figured MJ had hit a dry spell. She's a trooper, highly motivated, and I hadn't worried about her productivity. But she hadn't told me that she'd lost sales when she'd had an interested buyer on the hook. If she had, I might have been more concerned. In fact, I might have done something.

But I couldn't dwell on that. Not right now.

She went on, "At first, I thought I had a competitor. Maybe a dealer had secured a collection like Essie Feldman's treasure trove of landscapes."

I shrugged. "Maybe someone bought a few paintings and had to get rid of them in a hurry?"

MJ scowled at me. "Why would someone do that?"

"Could be anything. Could be a change of heart or a need for cash," I said, trying to be reasonable. "Could be a divorce and the need to divide up assets."

"But it's happened too many times, Cara. Six times in the past two months. Doesn't that make alarm bells go off in your head? Sure does in mine. I even wondered If another dealer and I were going head-to-head. Maybe it boiled down to price shopping by potential clients. But I knew, in my heart of hearts, that I was pricing our works correctly. Eventually I phoned Wild Will and asked him if my theory made sense."

Wild Will was a nickname for William Abernathy, a dealer who'd actually known most of the original Highwaymen. Wild Will had mentored Irving's mother, Essie Feldman, the original owner of The Treasure Chest. Back when she started her collection, Essie would confer with Wild Bill and get his opinion before making a purchase. These days, Wild Will was semi-retired.

"What did Wild Will say?" I asked.

"He thought my prices were right on the mark. I went into detail about the deals I'd lost. Wild Will listened carefully and promised to do a bit of snooping around. He called me back a few days later."

Her voice climbed to a higher register. I waited to hear what MJ had learned, but instead of telling me, she buried her face in her hands. "Breathe, just breathe," I crooned to her. "Take your time."

"I should have told you right away!" She lifted her head. "After everything I've been through with Essie's collection, I couldn't stand to tell you about this. Especially when I wasn't sure exactly what was happening."

"And what exactly is going on?" I asked, patiently.

"I'm still not sure!" she wailed. "I'm not entirely confident that I have an answer. Wild Will is puzzled, too."

"MJ, get a hold of yourself. What is it that you and Wild Will suspect?"

"We suspect that someone is copying Highwaymen paintings and selling them at a discount," said MJ.

I needed a minute to process what she'd said. I asked, "So how would a scheme like that work? Where would the originals come from? The ones being copied?"

"I've given this a lot of thought. If you recall, we put high-quality photos on the website. Remember? The bill for the pictures was not insignificant. I'm worried that those images have come back to bite us on the butt. There's probably a forger out there who's using the photos on our website as templates. He or she enlarges the images and then copies them with small alterations. A talented forger could make several copies of the same painting, and no one would know because the High-waymen painted many of the same scenes over and over. If you weren't an expert, you wouldn't realize what you were seeing. To check my assumptions, I kept digging. I went back to my 'almost' customers a third time. I showed up on their doorsteps with a bottle of champagne, offering to celebrate their purchases."

"And?" I prompted her. "Did you get anywhere?"

"It was like pulling teeth out of an angry chicken, but the champagne worked wonders. Bit by bit, I pieced together enough information to convince me there's definitely a new seller out there. And get this, the new seller is either a person with an extensive collection of Highwaymen art or a person with an extensive collection of copies! What's more, this creep has the ability to dramatically undercut our prices."

"But what about the authenticity?" My question sounded like a whine. "Your reputation makes our paintings more valuable. Didn't these owners care about that?"

"My champagne guzzling friends eventually showed me their certificates of authenticity. Get this. The certificates are ones that I signed. *I signed!* That means they *think* they are buying paintings that I've vetted, but I didn't! Somebody copied the certificates and changed the relevant information. Of course, they didn't change my name, and they simply forged my signature." After exploding with indignation, MJ went silent. We sat there, thinking our separate thoughts, mulling over the problem. In the meantime, the only sound was water lapping against the banks of the St. Lucie River as a boat motored past. The movement sent up a spritz of water, ripe with the verdant fragrance of plants and fish.

MJ said, "You've seen that spreadsheet that Sid made for me?"

Sid could do anything with a computer. I have kept him on retainer to make it easy for my employees to use his services. I didn't know he'd created a spreadsheet for MJ. I admitted as much.

"Of course you know about the spreadsheet," said MJ, sounding disgusted. "You've even seen it. You just don't remember it. Here, let me pull it up on my phone."

She handed her iPhone to me. Simplistic in format, the chart included columns with the names of the 26 artists, a list of their paintings and coded identifiers, the size of the canvases, the type of canvases, a description of the image, any special features, the original frame if applicable, notes on provenance, and sales history. Basically, this exhaustive list was an encyclopedia of the work of 26 artists. She was right. I had seen it, but I hadn't remembered.

"I started this as a worksheet. Now I use it every day. I go over and over it, memorizing the information and updating it," said MJ as I returned her phone. "This is my cheat sheet, my textbook, and my guidebook, all in one."

Although I'd learned a lot about Highwaymen paintings, I would never be an expert like MJ was. She knew which of the Highwaymen were alive, how they signed their names, their favorite subjects, their typical canvas sizes, and so on. Using the spreadsheet as a study aid, she'd done a deep dive into their body of work.

MJ continued, "When I lost that first sale, I reviewed my notes. I went back to our original photos of paintings. Last week, I met Wild Will for lunch. He and I pored over the spreadsheet. He agrees with me. The photos on our website are being copied and later sold, using my authentication. I feel horrible about it! Not only is someone selling forgeries, but this creep is using my reputation to sell phony paintings."

"I think this is the reason Irving withdrew his mother's collection. I'm guessing that Irving stumbled onto this scam, and he's blaming us. Me, specifically. And you by extension."

She took a shuddering breath. "If I'd come to you sooner, you might have been able to talk things through with Irving. Maybe you could have looked into what's happening. You're good at snooping around."

"Thanks, I think." I stared out at the water. The puzzle pieces slowly took shape in my mind but I couldn't move them into place. "You are thinking that Irving removed the paintings because of...what? This new competitor?"

"Either that or Irving is in cahoots with the new seller." She tossed her hands in the air as if scattering confetti. "You know what a squirrel Irving can be! Who knows what he is thinking?

Could be that Irving knows someone is selling paintings at less than our asking price. Maybe he's worried that this new vendor will drive down the value of his mother's entire collection? Whatever he thinks in his little pea brain, I am positive that he blames me. And you. It's the logical explanation for why he didn't contact either of us, isn't it? He never forgave me when the collection disappeared the first time!"

Nearly ten years ago and before I moved to Florida, Essie Feldman's entire collection of Highwaymen paintings vanished. Essie was in the hospital when it happened. MJ had been told to close the store and take a vacation. When she came back, the paintings were gone. The authorities couldn't figure out where they went. Even though MJ hadn't been in town, she became the scapegoat. Everyone pointed the finger at her, including the police. Eventually, the cops gave up questioning her because there was no proof of her involvement. But that didn't matter. She'd already been branded as the thief. Her life must have been impossible. Tongues wagged whenever MJ walked into a room. She couldn't get a job in the area. Finally, to keep body and soul together, she took a position managing a laundromat.

When I moved here and bought the store, I quickly realized that I couldn't run The Treasure Chest without her. Her expertise was—and is—incredibly valuable to me. Beyond what she knows about the Highwaymen, she's a walking encyclopedia of Vintage Old Florida tchotchkes. Whether it's wicker or bamboo or maritime paraphernalia or unique items like painted window screens, MJ knows their value.

Shortly after she joined my team, I found the stolen paintings. Needless to say, Irving Feldman had been elated, as he was able to claim his inheritance. I'd hoped my discovery would remove the stain from MJ's name, but it didn't. Not completely. Even her marriage to Pete, a much-loved local veterinarian, hadn't washed her reputation clean. Worst of all, we now had proof that Irving still didn't completely trust her.

I said, "Irving is a nutcase. Even his late mother despaired of his ability to think things through. I'm not sure how he can blame you for the forgeries, if that's what's really happening."

"Of course he blames me!" she shouted. "Given my track record and the fact my name is on the certificates of authentication, he'd be stupid not to point the finger in my direction."

I considered patting her hand, but I had the strong sense the gesture would backfire.

"I hear what you're saying," I began, "but we don't know for sure if that's what's happening. Let's not jump to conclusions. We need more information before we move forward."

MJ's head drooped. "I should have brought this to you sooner," she repeated. "But my ego got in my way."

A mosquito landed on my knee. I shooed it away. It responded by dive-bombing my neck. If MJ and I stayed here much longer, we'd both get eaten alive. Time to move on down life's highway. "You did your best, MJ. That's all that matters. We'll figure out what's really going on. No one has been a better steward of Essie Feldman's Highwaymen painting collection than you. You know that. I do, too. Tell you what. Let me make sure that Honora is doing okay. If she's fine handling the store, why don't we go to Pumpernickel's Deli for a pot of tea? Hmm? We can pick up lunch and take it back to The Treasure Chest for later."

"Huh," MJ said. "You're right about one thing. We need to move away from the water. Bugs are biting me." She smacked her arm. When she removed her hand, her palm was wet and crimson. Raising an eyebrow triumphantly, MJ said, "And now I have blood on my hands. Things couldn't get much better."

CHAPTER 9

Honora answered my phone call in a chirpy, upbeat voice. Yes, she was fine handling things by herself, but could we bring her a bagel from Pumpernickel's for a late breakfast? Of course, we could. I would also bring her lunch for later.

"Oh, and by the way," Honora added, "Katrina called. They'll be here tomorrow. Today they need to coordinate paint colors for the mural."

"Thanks," I said. Nothing was moving along as it should. On the other hand, I knew why Eddie was ducking out. He probably thought I'd question his courage.

Rocky waved to MJ and me when we walked inside his small restaurant. Minutes later, a new server, a woman with bleached blond hair and a tired expression, took our order and promised to be right back with a pot of Earl Grey tea. Like all of Pumpernickel's employees, she wore black slacks and a white Pumpernickel's tee shirt. The waitress didn't wear a nametag which I took as confirmation that she was new. My heart went out to her. Being on your feet all day long is enervating. Even worse, if you wind up serving cheapskates who don't tip.

MJ seemed lighter after all she'd shared. The set of her shoulders wasn't nearly so stiff. Leaning her head on one hand, she spoke quietly, "At first, I thought I was having a streak of bad luck. As you know, I've done really well selling Essie Feldman's collection. But it was like a tap turned off. I thought I needed to ride it out, and then my bad luck kept on coming."

"We'll get to the bottom of this, MJ. It might take a couple of days, but we'll get there," I said.

Our server came back with a list of the day's pies, MJ shook her head. "Not for me. I'm cutting back on sugar."

I decided to take a pass, too. Instead, I ordered tuna fish sandwich lunches for the three of us plus a plain bagel for Honora. When the tea came, MJ poured. I stirred a packet of sugar into my cup. The bergamot in the tea leaves filled the air with a perky scent. MJ dumped three packets of sugar into her cup.

So much for cutting back on her sugar! Was everyone in my store trying, and failing, to cut back on sugar? I refused to participate. I consider sugar to be one of the major food groups. I opened three more packets and dosed my drink. It tasted like a dessert.

We drank our tea quickly because we needed to get back to the store. I made a signal to Rocky, and he brought me our lunches and Honora's bagel. Shortly after Rocky bought the place, he and I agreed that my store would run a monthly tab. That works for both of us. After signing the bill and tipping our server with cash, I told MJ I was ready. We walked out of the deli carrying four paper bags. Three of them smelled distinctly of tuna.

The stoplight on the corner had turned red, forcing us to wait at the curb. Trying to sound casual, I said, "About Mrs. Morrison. Um, I guess I should show you the pictures I took yesterday."

"Yesterday? When did you take pictures? What pictures?" MJ frowned at me.

"I took them while I was waiting for the EMTs and the cops to show up. I needed a distraction." I shuddered.

"EMTs? Oh, my lord! Cara, you were there when they found the dead body?" MJ practically shrieked.

"Shhhh," I said. People stood behind us on the curb. I didn't need them to freak out along with MJ. "Keep your voice down. Please! Yes, I was there. I'm the one who called 911."

"And you took photos?" Her beautifully arched brows had climbed to her hairline. MJ's expression had gone from horrified to curious. Leaning close enough that I could smell her Chanel No. 5, she whispered, "Please tell me that you didn't take a photo of Mrs. Morrison's corpse? Like they did of Marilyn Monroe and John F. Kennedy?"

"Of course not. I would never photograph a corpse. That would be gross!" I didn't think I had pictures of the dead Mrs. Morrison. If I did, I'd taken them accidentally while trying to capture the interesting décor. "The scene made me sick at my stomach. The dispatcher ordered me to stick around. I had to do something as a distraction, and I didn't want to disturb evidence. I couldn't sit down. Couldn't touch anything. Her decorating was exceptional, and I decided to share it with Skye. I figured taking pictures would give me a way to stay in control of myself."

MJ gave me a curt nod. "All right. I can see what you mean."

"In one room, the Morrisons have a Highwaymen painting. I took a photo of it. Their decorator chose colors for the sofa and the accessories in concert with the landscape. I'll show you when we get to the store."

The light changed. "But why were you there in the first place? Inside the house?" MJ asked.

"To collect our bill, of course." I explained about the dog going without water and the open door to the house. "I yelled and yelled, but no one answered. Since the dog didn't even have a bowl, I couldn't get water for him unless I fetched a container. After trying to rouse someone, I gave up and walked inside. I wasn't about to leave that poor dog without anything to drink."

"Finding a dead body must have been a shock." MJ and I paused outside the store rather than going in. "But for heaven's sake, Cara, going inside that house was a dumb idea on so many levels. What if the killer had attacked you?"

"I didn't know Mrs. Morrison had been hurt, much less dead. Her car was in the driveway and her back door was standing ajar. There were glasses of champagne gathering condensation on the poolside tables. I figured she was in the bathroom and hadn't heard me hollering."

I didn't tell MJ that Eddie's truck had been parked at the curb. No need to drag him into this. Not yet. He'd have enough explaining to do when he talked to Chief McHenry.

"You must have been surprised by what you found," said MJ. "I would have vomited."

"I did. Let me tell you, it's miserable when you're trying not to puke and you can't find the powder room. I opened a lot of doors. I found a butler's pantry and an electrical closet and a regular closet, but I needed the bathroom. I have never been so relieved in my life when I finally discovered one. Running outside seemed like a good option, but the dispatcher demanded that I stay put. I was stuck. I tried playing a game on my iPhone as a distraction, but I couldn't concentrate. That's how I came up with the bright idea of snapping pictures of the house. Anything to avoid staring at that corpse!"

"I guess," said MJ. "And you're telling me she has a High-waymen painting? I didn't sell one to her. Let me look."

I opened the photos section of my phone. The pictures from inside the Morrison house came up right away.

"For crying out loud," MJ leaned close. "Is that a bust of Stalin?"

I jerked back the phone, fearful that I had, indeed, captured Alicia Morrison's dead body. But I hadn't. Only a clean portion of the bust was visible. "Stalin? How'd you know who that is?"

"Because I keep up with trends. That's my job. These stupid busts are what the kids call 'a thing.' You can buy one from China for less than fifty bucks. On the other hand, that big desk is fantastic. It's modern but not too modern, you know?" MJ wrestled the phone from me. Using her fingertip, she swiped the photos. Then she stopped. "Wait a minute. You took this in Mrs. Morrison's living room? While you waited there with a corpse?"

First she gave me the bags she'd been carrying. Then, using two fingers like an expert, she tugged on an image and enlarged it. With her index finger she moved the photo of the painted landscape around and around. All the while she squinted at the painting. After what seemed like forever, MJ muttered, "This can't be."

"What do you mean? I asked.

"I sold that particular Al Hair more than a year ago. But I didn't sell it to Alicia Morrison."

"Are you sure?"

"I am positive. Absolutely, totally positive."

"If somebody out there is forging those paintings, how can we track that person down?" I asked MJ.

Her unlady-like snort signaled the futility of my question. She coughed, got ahold of herself, and said, "I have no idea. This is above my paygrade. You're the one who likes playing amateur sleuth."

There's nothing I love more than a challenge. My brain kicked into high gear. I said, "Finding the mysterious seller would be easier than finding the forger. The seller has to do his or her work out in the open. I guess I could poke around. But you're sure? You're positive that the painting I saw at the Morrisons' house is a forgery? That has to be a forgery, right?"

This time, MJ's face turned sour. "It has to be. I know the couple who bought the original. They've since moved to Maine. They wanted the landscape as a souvenir."

"I could share my suspicions with the Jupiter Island Department of Public Safety."

MJ glared at me. She talked with her hands, waving them around her head. "Be serious. First you show up at the scene of a murder. Then you take photos at the scene, and now you plan to tell the cops that one of Alicia Morrison's paintings might be a forgery? You want to announce that Alicia owned a copy of a painting exactly like one from the collection of the late Essie Feldman? The same collection that's been removed from your premises by Essie's son, Irving? For reasons unknown? A man who is now avoiding you? Earth to Cara? You think you're in trouble now, but you ain't seen nuttin' yet. You share all of this with the Jupiter Island cops, and you'll be busy defending yourself for the next six months at least. How on earth do you plan to defend yourself? If the cops think you found a forgery, doesn't that give you a motive?"

I threw all restraint out the picture window. MJ had neatly voiced all my worries, and she'd included a few I hadn't thought of. The world grew fuzzy. My pulse hammered in my head. I staggered. She caught me by the elbow and hissed in my ear, "Don't you dare faint on me."

"But the cops cannot blame me for this! I am not the only person who was there!"

"What?" MJ shook me lightly. "What do you mean you weren't there alone? You didn't tell me you had company."

"Eddie and Skye were both at the Morrison house on the morning Alicia Morrison was killed. I saw Eddie, but I didn't see Skye. The police told me she'd been there. See? I have a lot of company when it comes to visiting crime scenes. They should be able to vouch for the time I arrived. The blood was starting to dry. Mrs. Morrison was clobbered hours before I got there."

MJ turned loose of my arm. Her lower lip poked out like the mouth of a sulky child. "Rats. I wasn't supposed to say anything."

"Say what?" I thought I'd misheard MJ. I was close to hyperventilating, and I knew I wasn't thinking straight.

"I wasn't supposed to tell you Skye's secret," MJ admitted sourly. "She dropped by Mrs. Morrison's house on Sunday morning to see if she could convince the woman to pay her bills. No one answered the door so Skye left. Cara, you know perfectly well, that Skye wouldn't hurt a fly. And I doubt that Eddie would have hurt that woman either."

"What a mess," I said. Keeping a grip on the lunch bags, I leaned against The Treasure Chest, the building I'd bought on an impulse. In my mind, I ran a tally. By my count, I knew no less than seven people with motives for killing Alicia Morrison. Honora hated the woman because she'd teased EveLynn at the art fair. EveLynn hated Alicia Morrison for making fun of her and getting her banned from future art fairs. Skye was angry that Alicia hadn't paid her bill. Rocky was upset for the same reason. Eddie and Katrina were angry because Mrs. Morrison had stiffed them and taken their ladder. And I was angry with her for leaving her dog without shade or water, as well as all the same reasons my friends were peeved with the dead woman. I might even make a case for MJ being frustrated. After all, it looked like Alicia Morrison might have owned a forged Highwaymen painting.

"What a mess," I said again.

The Treasure Chest sign hung above our heads. The colorful legend never failed to bring a smile to my face. Except today. Today I wished I'd never bought this shop. Right at this moment,

I wanted to be somewhere far away, and I had a full tank of gas. Maybe I could pick up my pets and hit the road. Key West was famous for the bums and criminals who took up residence there. I would fit right in.

MJ stared at me, waiting for an answer. She shook me again. "You know that Skye didn't do it, don't you? You know that Eddie is innocent?"

"I know that neither Skye nor Eddie could have killed Alicia. But I also know that somebody did. I know that because I saw the woman's body. Until the authorities find a credible suspect, the police might consider all of us as suspects."

"Considering that Skye has already done one stretch in jail, I can almost guarantee the cops will point their fingers at her," said MJ.

That was exactly what I'd concluded, too.

CHAPTER 10

My store is located on a corner of downtown Stuart, Florida, the Sailfin Capital of the World. The apartments upstairs boast a lovely view of the Intracoastal Waterway. A stoplight holds up traffic, and drivers get a good, long look at my big display window. Twin terra cotta pots stand as sentries by the front door. Geraniums, petunias, and Creeping Jenny spill over the sides in a riot of color. The structure itself is brick, and strong enough to have weathered many hurricanes. I have always loved The Treasure Chest, even when I was a kid, staying upstairs during summer vacation. Adding a mural to one side would be yet another enhancement to the property.

The clatter of metal against brick caught our attention. MJ and I turned toward the noise. She arched a brow. "Sounds like Eddie and Katrina are working on the mural."

Relief ran through me. If Eddie was here, then he couldn't be a suspect. The cops would have tossed him in jail. Pumping my arms, I race-walked around the building and saw a tiny figure on a short ladder. "Katrina?" I called out.

With a paintbrush in hand, she stopped mid-stroke. My eyes

moved to a graceful palm tree that was taking shape under her fingers. The scene I'd approved was coming to life.

Too bad Mrs. Morrison couldn't be revived as easily.

"Hey, there," she called down to me. Katrina wore faded jeans and a tee shirt. When she turned my way, I read the wording across her chest: *Warning: I am a Jersey Girl.* In fine print, the legend continued: *I know where the bodies are buried because I planted them myself!*

"Where's Eddie?" I asked.

"He has a headache." Katrina came down the ladder, one step at a time. Glancing up, I saw an unfinished section about two-by-two feet square. "What do you call an unpainted area that your painter missed?" Katrina had asked me with a mischievous gleam in her eyes.

"I dunno," I'd said.

"A vacation spot," she said with a grin, "because that's where your painter quit working. Eddie is being naughty."

"Um, okay." I was fed up with Eddie. At a critical juncture, he'd run off and left me holding the body bag. Sort of. But complaining to Katrina wasn't an option and it wouldn't be fair.

MJ leaned close and whispered, "I'll take the food inside." She took possession of the bags from Pumpernickel's. With a brisk walk, she left me with Katrina. How could I move this situation along? No one could overhear our conversation, so I asked, "Katrina? Did Eddie mention that we were both at the Morrison home? We found Mrs. Morrison's body. I was busy calling 911 when Eddie split. I'm not too happy with him. He left me to face the cops all by myself."

She screwed up her mouth. "Join the club. I'm ticked off with him, too." Setting down her paintbrush, she said, "Yeah, he told me about Mrs. Morrison. I was not happy. That's probably why he stayed home with a headache today. Last night, after he told me, I went all Jersey on him. First, he loaned the woman that ladder, and next he goes by himself to get it back. I specifically warned him not to do that. She was not a nice person. You know how you get a vibe? She set my spider senses tingling. I could tell she was not the type of woman a man should approach by his lonesome. A person like that always takes things the wrong way. I warned him. He came home with his paintbrush tucked between his legs. Look, let me put away this can of paint so we can talk."

"Sure." I motioned to the back of the building where we could sit on the parked cars. The sun had moved, granting us a bit of shade. Being away from the rays beating down guaranteed we would be a tad bit cooler. Not much, but some.

Katrina rolled her shoulder muscles to loosen up. Reaching above her head all day had to be tiring. I waited. When she'd finished stretching, she turned to me and said, "Eddie has a heart of gold. He can't say no. That's why we make a good team. Up in Jersey, you learn that people can be sneaky. You've got to tell it like it is, or people will walk all over you. You know what I told you? We keep losing our tall ladders because Eddie allows people to 'borrow' them." She put quotation marks around the word "borrow." She continued, "Do you have any idea how much a good aluminum ladder costs?"

"Not a clue." Using the building's back wall as a prop, I pressed the soles of my feet against the bricks. That kept me from sliding off the front hood of my Camry. Katrina leaned her back against the same wall. The relaxed postures made us both feel comfortable.

"Cheap ones are a couple hundred bucks. Good ones can cost up to a grand. Average ones are five hundred. We lose a ladder, and that wipes out our profit on a job. But Eddie can't say no. Even though people don't bring them back or don't return them in a timely manner. It makes a big hassle for us. He knew I was already upset about him letting Mrs. Morrison sweet-talk him. She promised she'd get the ladder back within 24 hours, but it'd been two weeks."

"That's a long time. Especially when your business depends on a piece of equipment," I said.

"You've got that right. I was angry enough after he told me he'd loaned it out that I had to take a walk and cool down. I wanted to shout at him. Ever hear the definition of insanity? Doing the same thing over and over and expecting different results? I told Eddie he was out of his mind. That was before we heard how she'd stiffed you. He likes you a lot, Cara. So do I. Knowing that Mrs. Morrison practically took money out of your wallet made us both furious. I could tell that Eddie was agitated. I warned him, 'Do not under any circumstances go to that woman's house!' But he moped around. I can always tell when he's depressed, and he was miserable, feeling he'd make a mistake and couldn't correct it. Finally, while I was taking a nap, he decided to sneak over to Mrs. Morrison's house and beg for the ladder. He knew I'd be furious. When I woke up, he was sitting on the end of the bed and shaking. His face was as white as the bedsheets. He didn't want to tell me what had happened, but I refused to let it go. Finally, he told me that he had noticed the dog was without water. You know Eddie. He loves animals. Like you, he walked all around the outside of the house, trying to find a bowl. Eventually, he found the back door to the house was unlocked. He figured he could slip in, grab a bowl, fill it with water, and sneak back out. As he searched for something suitable in the cabinets, he couldn't figure how come there wasn't a dog bowl anywhere. After all, we have one dog and several bowls for Chloe. How come Mrs. Morrison didn't even have one?"

I stayed perfectly still, balanced as I was on my car hood. What would Katrina say next? Would she confess to me that

Eddie lost his temper and struck out at Mrs. Morrison? Lord above, I hoped not.

"Eddie told me that he kept trying to find a bowl and got more and more frustrated. He figured maybe Mrs. Morrison crated her dog. So he walked out of the kitchen. That's when he heard a gurgle, a sound like water running. He followed the noise and found Mrs. Morrison, lying on her back and dying. That noise had been her last breath, I guess. He could see her brains splashed on the carpet. No way could she have survived. Anyone else would have called 911 or hightailed it. But Eddie's been through a lot that he doesn't talk about. I think he has PTSD, although he'd never admit it. I figure he had an episode when he saw her. He simply froze in place. If you hadn't arrived on the scene, he might still be there, staring at her body. Now you know all of it."

The silence between us felt like compassion. Katrina was clearly distressed. I felt awful, too. Dan and I had talked about PTSD. When he first slept over, he warned me, "Never shake a soldier awake. Always touch his foot lightly." While I didn't know if Eddie had been in the military, that didn't matter. You didn't need to be in the service to suffer PTSD. I'd seen Dan go dark twice, but that had been more than enough. I would never forget how he'd fled his body and gone to a nightmare place. It was spooky and painful for both of us.

Katrina was being honest with me. She'd told me why Eddie had bolted.

I patted her shoulder. "Thanks for sharing this. I am sorry he was in that situation. It's a shame we're both caught up in this. I'm assuming he grabbed the ladder before he left?"

She chuckled. A mischievous glint lit up her eyes. "You bet he did."

I couldn't help but smile. Good on Eddie. At least one of us had gotten what we'd come for. I said, "I also assume the police don't suspect him?"

"We hope not. Eddie didn't touch anything but the kitchen cabinet handles."

"I'm glad to hear that," I said.

"Okay," Katrina said, "back to work. By the way, who's that guy who's been hanging around? A friend of yours? Or is it someone casing the joint?"

"If he's casing the store, he's going to be disappointed. The only items of real value were the Highwaymen paintings. If he knows where they are, I wish he'd tell me!"

The minute I walked through the front door, Honora buttonholed me. "I'm glad you're back," said Honora, guiding me by my elbow. "The chairperson for the Jupiter Medical Christmas in July fundraiser called. She's still hoping for a donation. I told her you'd been busy, but that I'd jog your memory."

A fresh panic engulfed me. "Crud. I'd told them I might be able to come up with a Highwaymen painting. I figured that Irving and I could divide the cost. What am I going to do?"

"You are going to track down Irving." Honora gave me a calm smile as she folded her hands over her waist. "Meanwhile, why don't we offer them one of my miniature scenes? It won't bring as much as a landscape would, but it would be good publicity."

"What would I do without you?" I hugged her. "Since you've solved one problem, care to take a swing at another? How am I going to track down Irving?"

Honora cocked her head in a manner that reminded me of a robin eyeing a worm. "Cara, darling. You signed a legal agreement with Irving, didn't you? Have you contacted your lawyer?"

That was an excellent suggestion. If hadn't been so rattled, I would have thought of it myself. After all, that's exactly why I'd paid the lawyer to write up a contract. I reached in my pocket for my iPhone, but I didn't get to make the call at that moment, because four customers streamed in through the front door, and they needed help.

When I had a break, I called Allison Edwards, my attorney. Allison looks like a high school girl with her strawberry blond hair and sunny smile. But those youthful features hide a brain like a huge computer. She's smart, tough, and fair. She listened to my complaint about the Highwaymen paintings and said, "I don't even need to look up the contract. This is exactly why we drew up an agreement with Irving. He can't do this. Not without proper notice. Not without reimbursing you for the substantial improvements you made to your store. You bent over backward to build an environment that would safeguard those paintings. Furthermore, we've documented the time you spent to list the artwork on your website. That's a cost he'll need to reimburse you for, if he is committed to this course of action. Do you want me to start proceedings? I can, but it's always best for you to talk to him first. Remind him of his obligations."

"I'll talk to him." I leaned back in the office chair and groaned. "If I can find him."

When the call ended, Honora knocked on my door.

"Hey, Honora. What is it?"

"You're familiar with the saying, Follow the money? I decided you should follow the movers to find out where they took the paintings. Here's the number for Hercules Movers," she said and smiled at me. "See? An old dog like me can learn new tricks. I goo-gooed Hercules Movers to get their phone and address. I've never used Goo-goo before."

"Well done," I said. I didn't bother to tell her I already had their number. Nor did I want to correct her about Googling. What did it matter? Instead, I stood up and grabbed my purse.

Suddenly, I needed fresh air. The walls were closing in on me. "Can you and MJ watch the store? Rather than phone the moving company, I think I'll pay them a visit."

"Yes, we can mind the store," said Honora. "I have plenty to do. I'm stapling together the handouts for my fireworks stall. Skye comes in at two. She can help me if we have customers."

"That's right. Of course, you need to work on your stall kits. Your Independence Day classes are only a week away."

"I have a countdown on my phone." Honora beamed with pride.

If only I was as organized as she was.

Once the address for Hercules Movers came up in my phone's GPS, I could let my mind wander. It was pleasant to follow the directions as spoken in a plummy British voice. My son Tommy had programmed the Brit into my phone as a bit of a joke. He'd teased me about following the royal family. When I protested that I wasn't really interested in them, he listed all the times he'd seen me reading articles about the royals. Faced with the evidence, I had to admit I was a fan girl, although a part of me knows better than indulge in such nonsense. But what's life for, if not a bit of fluff now and again?

In short order, I found myself on State Road A1A, meandering along the coastline and pointed toward the Town of St. Lucie Village. Once I reached the downtown, emotion hit me hard. Tears welled up. I was nearly forced to pull over and find a parking space. Dan and I had spent many pleasant afternoons wandering through the shops that featured local artisans. A favorite activity was dawdling over the Louisiana-style cuisine in the outdoor seating area of a funky little restaurant. After eating, we'd meandered along at a leisurely pace, enjoying each other's company. Remembrance caused a sharp ache in my chest. I could barely catch my breath. Once again, I pinched my upper thigh. This was entirely the wrong time for a panic attack. I told myself sternly that I was on a mission. The upshot of this trip could determine whether or not my store stayed open. I had to track down Irving and get the paintings back. Time to focus and rehearse what I would say.

My GPS told me, "Your destination is on your right." An egg-yolk yellow awning announced I had found Hercules Moving. A squat concrete building sat surrounded by a cyclone fence. The mesh started at each end and made a large rectangle, enclosing several warehouses. Metal signs with warnings about guard dogs and security cameras dotted the crisscrossed wires. I took that to mean Hercules Moving was a provider of storage as well as packing and transport services. Surely, Irving didn't store those valuable paintings in one of these buildings!

I turned my attention to what I figured was the office, as designated by plate glass door and windows spanning the front of the building. Signage indicated that the business was open, but when I walked in, I found the place to be empty except for a desk, an office chair, and two folding chairs. The floor was a tired linoleum, manufactured to look like white tiles.

Not again, I muttered to myself. Was I about to stumble over yet another dead body like I'd done with Mrs. Morrison? I sure hoped not. "Hello?" I called out. My heart raced as I waited for a response.

The brisk click of footsteps came as a relief. They heralded the arrival of a young woman, probably in her late twenties, who headed toward an empty metal desk. Like most girls that age, she wore tons of heavy eye makeup. Her arms displayed "sleeves," tattoos that covered her skin from the wrists to the shoulders. Confession: Until I moved to Florida, I'd never seen so many tattoos in my life! They're as ubiquitous here as flipflops. Because it's rarely cold here, a person can display the inkers' art all year 'round. Still, I flash back to my father and his refusal to hire someone with tatts. He thought they signified gang affiliations or time in jail. He'd have to change his mind if he opened a restaurant down here.

"Help you?" The young woman spoke in an abbreviated style. She took a place behind the desk and rocked back in the office chair. Instead of giving her gravitas, the setting made her look childish. Given that she smelled of strawberries and vanilla, I revised her age downward.

"I'm here to speak to the owner. I don't know his name."

"Salespeople have to make appointments." She managed to look both curious and slightly bored at the same time.

"I'm not a salesperson. I need specific information about a move that you did."

She moved a piece of gum from one side of her mouth to the other. I hoped she didn't drop it onto her lap. "How come you're here?"

I guess they didn't cover this in Business School 101.

"Like I said, I need to know about a particular move. Your crew crated a bunch of paintings and took them out of my store."

After a languorous chew, she perked up. "Yeah. You own that treasures place?"

"The Treasure Chest."

"Yeah, but you didn't pay for the move."

"No, I didn't. That's the problem. I need to track down the person who did pay for it." Seeing how skeptical she looked, I recognized this as a time for fancy footwork. What could I say to convince her to give me the information I needed? I suspected I'd need to bamboozle her, and I hated myself for even giving that idea consideration. But I had to do something and I had to do it right away.

"See, when the workers crated the paintings, they boxed up two that belonged to one of our customers by a mistake. We were simply storing them for the MacDonalds." I'd said MacDonalds because I was getting hungry. As I finished, my stomach rumbled. Belatedly, I realized I hadn't eaten my tuna fish salad sandwich.

"You sure about that?" The girl lifted an eyebrow at me, trying to be both polite and skeptical.

"Pretty sure. That's why I'm here. I figured I could peep into the crates and find out if the pictures are there. That would save everyone a lot of fuss and bother."

"Uh-huh." She looked skeptical, but she was warming up.

"Right. I'd hate to be wrong. I mean, I want this not to be a big deal. If the insurance companies get involved, they'll phone lawyers, and it'll all get messy fast. It could impact your reputation, and that would be awful."

Her shoulders had been up around her ears. Slowly, as I talked and feigned helplessness, they returned to a normal posture. She repeated herself, "You own that cute little place? The Treasure Shop?"

"The Treasure Chest," I corrected her again. "Yes. It belongs to me and the bank."

"Okay, all right. I can't give out information on our customers. Big no-no. But I can go and get Hercules. He might help you out."

"There really is a Hercules?" I winced. Who named her kid Hercules? Actually, I had a friend back in St. Louis who gave her sons funny names. All three would need therapy when they got older.

"Yeah, there really is a Hercules. I'll go and get him. You can take a seat." She disappeared through a door marked "Employees Only."

CHAPTER 11

The folding chairs did not look comfortable. I'd been driving for forty minutes, so I chose to remain standing. My back was to the door when it swung open, but I heard the squeak of hinges. I whirled around to face the most muscular man I'd ever seen. His upper arms were the size of Honey Baked Hams. He wore his dark brown hair in a military buzz cut that accented his lean features. His jaw could have cut ice, it was that strong. His eyes were steel gray, the same color as the fencing outside, and his skin was a deep tan.

"Sandy says you want information." He didn't introduce himself. He crossed those huge arms over his chest and took a position called parade rest. If he was trying to glare at me and look menacing, he'd certainly succeeded.

I swallowed hard and stuttered, "Y-y-yes, please. Your crew came to my store last week. They crated up a lot of art and hauled it away. I'd like to know where those pictures went."

"Can't tell you that." His voice was cold, but not threatening. Just flat, like this was a boring recitation that he'd made a million times or more.

I tried again. "Those paintings meant a lot to my business. They're the property of Irving Feldman. Irving's attorney showed me a letter demanding that they be returned."

"And your point is?" Muscle Man raised a dark eyebrow.

"I need to get in touch with Irving. He sprang this on me, and it isn't fair." Slowly, my temper was rising. Why was I being put through this? Why hadn't Irving been an adult and talked to me. I continued, "I have a legal agreement with Irving, and he didn't even have the courtesy to call me in advance. Instead, he hired your minions, and he sent his lawyer, a little chipmunk of a man, to present me with paperwork."

"A chipmunk?"

"A chipmunk. Fat cheeks, and a wide skunk-like stripe down his back because he's a coward."

"So not a chipmunk. More like a skunk. Maybe it was a badger," he said, keeping his face perfectly straight.

"Or a squirrel or a snake. Point being, I deserved a call from Irving. We've sold thirty-two of his mother's paintings, and he should have given me a heads up. Instead, he sent his minion to my store with a legal document. Then your goons showed up—"

"Goons? I thought we were minions."

"Whatever. Point being, this is not the way a business person operates. This is causing me all sorts of grief—and now Irving has disappeared, darn it," I knew I was babbling like I'd taken an Adderall, but I couldn't help myself. I kept going, "I've known Irving since we were kids, and I always stood up for him, and this is how he repays me? He scuttles off in the night like a thief?"

"How can he be a thief if those were his paintings to begin with?"

"I said 'like a thief.' That's a simile or a metaphor, I forget which. Again, I'm making a point. I can't find Irving, and I want an explanation and I won't leave until you give me his contact information!"

Muscle Man had gone from amused to peeved. A clock ticked somewhere, measuring the silence as he worked his jaw. Finally, he said, "Is that your car out there? The black Camry?"

"Yes."

"Would you prefer for me to escort you or would you like to leave under your own power?"

Now I was smoking hot. How dare he throw me out of his business! The gall of the man! I nearly spat out the words, "Make me!"

"Yes, ma'am. That I can do," and he threw me over his shoulder faster than I could blink. One minute I was standing on the fake tile floor and glaring at him. The next I was looking at the world from an unusual vantage point as each step bounced me up and down. He moved with unusual grace, out the door and into the parking lot. He set my feet on the ground gently and held out his hand. "Keys?"

I was flustered. I handed them over. He unlocked my driver's side door and froze. "My stars. Is that what I think it is?" He stuck his head inside my car. When he moved out, he turned to me with an expression I couldn't read. His eyes were soft and his shoulders slumped. "That medal? The mariner's cross? Where did you get it?"

I sniffled. *I would not cry, I would not cry, I would not cry.* "From a friend."

"That friend wouldn't happen to have been Dan Pateman, would it?"

I didn't trust myself to speak. Instead, I nodded.

"You're Cara Mia. His lady. Aren't you?"

I nodded.

Hercules led me gently back the way we'd come. Sandy had resumed her place behind the desk. I could see her surprise. After being unceremoniously carried away, Hercules had shepherded me with all the gentleness of a nurse toward a patient.

"Sandy? Hold all calls. I don't want to be disturbed," he barked and pointed me toward the swinging door.

His office proved a surprising treat. On one wall was a mounted rack of antlers, too big and too thick to belong to deer. Behind his utilitarian desk was a map of the Middle East, dotted with red-headed pins. A tall bookshelf was packed with thick hardbacks, classic literature to law texts. In a convenient corner sat a small refrigerator. Once he'd escorted me to a comfortable leather club chair, he opened the fridge and withdrew two cans of Diet Dr Pepper. Seeing Kiki Lowenstein's favorite beverage, I hiccupped, swallowing down a sob. Life was conspiring to breach my carefully constructed wall of strength, to sabotage my efforts to stay in control, and to move past the problems confronting me. In short, I was a basket case.

Hercules popped open a can and handed it to me. "Sorry. This is all I drink. You might want something else. Can I have Sandy brew you coffee?"

"No."

He rubbed his hand across his mouth. His face was dark with concern. Whereas before, he'd seemed like a total hard dude, now he was flummoxed. He sank into his desk chair and stared at me, unsure what to do next.

After a few sips of the cola, I said, "You knew Dan?"

"Heck, yeah. He and I were good buddies. Did missions together. That's how I heard your name. He spoke of you often. Man, oh, man. He sure loved you."

That caused all sorts of emotions. I finally regained control and said, "We fought. That last time I saw him, we had a bad fight. It was awful. I can't believe we were upset with each other when he left."

The cause had been Covid. Dan was leaving on a mission, one of those secret jaunts that took him away and brought him back with a new set of nightmares. This, he had told me, was his duty. Our country had given him a set of skills second-to-none. Of course, he couldn't share where he was going or what he'd be doing. All I knew was that he would lead other men in a high-risk venture. They would fly somewhere, bunk up together, plan their course of action, and hopefully, survive by relying on each other.

The problem was that I wanted him to wear a mask. We didn't know much about Covid back then. Certainly, we didn't know enough. The Jupiter Island newsletter shared statistics weekly, tracking the number of residents who'd been diagnosed, and those who died. At the store, we'd gone almost entirely to online sales. Yes, we still opened our doors, but only to three customers at a time and only those who wore the approved N-95 masks. In my heart of hearts, I doubted these precautions made much difference, but I couldn't risk Honora or Bippy or Poppy or even Nick catching the virus because of my business. To safeguard his aging mother and his young son, Lou moved back into his trailer, his home during his bachelor days. Although Skye understood his reasoning, she hated being parted from him.

I counted myself lucky because Dan was able to teach remotely. I wore a mask when my turn came to open the store. Since Dan taught history, he was able to relate this pandemic to other similar scourges in the past. Having so much time together was actually delightful, although I worried a lot about my grandfather. But Poppy was more than happy to stay home and have food delivered from Publix. He'd recently acquired a wreck of an Alfa Romeo, and he'd decided to take the antique auto apart, disassembling every inch and rebuilding the sportscar.

Dan's orders to leave came as a shock. Never having been a military wife, I wasn't used to a quick summons from on high. We'd been drinking coffee on my deck and enjoying the lapping of the surf just beyond my lawn when his phone rang, the one he never used for personal calls. Taking his mug with him, he went inside while I sat with Jack and Gerard. Jack had lost weight, and for a dog that clocked in at two pounds, that was bad news. Pete had warned me Jack was headed for the Rainbow Bridge. "What should I do?" I had asked.

Pete reminded me that animals don't think ahead like we do. It wasn't like Jack was contemplating his mortality. Pete said, "Jack won't understand it if you're sad. Try to live in the moment, as he does."

Dan and I decided we'd spend as much time with Jack as possible, taking the little Chihuahua for as many rides as we could because next to me, he loved car rides most of all. This from a dog who'd been tossed out of a truck! Crazy.

Jack's condition was foremost on my mind, not the substance of Dan's phone call. In fact, I barely noticed that his absence was prolonged while I sat there on the deck. I figured Dan had slipped into the bathroom or taken out a steak to defrost. Blissfully, I'd fallen into the trap of thinking that our lives were continuing as normal. A new normal, but a normal at last. Looking back, I would divide my life into then and now. The call Dan had answered would rock my world. The reason he hadn't come directly back to join me on the deck was the immediacy of the request. He'd gone to grab his go-bag, tossing in a paperback and a new tube of toothpaste. When Dan reappeared next to me, canvas tote in hand, it felt like a fist slammed into my stomach, knocking all the wind from my lungs.

Maybe that's why I fought with him so angrily, demanding a promise that he would mask up. Maybe my nasty attitude explains why he was entirely dismissive of my request. Maybe, if we'd had more time to work through his hasty departure, we would have regained our common ground.

Instead, he told me haughtily, "Cara, that's not how this works. My men have to be able to see my face."

"You can take it off when you need to, but at least you should wear it when you're in close quarters," I'd countered.

He'd given me a disgusted huff of dismissal. That stoked my fury. "You don't get it, Cara. These are macho guys. I can't show up wearing a mask! They wouldn't have any respect for me."

"You're suggesting that they aren't very smart?"

"They're the finest soldiers I've ever had the privilege to know," he snapped, pivoted, and stomped away.

That's how he left.

Two weeks later, he was dead.

Since I wasn't his wife, I didn't even learn of his passing through official channels. Instead, my phone lit up with a text from his stepson, Gavin. Never much of a communicator, Gavin simply wrote: *Dad died of Covid while on a mission. Mom and I will bury him. She doesn't want you to come.*

Now, sitting in an office in Port St. Lucie, I told Hercules my story. He scrubbed and scrubbed at his face until the skin was rash-red. When I finished, he let the silence build. Finally, he said, "Doesn't matter one bit. Not one little bit. He loved you. He wanted to marry you from the get-go. That witch Sonya kept him hopping. She promised he'd never see Gavin again if you two made it legal. I kept reminding him Gavin was old enough to make up his own mind. But man, that Sonya could be devious. She could really twist that kid around her finger, and Dan knew it. She was a piece of work."

I had understood Dan's dilemma, and I'd consoled myself with the fact we didn't need a ceremony. He was my life partner, until he wasn't. We would have married, despite Sonya's threats, but Covid had made a celebration nearly impossible, and we wanted a real party. In that way, Sonya actually had managed to thwart us. In the end, she got her wish. She was accorded the courtesy of a widow, despite their divorce. Dan had never bothered to remove her name from his papers. He'd hoped his military benefits would go to Gavin, helping the boy with his education. I heard through my son, who had befriended Gavin, that Sonya had other ideas. She figured Dan owed her the money, and she spent it without concern for son.

"I hate to switch the subject, but why don't you tell me more about what brought you here? Maybe there's a way I can help," said Hercules. He'd started on his second Diet Dr Pepper.

I explained what had happened with Irving, how he hadn't given me advance notice, and how we had a legal agreement. "But without any way to contact him, there's nothing I can do. Like I said, I've known him for decades. He's never been a tower of strength. I have a hunch that when I talk to him, he'll change his mind. In fact, I'd bet money he's done this in response to lies he's been told or..." I stopped. There might be one other reason Irving had removed the paintings. Perhaps MJ had been right. Maybe Irving knew about the fake landscapes. Could it be he thought we were the ones copying and authenticating the phony paintings? Yes, that was entirely possible. That was exactly the way that Irving's mind worked. He could have easily been convinced we were the culprits. Given that MJ had once been accused of stealing Essie's collection, Irving would have found it easy to pin the blame on my friend, given that something similar had happened before.

Hercules folded his hands and rested them on his desk. "I met Irving Feldman only once, when he came to check us out. I'm pretty good at reading people, and he didn't tip the scales as being someone with a lot of character. I can't, in good conscience, hand his address over to you. But I could drive you there."

This was totally unexpected.

I said, "Yes, please."

CHAPTER 12

Hercules opened the car door of his Tesla for me. I was amazed by the comfort and quiet. I'd never ridden in one, and I was amazed by the comfort and quiet. We took a couple of back roads, gliding past scenery that must have inspired the Highwaymen painters. Herk, as he suggested I call him, was a thoughtful driver, never jerking me about and solicitous of my comfort. Classical music played quietly, another surprise in a day full of them.

Herk asked how I'd come into possession of the Highwaymen paintings. I explained about coming to Florida as a kid, renting the apartment above The Treasure Chest, getting to know Essie, and learning about the artists directly from her. Back then, there'd only been one big apartment upstairs. Now the space boasted twin apartments, occupied by Bippy and the Murray family.

When we pulled into a subdivision outside of Port St. Lucie, Herk nodded at a modest white ranch house. A flattened stack of cardboard boxes rested on the curb, signaling the occupant had done a lot of unpacking. Herk said, "That's where Irving lives. At least, it's the address where we delivered his furniture."

"Can you wait while I go and talk to him? Or should I come back later alone? I think I can find it again."

Herk rubbed his chin. "Let's compromise. I'll drive around. You can text me when you decide to leave. How about if we meet at the corner so Irving doesn't see my car? It's not my style to squeal like this, but I'm doing this for Dan, okay?"

"For Dan," I repeated.

"Yeah, and I have to admit, this stunt that Irving pulled was low. I don't like how he handled things."

"Got it."

The front door of the white ranch house had a Fourth of July wreath on it, a rather tired and tatty piece. I knocked and no one answered. I knocked again.

"What?" Irving yanked the door open and stared at me. "Oh, you."

"Yes, oh, me. We need to talk."

In the background, Irving's wife sang out, "Cara! How good to see you."

That was all the opening I needed.

"Let me get this straight. Irving believes you are copying paintings and selling them? Why would you do that?" Herk's Tesla glided to a stop. He'd volunteered to run us through a drive-up window to get something to eat. It was nearly five o'clock and I was famished.

"I have no idea. It doesn't make sense. A scheme like that would undercut my prices, ruin my reputation, and be pointless," I said. "Is there a Chick-fil-A nearby? I love their peach milkshakes, and I skipped lunch."

Tapping the navigation button on his computer screen, Herk found a Chick-fil-A five miles from our location. Worked for me.

"Were you able to convince Irving that he was wrong?"

"Nope."

"What are you planning to do?"

"Track down the source of the fake paintings. That's all I can do. Irving dug in his heels. He says he got an anonymous tip that I was selling fakes to undercut his prices. Like I'd do that! Of course, he wouldn't tell me more about the tipster, and he didn't bother to make the sneaky piece of dog poop prove the accusation. This is the sort of nonsense that would have driven Essie wild. Irving certainly didn't inherit his mother's brains."

"How can I help?" Herk turned gray eyes on me. They had warmed from steel to slate. Good, I thought.

I hesitated. "Are you serious?"

"Yeah. I've got this Superman complex. Dan teased me about rescuing people all the time. He even called me Supe. Besides, running a moving company is boring."

"Boring?"

"Compared to helping damsels in distress and tracking down forgers, heck yeah. Let's work up a plan."

"I appreciate the help, and I do need to get to the bottom of this, but it might have to wait."

"You got something more important to do? Like what? Wash your hair?" Herk's voice was teasing.

"Like finding a murderer. See, I paid a visit to a customer who stiffed us, but the situation went sideways."

"Sideways? Like how?"

"The customer was dead. She'd been bashed over the head with a statue."

Herk frowned. "No wonder you kept Dan's interest. I can hardly wait to hear what you do in your copious free time."

Herk and I discussed a variety of options for uncovering the source of the forged paintings. In the end, we decided our best strategy was for him to pose as a buyer. He would put out the word that he was in the market for a large Highwaymen landscape. "I can send an email to a few former customers. Most of our residential clients are high net worth individuals with connections. Exactly the type of people who'd buy a Highwaymen painting. Better yet, I'll run an ad or two. There are several neighborhood newsletters online that reach fancy zip codes. Ads are cheap."

Once the seller contacted Herk, I'd go with him to examine the piece.

"It would be better to have MJ look at it," I said. "I'm not an expert."

"You really think that would work? She's pretty well-known for being an authority on their work. I remember seeing her on one of those local TV shows."

"No, you're right. I guess I'd better study her spreadsheet." I explained about the chart she was using to keep current with the market.

"Why not load that information onto your phone? You can pretend you're checking your messages and pull up the spreadsheet?"

We arrived back at his business. Herk hopped out and opened the door of the Tesla for me. Holding out his palm, he said, "Your keys." I handed them over, and he unlocked the driver's side door of the Camry.

It was a small courtesy, but one I'd missed since Dan had gone.

"Excellent idea. I should do both." I slid into the driver's seat and took my keys. "Herk? Thank you. I very much appreciate your help. You're going above and beyond."

"No problem," he said as he slammed the door closed. "A

word of caution: This won't happen overnight. The hardest part of any operation is being patient."

"I understand," I said. I made a mental note to cook a big pan of lasagna for him. My mother always said, "There's no man alive who can resist lasagna. You have my word on that."

Skye was scheduled to work on Wednesday, but she sent me a text message late Tuesday night saying she wasn't feeling well. I shot back that we needed to talk. She responded she would see me in the afternoon on Wednesday, if she felt better. I stared at her message for a long time, debating what to do. Should I force her to talk to me? A surge of desperation rose inside. Why was she avoiding me? A new pain of loss followed. These two emotions nearly crippled me. My fingers twitched, hovering over the keyboard. I considered pressing the point. I could ask her if she wanted to continue to work for me, and with that threat, I could force her to meet with me. But that wasn't my way. I have a temper and I get mad, sure, but I would never hold my position as boss over the heads of my employees. Threatening people wasn't my style. Skye had worked for me before I could even afford an employee. Pulling rank would be petty. Maybe I could corral Bippy and ask her if Skye was feeling better? That would be a sneaky way to check out what Skye was doing. Was my friend purposefully avoiding me? Or was she dealing with a problem of her own?

Skye's absence wouldn't hurt coverage of the store because MJ was scheduled to work all day. Honora had been scheduled as well. I was eager to talk with MJ about my meeting with Irving and about Hercules Vaios, the mover, but I didn't want to leave our discussion to chance. I texted Honora to be sure she'd be available to watch the sales floor. She responded she'd planned to iron out details on the miniature fireworks stall class she was going to teach, but she only expected that chore to take an hour. The rest of her text read: *Sent out another email. Hope to get the class filled.*

Without revenue from the Highwaymen paintings, Honora's contribution would be more important than ever. In fact, her text reminded me of a new item for my "to do" list: *Find a way to immediately increase revenue.*

Although the fluffy little dog seemed to be settling in, I didn't want to chance a disastrous encounter with Gerard or Luna. Better safe than sorry. Joyce the Petsitter would let my fur babies mingle for a while when I was gone and monitor their interactions. However, they seemed to be making friends. While I got dressed and ate a blueberry muffin for breakfast, Bailey and Gerard romped through the house. Occasionally they playfully chased Luna, who responded by sticking her tail in the air and stalking off indignantly. Looking around, I realized what a mess the place was. Oh, well. I didn't have the energy to clean. Getting a cleaning person moved higher on my list of things to do.

Before I left for work, I closed Bailey up in my bedroom. The sweet little dog hopped nimbly onto my bed. Once there, he plopped down on a pile of clean clothes that needed folding. I shook my head at him, but I had to smile. He looked supremely comfortable.

On my way to the store, I phoned Chief McHenry. "Hiya. I'm wondering if I need to return Bailey to someone?"

"Good question. I'll make a note to ask. No one has mentioned the dog. Mrs. Morrison's next-of-kin is a cousin in Miami. We've yet to get instructions from him. Probably has too much on his mind. Is the dog an inconvenience?"

"Not at all. Bailey is fitting in with my pets. I don't mind having him, as he's a sweet boy."

"You're doing me a solid, Cara."

"Speaking of which, are you making any progress?" Realizing that the chief couldn't update me on the case, I added, "Just tell me if I need to make sure my doors are locked at night. Is a killer roaming the island?"

"Cara, you should always lock your doors. You know that. Most criminals are opportunists." He stopped, as if thinking, and then added, "But yes, you do need to be vigilant. We've had reports of a young man, wandering around and peeping in windows. We've stepped up patrols in an attempt to find him."

My stomach twisted. Back in St. Louis, several neighborhoods had been terrorized by a serial rapist who started his crime spree as a Peeping Tom. Friends in the police department told me that this was common. Voyeurs tend to escalate their behavior, moving from looking to doing.

"Thank you for the reminder, Chief. I do lock my doors, but I'll double-check them from now on. Stay safe."

"You, too, Cara."

I put down my cell phone feeling relieved. Our conversation had been incredibly civilized. Maybe Chief McHenry would come to trust me like Chief Fernandez had done.

I had promised Hercules I wouldn't tell anyone that he'd taken me to Irving's new house. If anyone asked, I'd say I'd gotten the information from Irving's lawyer, Mr. Grassley. That attorney was a miserable worm, and I didn't mind throwing him under a moving lawn mower. However, my desire to talk to MJ about my meeting with Irving became imperative. She needed to hear about the plan that Hercules and I concocted to track down the seller of the fake paintings. Once Honora was out on the salesfloor and busy with class preparations, I ushered MJ into my office and closed the door. I reported my efforts to find the paintings, blaming Mr. Grassley for giving up Irving's address. "As I drove to the Feldman's home, I drove right past Hercules Movers," I said, doing my best to sound innocent. MJ's eyes bored holes in me. Could she tell I was lying? I hoped not. "Seeing I was, literally, right there, I decided to talk to the owner of the moving company directly."

A blush was creeping up my neck. I hoped MJ didn't notice. I'm not a good liar.

MJ listened carefully, which was unusual for her as she tends to jump in and interrupt. After I finished, she totally surprised me by saying, "I think there's a way that I can help."

"What do you mean?" I was cautious because MJ wasn't usually this agreeable. She was a "no first" and a "yes later" type of girl.

"Everybody knows that we don't have the paintings anymore."

I must have looked horror-stricken. My face felt hot with shame, like I'd been caught doing something wrong. I've never been slapped, but this must have been what it feels like.

"Oh, come on, Cara. We live in a hotbed of gossip. The Treasure Coast is populated with retirees who have nothing to do but talk about each other all day long. The minute that moving van pulled up out front, tongues started wagging. We should have asked the movers to go around back."

My temper flared. "I would have but things came as a surprise. I was blindsided." Yes, this was a pointed criticism aimed at her keeping secrets from me. If MJ was going to give me grief, I would give it right back with a bow tied to the top.

"Me, too, and I'm not blaming you. I should have thought about how bad everything looked. A crew of beefy guys in Hercules Movers tee shirts parading in and out while carrying custom-made crates? What else could it mean but we lost our famous collection of paintings? Anyway, the point is this, it's common knowledge. Rather than fight it, maybe there's a way we can take advantage of it."

"How?"

"By piggybacking on what Hercules is doing. See, I have a big list of every prospect who's called asking about Highwaymen art, plus a roster of all my previous buyers. What if I send those people an email? I'll tell them we're looking to replenish our stock of Highwaymen paintings, and that we're willing to pay top dollar. I'll ask them to contact me and tell me what they have. As a sweetener, I'll offer to appraise whatever they own so they can update their insurance."

"And then?"

"And then, I'll compare what they own to my list of sold paintings. If they have one of the paintings from our website, but we didn't sell it to them, we'll know they probably bought a fake."

"Can you tell by looking at the painting whether it's a fake or real?"

She gave me one of her MJ looks, a combination of irritation and pity. "Of course I can, but I won't have to. I'll ask to see the authentication. Every authentication letter that I signed has a code on it. I can check it against the list I made."

"You put a code on the authentication letters?"

"I sure did."

"MJ, that was brilliant."

She shrugged but I could tell she was pleased. "They put codes on gift certificates. When I shop at Sephora, they check the code on the gift certificates that Pete's mother gives me. It seemed to me that using a code was a logical way to track what I sign. The code is simple enough. There's a coded date of sale and a coded name of the painter."

"I always knew you were smart, but this is outstanding."

Getting to her feet, she swept her arm to one side and curtseyed. "I get underestimated all the time. That's the price I pay for being beautiful."

I couldn't see any downside to her plan, but I was curious. "What are you going to do if you discover a fake?"

That wiped the big smile off her face. She frowned and said, "I don't know. I'm gonna have to deal with that as it happens." Her expression grew even more cloudy. "Cara? You realize that I've sold a lot of paintings to buyers who live out-of-state."

"Yes." I wondered where she was going with this. Doing a quick mental recap, I reminded myself that we hadn't sold any forged paintings. As far as I was aware, every landscape we'd sold had come from Essie Feldman's collection.

"If the forger has sold fake landscapes to buyers in other states, they've committed a series of felonies. We need to contact the FBI."

"Crud," I said. "I guess we need to make a police report to the local authorities before we call in the big guns."

Her cupid bow lips quirked in a half-smile. "Maybe, maybe not."

I almost rolled my eyes. MJ had a habit of keeping secrets. What was she keeping from me now?

"I wasn't going to bring this up," she began, "but one of my ex-boyfriends is an FBI agent. He works out of their office in Miami."

"Of course!" I threw up my hands. Why hadn't I thought of this before? Before her marriage, MJ jumped around like a flea in a kennel full of dogs. She dated a huge percentage of the men in our area and wound up marrying five of them.

As if reading my mind, she arched an eyebrow at me. "Go ahead. Be jealous. Naturally, I didn't content myself with local talent. Why would I?"

"That's an excellent question," I said. "Actually, it makes sense that you would cast a wide net."

"What a poetic way of suggesting that I got around," she said, batting her thick eyelashes at me.

We both laughed. She added, "I didn't tell Pete about the beaus. Especially those who were exceptionally good-looking like Rafe. Rafe Caruso."

"Rafe as in rake?"

"Ha! Funny, isn't it? Rafe definitely is a rake, a gorgeous Italian whose real first name is Raphael. Both his parents are from Italy, and he's a dreamboat. I'll give him a call."

"Does he know you're happily married?"

"Ah, Cara, you are such a child." MJ gave me another pitying look as she tapped a message into her phone. At this rate, her face might freeze. That's what my mother always warned me would happen. I bit my tongue instead of sharing Mom's advice with MJ. Maybe Mom had been wrong.

"Rafe's currently in Jacksonville, but he'll be driving through Stuart on Friday, and he'll meet us for lunch," MJ said, with an air of triumph. "He can't visit for long. I suggested we meet at Lola's Seafood. It's close, they serve wine, and the food is always good."

Sounded like a plan.

CHAPTER 13

Finally, it looked like we were poised to move forward. I'd done as much as possible to solve the mystery of the forged paintings. But would our efforts yield results? I couldn't be sure, and I didn't want to leave it to chance. On the movie screen in my brain, the projector showed a close-up of a Nancy Drew book titled *The Mystery of the Fake Paintings*. Good old Nancy Drew. She'd influenced an entire generation of amateur sleuths. What a gal! I don't think she gets enough credit for how she changed the world, one reader at a time.

But what should I do next? Hercules had promised to text me with an update later in the week. Maybe I'd have more information to share when we met with Rafe. Or not. Meanwhile, MJ had gone into my office where, with the door closed, she was calling old customers.

As for my next move, I'd have to think on it.

"Done for the day," said Katrina, walking in and wiping wet hands on an apron. "Eddie is doing the clean-up."

I considered popping out to talk to him, but what was the use? Instead, I thanked Katrina and said I'd see her tomorrow.

It was quarter till five when Skye finally came scurrying

down the stairs from her apartment. I'd been lying in wait for her. When she stepped onto the salesfloor, I took her by the elbow. "Whoa," I said, "stop right there."

She turned crimson and glanced around, hoping for a distraction, but I'd warned Honora to leave us alone if Skye and I had the chance to talk. Sure enough, my oldest employee noticed Skye's arrival. Honora nodded, signaling that she wouldn't interrupt us. She hustled over to wait on two customers who were examining wooden pallets painted like American flags.

"There's no escape, Skye. You can't avoid me forever. This is crazy. What is going on?" I maintained my grip on her arm.

She couldn't meet my eyes. Long curling strands of her hair veiled her face. As always, she smelled like freesia, sweetly floral. I had her physically pinned against the stair railing. "Skye? Spit it out. What on earth is going on?"

She pulled her bottom lip over her teeth and chewed the flesh. Her pale skin pinked up from the neck to her cheeks. Still, she said nothing. She kept staring at the tips of her toes.

I leaned close enough to whisper. "As friends, you and I have been through all kinds of problems. I've always had your back and you've had mine. That's what I don't understand. I thought we'd tested our friendship, time and again. Whatever's going on, I need to know. I can't run the store like this. I need your help. I need my friend. I need my coworker. I need my creative person. Where did she go?"

Tears slipped from the corners of her blue eyes and ran down her cheeks. The drops slid off her chin and splashed on the front of her thin cotton top. I waited. I'd said my piece.

"I've been meaning to tell you something, Cara," she said, "but I couldn't. I really couldn't."

"Look it's the end of the day. What do you say you and I have a glass of wine? I've got a really nice bottle of California red back in my office. Let me toss MJ out from behind my desk, and we'll have a chat. Okay?"

"Let me check with Bippy to see if she's okay watching Nick, and I'll meet you there." Using the back of her hands, Skye knocked away the tears.

"Only if you promise not to bail on me," I said. "If necessary, I'll barricade the front door."

A hint of the old Skye came back as she said, "You've got two doors. How are you going to cover both of them?"

"I'll manage."

She went upstairs as I went to my office and told MJ to skedaddle. "Call it a day, MJ. Skye and I need to have a talk," I said.

"It's about time," grumbled MJ. "Keeping her secret is giving me heartburn."

"Thanks heaps," I said sourly.

"I'd say you're welcome, but you're not. This has been a major pain in the *derriére*."

"Tell me you had some success," I said as I tipped my head toward the notepad in front of her. She'd taped a spreadsheet between two pages. Pencil marks were neatly made in boxes.

"Some, maybe. A few people flatly refused to talk and acted suspicious. One man, a guy who bought a major piece, said he wanted to think this over before he told me more. Two others acted offended. I'll talk to more tomorrow. I started with the least likely to cooperate, figuring that I'd polish my pitch on them. But I have run into one problem."

"What is it?"

"These people don't want to talk to me. They regard me as a snoop, which I guess I am, and they don't want to air their dirty laundry in front of my house."

This tired me out. I rested my body against the door jamb. But I couldn't lounge around for long. I walked to my desk drawer, opened it, and found the bottle of red wine and a corkscrew. I opened the wine to let it breathe, making it ready for Skye and me. MJ continued to occupy my chair.

"I'm leaving as soon as I get my hat on," chirped Honora, poking her head in. During the summer, she wears a straw boater that she secures to her hair with hatpins. The hatband ribbon changes to match her outfit and her mood. It's charming and distinctively Honora.

MJ and I bid Honora good evening even though she hadn't left yet. MJ started gathering her paperwork and her purse, while I contemplated what she had said. The bald truth was that I should have realized no one would tell MJ that they'd bought a painting from a fly-by-night dealer rather than working with an expert like her. They'd depended on MJ to educate them and later gone behind her back to buy art from someone else. Under the same circumstances, I would have been embarrassed to talk about my purchase, too.

"What's the solution?" I asked as MJ dropped her phone into her Kate Spade purse.

"Find another person to make the calls."

"Herk is on it. He's running ads in the online newsletters that go to pricey neighborhoods. They should be appearing any time now."

"You need a script so he sounds like a person who knows about Highwaymen art," said MJ. "Otherwise the questions will sound phony."

"I know exactly the right person for the job," said Honora, poking her head back into my office. She has a bad habit of eavesdropping.

"Not EveLynn," I said, thinking of her daughter's inflexibility and lack of social skills.

"Not EveLynn," Honora assured me. "Let me ask this person, and I'll report back tomorrow."

At ten after five, Skye came into my office, wearing a pair of knit harem pants and a tee shirt. She still couldn't look me in the eye. Her face was blotchy from crying. In one hand, she carried a charcuterie plate. "Bippy put this together."

"Bless her," I said. Bippy was a Grecian goddess. That tiny powerhouse could cook like no one I'd ever met, and I come from a family of chefs. In fact, Bippy was so accomplished that my son, Tommy, had spent hours at her side, learning to make various Mediterranean dishes. Since Tommy wants to open his own restaurant one day, this was time well-spent.

The beautifully arranged platter showed off paper-thin slices of cured meat, olives, artichoke hearts, Tom Thumb tomatoes, and an array of cheeses. Under her arm, Skye carried a box of crackers. With the addition of my bottle of wine, a feast was spread before us.

I poured a glass for Skye and one for me. Before she sipped, I made a toast. "To friends," I said.

She brushed away fresh tears before taking a long gulp of wine.

"What is going on?" I asked.

"Well," she said, "you know that I was married before?"

"Uh-huh. And I know the guy was abusive. Right?"

She nodded. "You know that I did time in jail."

"Uh-huh, and I know that had something to do with your first husband. You took the fall for him. He had a record, and you didn't. The prosecutor told you that you'd get probation. The judge decided to make an example of you and send you to jail."

"Right," she said, playing with a cracker. "My first husband is out of jail."

"Oh?" I said. "I didn't know he was in jail. I thought that's why you took the rap."

"I did, but Bucky being Bucky, he only stayed out of trouble for exactly one month. Then he jacked a car, drove it drunk, and smashed into an adult toy store. Luckily, he pulled this stupid stunt around six a.m. and the place was closed. No one was injured."

"When did they release him from jail?"

"Three weeks ago. The notification wasn't processed due to a clerical error, or so they say. Lou only recently heard about Bucky getting out on parole." She nibbled on the edge of the cracker.

"All right. Bucky's out and about, but you're married to a cop. Wouldn't that be a good reason for your ex to steer clear of you?"

"Yes, that's exactly what a sane person would do, but Bucky isn't sane, Cara. He was never an intellectual giant, and after spending time in jail, his brain has been scrambled by all kinds of drugs."

"Drugs? In jail?"

"They're easier to get there than on the outside." Giving up on the cracker, Skye put it on her plate. "Bucky has always had a chip on his shoulder. When we were married, he often accused me of being unfaithful. Once he heard that Lou and I had a baby, Bucky went crazy. He actually phoned me and called me names for having a child with another man. He is determined to make me pay."

"For what?"

"For leaving him. For not staying faithful." This last word she emphasized with air quotes. "Bucky says if I hadn't divorced him, he wouldn't have stolen that car. His story is that he needed a car to talk to a lawyer about how to stop our divorce proceedings. When he couldn't borrow one from a friend, he had no choice but to steal one. According to Bucky, this latest rash of problems is all my fault. Even so, he's told his friends that all will be forgiven if I go back to him."

This was the sort of twisted logic that occurs when a narcissist builds up a head of steam. I'd heard similar nonsensical garbage from my own ex-husband, and while it still had the power to surprise me, I didn't find this narrative hard to believe. When you cast yourself as a victim, you correspondingly need a villain, a person who is persecuting you. For Bucky, that was Skye. She had to be the source of everything gone wrong in his life, otherwise it might be his responsibility. And gee, taking responsibility means taking risks. When you're responsible, you might fail, and that's terrifying. Better to cut to the chase and say, "Yes, I failed but you can't blame me! It wasn't my fault."

"What does this mean in practical terms? What does it look like?"

"It means that you've probably seen Bucky hanging around the store or watching us from across the street."

With a flash, I remembered the slender young man Katrina had spotted walking behind the store. "Is he thin? Built like a pencil?"

"Yes. That's Bucky."

"What can I do to help? What are you doing about being stalked?"

"Lou has talked to an attorney about this. Unfortunately, Bucky's behavior is protected here in the Sunshine State by the First Amendment. The court would be more likely to penalize him for harassment than stalking, and that penalty would be a first-degree misdemeanor. In other words, he could get in more trouble for a series of parking tickets."

"Skye, that can't be right!"

"Oh, but it is. The severity of punishment only changes if Bucky actually harms me." Skye shivered. "To top it off, Bucky is acting the part of a model citizen. He has a steady job. He's working for a pool service company. He delivers chemicals, tests the pH of the water, and cleans the pools. The business owner is happy with him, which means the state considers Bucky a rehabilitation success. That's fine as long as he doesn't hurt Nick or Bippy. I can take whatever Bucky doles out."

"Would it help for me to file a complaint?"

"Not unless you love wasting money on legal fees," she said. "Remember, Lou and I have already paid a top-tier criminal attorney for advice."

I drummed my fingers on the desktop. I'd thought that by talking to Skye I could cross a problem off of my bucket list. Instead, I'd added a new one. Still, there were ways to manage Bucky by staying vigilant. If he crossed a line, even a thin one, I would pounce on the creep. Taking a long, deep breath, I moved to my second question, "Why were you at Mrs. Morrison's house?"

"Because I am stupid and a sucker." Skye raised her chin but her voice trembled. "I've avoided you rather than admit what a dope I've been."

I poured her a second glass of wine. "Back up. I've never thought of you as stupid or a sucker. You're going to have to explain yourself because I'm lost."

Skye bowed her head. Her knuckles turned white as she tightened her grip on the wine glass. Worrying that she might break the stem and cut herself, I got up, reached over, and took her free hand. After what seemed like hours, she squeezed my fingers and looked at me. "Cara? I'd do anything to protect the people I love. Lou, Nick, Bippy, and you."

"I know that."

She gave a sigh that came from the soles of her feet. "After the attorney told Lou that we're basically helpless, and I saw the bill for our visit, my emotions were all over the place. I went from angry to scared to ashamed, and finally, I became determined to find a way out from under Bucky's shadow. That's when he called me. Bucky told me that all he wanted was for us to be friends again. He explained that he'd been incredibly lonely after getting out of jail. I understood that. See, when you're incarcerated, there are people around you all the time, unless you are thrown into solitary confinement. You eat with your elbows touching other inmates. You shower and use the toilet as part of a crowd. All decisions are made for you, and that means you never have to think through a problem on your own. I could see what he meant about loneliness.

"But I knew I needed to keep my distance. Bucky promised on his mother's life that all he wanted was to talk, to clear the air. I told him no way and quit texting me. I blocked his number."

"Good for you," I said.

"In the meantime, MJ got upset about the paintings, and I felt incredibly guilty. I couldn't do anything to help MJ, but getting Mrs. Morrison to pay her bill was my responsibility. I'd put you and Rocky in a tough situation. You said you'd take care of it, but I knew you were going to have your hands full getting back the paintings. I couldn't let things rest. I texted Mrs. Morrison and asked if we could talk. I figured if I groveled, maybe she'd give me a portion of what she owed. She messaged me to say she might be able to meet me on Sunday, early. She had an event to attend in the afternoon."

Skye stopped talking. She swallowed repeatedly. "A text came through Saturday night. Mrs. Morrison agreed to meet me at eight a.m. What a fool I am! It never occurred to me that Bucky might be there, cleaning Mrs. Morrison's pool. Actually, I think he was more like her cabaña boy than a contract laborer. See, Bucky can be quite charming. He's buff after working out in jail. Alicia Morrison would be everything he wanted in a sugar mama, and he could play the part of her young stud. Judging from her tan, she spends a lot of time lounging around her pool.

If she fell asleep in the sun, he would have had total access to her cellphone!"

My hand flew to my mouth. "He lured you to the Morrisons' house!"

"Mrs. Morrison's house. Yes." Hot tears ran down her face. Skye cried so hard that she couldn't catch her breath. She sobbed until she hiccupped. I ran to the refrigerator, grabbed a cold Diet Dr Pepper and passed the can to her. A few swallows later, Skye was back in control.

"Bucky tricked you?" I tried to sound nonjudgmental, but in truth, I wondered how Skye could be so dumb.

"He's been writing me nonstop, begging for us to meet. He swears he only wants to see me. That he wants to talk, and that's all, but I don't believe him."

"How long has this been happening?"

"A year now. He began writing me from jail. He knows how to wear me down."

"What?" Here I thought she was my best friend, but she hadn't shared any of this. I scowled, feeling hurt. "Why didn't you tell me?"

"Because this is my problem. My cross to bear. No one else's."

"Isn't that what friendship is all about? Being there for each other?"

She had the good grace to look embarrassed and another round of tears started. This wasn't the time to have an in-depth discussion about how friendship worked. I shook my head and plastered on a bland expression. "How'd you wind up meeting him at Mrs. Morrison's house?"

"There was a message. I thought it was from her. Like I figured out later, he must have had access to her phone. I was desperate to get you a check from her. Especially because of the problems with the Highwaymen paintings. I know we've lost an important portion of the store's earnings. Then came a text message from Alicia Morrison with the promise of money she owed you. I ignored all the little warning signs because I was too eager to make things right."

"Something made you suspicious?"

"Bucky has dyslexia. The text shared Mrs. Morrison's home address, and two letters of the street name were transposed. That's the sort of problem Bucky always had. A part of me knew better than to go. The other part said this might be my only chance to get you your money. When Sunday morning rolled around, I told Lou I'd forgotten to buy craft supplies for Honora's Independence Day class. I didn't tell him the truth because I didn't want him more involved. If Lou'd known I was going to see Mrs. Morrison on my own, he would have stopped me. He's been in a protective mood ever since we learned Bucky is out on parole. Lou is furious because we weren't warned about Bucky's parole hearing. I hate seeing Lou upset. I figured I could fix this all by myself."

This was a long speech for Skye. Some of this, I already knew. I'd witnessed her tackling problems herself, like finding a person to detail her car and tracking down an errant tax refund. Lou handled such minor snafus without the blink of an eye, while Skye, with her wildly creative brain, found it difficult to stay focused. But she'd learned the hard way that a woman needs to stay independent.

She took a swallow of cola and said, "I should have guessed that Bucky sent the text. But I talked myself into believing it was Mrs. Morrison, justifying my trip to her house. When I got there, a Bentley convertible sat in the driveway. I recognized her car. Since it was the only vehicle, I figured that Mrs. Morrison and I could talk in private. But when I rang the doorbell, I thought I heard two people arguing. Nothing vicious. Only disagreeing in an active way. I figured it was the television."

Skye paused, gathering her thoughts. This was hard for her.

She'd tried to fix a bad situation and only made matters worse. "I was totally determined that I would confront Mrs. Morrison. For once, I had a singular focus."

That made us both smile.

"I considered going home," she continued, "but I figured this might be my one chance. Rather than ring the doorbell a second time and give her a chance to ignore me, I walked around back. There, stretched out on lounge chairs were Bucky and Mrs. Morrison. They both looked very relaxed. Although rain threatened, she was in a bathing suit, and he was in swim trunks. At first, they didn't even see me. Was I sneaking around? You bet, and since I wasn't sure about the cause of the disagreement, I hesitated long enough to watch and listen. They were both holding glasses of champagne. There was an ice bucket with an open bottle of champagne between them. Mrs. Morrison asked Bucky if he'd made his deliveries. I guess she meant dropping off chemicals for the customers. He told her she was being a nag, and she sniped back at him. I've seen Bucky's temper escalate, so I coughed. Mrs. Morrison turned to stare at me and asked, 'What are *you* doing here?' Before I could answer, Bucky said, 'I invited her.' That's when I knew for sure he'd tricked me. I turned and ran to my car. Bucky wasn't far behind but I locked the car doors and drove away. I'm guessing he parked the truck for the pool service in the club's lot. A lot of Jupiter Island residents don't like service vehicles blocking their driveways."

"Do the police believe you?" I asked. "I'm assuming you told them all of this."

Her brows shot up. "You don't?" Her fingers worried the rim of the can.

"I do. I asked because I don't know what they're thinking. Chief McHenry is new to me, and we don't have a history. Are they satisfied with your story? How can I help?"

She chewed on her bottom lip. "You can't. I got myself into

this mess, and I have to dig myself out. I've turned over my phone to the county sheriff's office. They have the technical know-how to read my messages. Since it'll take them a while, Lou got me another phone. I'll give you my new number. Once the forensic analysts trace the text messages to my old phone, they'll see I'm telling the truth. Besides, Mrs. Morrison was found dead inside her house. I didn't go inside, so I couldn't have touched anything. When they finish processing the crime scene, they won't find any physical evidence of my presence. There can't be any."

"What's Bucky doing now?"

"I have no idea."

She was lying. I could see it in the way she avoided my stare. "Skye? What aren't you telling me?"

"Bucky put a note under my windshield wiper yesterday. He did it while my car was parked behind the store. He says that if I don't talk with him, he'll kidnap Nick."

That nearly knocked me off my chair. "He what? Skye, you should have told me sooner. We need to ramp up security in this building."

"Lou's already taking care of that. He has ordered security cameras, one for the stairway, and one for the hall and a couple for the rest of the store. He's also expecting a delivery of panic buttons that he plans to install. The supplies should arrive in the next few days. We were going to ask your permission, but we wanted to wait and show you what the gizmos look like. We didn't want you to approve a pig in a poke."

I waved that away. "Anything to protect Nick. But let me get this straight. Your ex-husband is a felon and a jerk. Now he's threatening your baby? Skye, I'm so sorry. How on earth did a creep like that get out of jail? Isn't he in danger of violating his parole by harassing you?"

"Bucky's father is a Florida Congressman," she said.

CHAPTER 14

That left me gasping for air. Florida politics have gotten crazier and crazier, thanks in large part to gerrymandering. Like politics everywhere in the US, ours have gotten increasingly virulent. The lack of term limits has given our elected officials a sense of entitlement. I could imagine the strings Bucky's father had pulled.

Skye tossed her can into the recycling bin. She dropped her gaze to her hands. She'd been picking at flecks of light pink polish, leaving her manicure a blotchy mess. "I can't be certain, but I imagine that Bucky's dad worked with the parole board to get him out. That's not surprising. In fact, that explains why Bucky turned out like he did. His dad would ignore him, Bucky would misbehave, and his dad would give him attention. When and if they take Bucky in for questioning, you can bet your last dollar he'll be lawyered up. Nothing's too good for daddy's little boy if it keeps the family name out of the papers."

"Great," I said. "Just wonderful."

She turned those pretty blue eyes on me. "Look, Cara, I'm sorry about all of this. Not only are you out the money for the supplies that went to Mrs. Morrison, but you also stumbled into the scene of her murder. That's on me, and I feel miserable about it. You wouldn't have gone to her house if you weren't worried about her bill."

I hugged Skye. "All I care about is you and me. The rest is small potatoes. When you avoided me, I was miserable. Please don't do that again. Tell me if something's going on in your life. What else can we do to protect Nick?"

A bright yellow pickup truck dominated my driveway. I didn't get close enough to read the lettering on the tail gate. Could it belong to Bucky? Was the Ford F-150 his pool service vehicle? Who else could be visiting my house? The hairs rose on the back of my neck. I backed out of my gravel drive and swung over into my neighbor Aurora's brick driveway. I phoned the Jupiter Island Department of Public Safety as I collected the Hamiltons' mail. She and I did that for each other, although she and Bill went away more often than I.

The dispatcher explained that a patrol car was down the block. The cruiser would swing by. If all was well and there was no problem, I could simply wave the police car past. No harm, no foul. But if Bucky was my uninvited visitor, help was at hand. In the meantime, I sat there in Aurora's drive, windows up and doors locked. My mouth went dry. Was it possible that Bucky had shown up at Seaspray? Or was my uninvited guest Mrs. Morrison's murderer?

A rap on my trunk nearly caused me to pee my pants. I looked up to find Hercules standing next to my passenger door. He must have cut through the foliage that separated my house from Aurora's.

He signaled for me to roll down my window. "Nice parking lot. Your place?" he asked.

I nodded. He loped back through the scaevola, crotons, and pothos that ran between my property and the Hamiltons'.

"What are you doing here? How did you know my address?" I asked him as I climbed out of my Camry once I'd pulled into the garage.

A white Jupiter Island police car came up my drive. Two officers jumped out, both with hands on their weapons. "Everything all right, Ms. Delgatto?" asked the older man in uniform.

"False alarm," I said with a friendly wave. "Thanks so much."

Herk watched the cruiser spit gravel as the cops backed out and drove off. "Impressive. Are they always that protective?"

"Yes," I said. "What happened to your Tesla?"

"It's at the office. This is one of my company vehicles. It's good advertising when I drive it around."

He had a point. Navy-blue letters on the doors spelled out Hercules Movers against the egg-yolk yellow background. I should have guessed from the color that the truck belonged to Herk. But I decided to grant myself grace, as I had a lot on my mind.

"I hope you like animals," I said as I turned the key in the door.

"Love them."

Herk walked in behind me. "Dan said your grandfather owned this place. He's selling it to you?"

"Yes." I put down my handbag. "Otherwise, I couldn't afford to live here."

Wandering around, Herk moved to the back windows with their spectacular view of the ocean. "Hmm," he said. He was impressed, but then, Seaspray impresses everyone. This is a calming oasis in a busy world. A psychic friend told me the Hobe Indians must have performed sacred ceremonies here. All who visit mention the incredible sense of calm.

I opened the guest bedroom where I'd been sleeping and

Gerard bounded out. He was delirious with joy, slobbering and pushing his nose into my hand. A double-take confirmed to the yellow dog that I was not alone, and Gerard turned his full attention on Herk. While Herk stroked Gerard's head, I opened the master bedroom. Out galloped Bailey, his plume-like tail bobbing along merrily. Bailey gave me a careful one-over before racing to meet Herk. The big man had sunk onto my sofa where he basked in the enthusiasm ministrations of both canines. Luna was nowhere to be seen, which wasn't surprising. She abhors any display of interest in humans.

"Would you like a drink? I have wine, beer, sparkling water, iced tea, and plain water."

"A beer would be fantastic," said Herk, trying to keep Bailey from licking his face.

I grabbed a Bud Lite for Herk and a can of Spindrift sparkling water for me. After serving my guest, I sat on the armchair across from where Herk and my dogs competed for space on my beige Pottery Barn sofa.

"Sorry to drop in unannounced and scare you," he began, "but I got to thinking about Irving Feldman and how he treated you. I got a little hot under the collar. Rather than stomp around my office, I went to visit him. He wasn't there, but this wife was. She's a nice lady. Smart, too."

I agreed. What Evie saw in Irving was one of life's great mysteries.

"Mrs. Feldman told me the backstory to all of this drama. Seems her husband has become a rabid pickleball player. In fact, he's even taken lessons to improve his game. She says he's really getting good, which means a lot to him because he's never been athletic. They joined a country club with a pickleball court. That's the major reason they moved, to be closer to the club. Irving has been climbing steadily up the rankings ladder, but the other day, he lost to another player. Naturally, Irving was upset. He went into the locker room to sulk. Her words, not mine. While he was there, another club member got in his face and shouted, 'You tried to cheat me!' Turns out, this guy wanted to buy a Highwaymen painting. Someone referred him to Irving. According to Mrs. Feldman, Irving gave the man a business card with his name printed on the front and MJ's name handwritten on the back. This was a predetermined signal that MJ should make the bearer a really good deal. After meeting with MJ, the potential buyer mentioned his planned purchase to yet a third club member. That person said, 'I have a contact that will beat The Treasure Chest's prices.' Sure enough, the guy wound up buying a Highwaymen painting at a steep discount."

I groaned. This was the worst possible scenario, and sadly, it made sense. No wonder Irving had been furious! He'd been embarrassed in front of his new friends.

Herk continued, "Mrs. Feldman explained to me that Irving is convinced you are robbing him. He thinks you substitute fake landscapes for the real ones collected by his mother."

"That explains why Irving hired you to come and clear out his mother's collection," I said, finishing the story for Herk.

"What're you going to do?" asked my guest. Gerard raised his head to stare at Herk.

"Where'd you leave it with Irving?" I asked.

"I strongly encouraged Irving to talk with you. I explained that I met you through a mutual friend, and therefore, I know you're above board. I even went so far as to say that I'd heard your side of the story, and you suspect that someone is copying both the artwork and your expert's certificate of provenance."

"Did she believe you?"

"Yes, she did. Mrs. Feldman is Team Cara all the way. She assured me that she'd even told Irving that he was being a jerk."

I laughed. "Did that convince him to talk to me?"

"Never underestimate the power of a lady over her man. I

suggest you give Irving a few days to think this over," said Herk. Bailey was curled up on his lap while Gerard rested on Herk's feet. "Thanks for the beer, Cara. I'm sure you had a long day. I'll leave you alone."

"I will still need to track down the forger," I said, accompanying Herk to the door. The dogs came bounding outside, hoping they'd get to take an R-I-D-E.

"Right and Irving needs to help you track down that forger. Otherwise, he'll never really believe you're telling him the truth." Herk leaned against his truck. "Tell you what. I'm kinda invested in this. Let me get back in touch with Irving. When he asked me how much I would charge for moving his junk, he acted intimidated by me. I can't imagine why. I was perfectly civil."

I giggled. The giggle turned into a belly laugh that left me gasping for air. "You can't imagine why? Because you're built like the Hulk? And because Irving is such a wuss? Herk, you couldn't be scarier if you breathed fire."

His smile didn't reach his eyes, and I could tell I'd hurt his feelings. "I guess," he muttered.

I hated the fact I'd hurt this nice man. He was taking good care of me, and I'd laughed at him.

"Herk, what are you doing to celebrate the Fourth of July?"

"Boiling hotdogs and surfing channels. Why?"

"How about letting me cook for you? I owe you a nice, home-cooked meal as a thank you for everything you've done. My grandfather will be here, too, so you don't need to feel like it's some sort of a date that I'm roping you into. Say you'll come, please."

He blushed. "Dan bragged about your cooking all of the time. We finally told him to put a sock in it."

"I guarantee that whatever I cook will be better tasting than a dirty sock."

The next day was busier than I'd expected. Customers streamed through the front door. By one in the afternoon, Honora had completely filled her Fourth of July Fireworks Stall class. At two, she and I had the chance to take a break. "Don't forget," said Honora, dunking her tea ball in hot water, "you need to make sure your grandfather's Uncle Sam costume fits."

Poppy had agreed to dress up like the iconic Uncle Sam and stand outside my store on July 2 and 3.

"I'll text him right now," I told Honora.

Poppy was his old grumpy self, but I promised my grandfather I'd take him to Cracker Barrel for dinner after his fitting if we could do it immediately after I got off work. Wearing a costume in July wasn't going to be fun for him, and I'd suspected Poppy had done his best to let this particular obligation slide. My offer to take us to one of his favorite places prompted him to agree we'd meet that evening. Honora was pleased with my progress report on the paintings, but she was horrified when I told her about Bucky's vow to kidnap Nick. "That explains why Bippy hasn't come downstairs to chat for several days," said Honora. "Usually, she puts him down for a nap, turns on the baby monitor, and joins me for a nice little break."

"Skye says Lou has ordered security equipment, and he's going to install cameras and panic buttons throughout the store. Meanwhile, we need to stay alert."

Honora nodded. "A very good idea. We'll be safer after Lou adds those gadgets. In the meantime, I shall carry my hatpin with me at all times."

Believe it or not, that hatpin was a fabulous weapon. "Honora? Do you own an extra hatpin I could borrow?"

"I'll bring one to work with me, one you can keep." Her papery skin felt cool as she patted me on the arm. The scent of lavender enveloped me like a cloud. "Every woman should own one. In fact, why don't I cruise the web to see where I can buy more? The hatpins I have are decades old. We should sell them as personal safety devices."

"You do that." A thought struck me. "Honora? I need a housecleaner. Can you find someone to help me?"

She smiled. "I'll get right on that. Not to worry."

———

On my way to Poppy's house, Honora phoned, "Cara, darling, I am waiting for a call back from a woman who cleans homes. She's not young, but she's very active and lives in Hobe Sound, only a couple of blocks from Jupiter Island. One of her older clients has died, and Connie is looking for work."

"She sounds perfect," I said. I thanked Honora and turned onto the street where my grandfather lives.

"Come on in," Poppy yelled. "It's not locked." Spread in front of him was a table filled with papers and faded photos. He was working on his scrapbooks, large binders filled with photos of his time in the service. "I figured the kids might want to see these pictures. I'll give them a history lesson, while Honora gets her project all set up," he said.

Flipping through pages, he narrated the photos until he got to pictures of himself during the Bay of Pigs. "What an unmitigated disaster. Men were dying left and right. I was on a transport ship, the Houston, as part of the CEF, Cuban Expeditionary Force. Our ship was one of five freighter ships chartered by the CIA and outfitted with anti-aircraft guns. Our mission was to transport about 1,400 troops and armaments near to the invasion beaches. But there were engine failures and damage by unseen coral reefs, reefs that the CIA had originally believed were nothing but seaweed. As a result, the unloading was delayed. On top of that, our landing spot, the Red Beach, was lit with floodlights. We'd run right into a hostile welcoming party. They knew we were coming. Things went from bad to worse. One hundred and eighteen men died. I was lucky to have survived."

I'm always shocked when Poppy talks about his military service. My parents never mentioned it. Maybe that's because Poppy and my mother didn't agree on much, and so my grandfather's personal history continues to be a revelation. As time passed, the two of them communicated less and less. When Mom was diagnosed with cancer, Poppy felt my dad was wrong to push for chemotherapy. As a consequence, my parents and Poppy became estranged.

Since moving down here, I've been forced to reevaluate my grandfather. When I first got here, I thought of him as a crochety old man. He's that, but he's also a war hero, a talented mechanic, and a generous soul. Sitting beside him and staring at the photos of him in uniform, my heart swelled with pride. I threw an arm around Poppy and hugged him while whispering in his ear, "I'm proud of you, old man. I can never say that enough."

"Pshaw," he grunted. Poppy hates expressions of emotion. His stomach growled. "I thought you promised me a visit to Cracker Barrel. Come on, let's get moving."

Over the meal, I told him about Mrs. Morrison.

"Mrs. Morrison was hit in the head with a bust."

"A bust? Like a woman's breasts?"

I snorted. "I wish. We're talking about an abbreviated statue of a man. MJ identified it as a bust of Stalin."

"That's a durn peculiar weapon, and I'm wondering if it had a special meaning to the killer." Poppy took a big bite of his meatloaf. The ketchup dripped off his fork.

I paused while chewing on a green bean. "I never thought of that. The Jupiter Island Department of Public Safety responded to my 911 call. Someone must have thought about the significance of the weapon, right?"

"Jupiter Island would've turned a murder investigation over to the county sheriff's department. I got friends there." My grandfather shoveled in a mouthful of the hash brown casserole we both love. After swallowing, Poppy said, "See here, young 'un, when we get back to my house, let's have a look-see through one of my books on military history. Maybe you can show me a picture of that-there bust. Once you do, I'll make a call over to one of my pals in the county sheriff's office. This-here being a murder investigation, it ain't smart to overlook something like that. People are people, after all. We mess up."

"I don't understand. Why would anyone own a bust of Stalin?"

"A person who came from Russia might revere him. A history buff might like a hoohaw like that," said Poppy.

"You're saying a communist killed Mrs. Morrison?"

"Not necessarily, but could be. Could also be a person with a hankering for old military paraphernalia. You know that outdoor farm market on the way to Stuart? That-there proprietor buys old Army gear. Pays top dollar, too. There's a Russian princess who lives in Palm Beach. I'm guessing she didn't move to Florida by her lonesome. Probably part of an enclave of Russian expats. If'n she had a sense of humor, she might own a bust of Stalin and dress him funny for the holidays. Most people favor gusseying up their statues of flamingos or manatees, but there's no accounting for taste."

CHAPTER 15

Bright and early the next morning, there was a knock on the door. Through the glass panes, I saw Aurora Hamilton, doing a goofy wave, the one she uses to announce her presence. "We're back," she sang out as I opened up.

Waltzing past me, Aurora threw herself down on my sofa. Before I could warn her, Bailey divebombed my neighbor. "Omph," Aurora said, doing her best to hold Bailey at bay. He was intent on delivering French kisses. "What are you doing with Alicia Morrison's dog?"

"Didn't you hear? Guess who found Alicia Morrison's dead body?"

Aurora sat bolt upright. "You have to be kidding! Cara! What is it about you and dead people?"

"Beats me. It's like those dousing sticks they use to find water? The Y-shaped branches from willow trees? My whole body is a dousing stick, but I'm tuned to find corpses. *Corpi.* Whatever."

"Tell me all about it."

While I gathered her mail and tucked it into a plastic bag

from Publix, I explained how Mrs. Morrison had stiffed Rocky and me. "Do you know much about the woman?" I asked.

"Yes and no. Alicia Morrison was a mystery. She didn't grow up here. Came here when she was a teen. Definitely someone who speaks English as a second language. I think she's a Latina."

Aurora alternated between present and past tense. Coming to grips with a death is always hard. My friend's recitation explained the corpse's dark brown eyes and hair. Alicia's skin had been deep mahogany, but tanning is a recreational drug in Florida. I'd figured she was a sun-worshipper. As a Latina, she might have had a head-start.

"Not a surprise," I said.

"Alicia was not exactly popular," said Aurora. "In fact, club members gossiped about her all the time. Bill told me Prescott's first wife was nothing to look at."

Bill was Aurora's husband.

"But Prescott was devoted to her. His friends thought he'd stay a widower for the rest of his life. They were shocked when good old Prescott walked in with an exotic beauty and told everyone that he'd married her. That must have been back in the early 70s. Prescott was teaching at Miami Dade College, when he met Alicia. She might have been a student. I'm not sure. How did you wind up going to her house? Was it the lure of another corpse?"

"Ha, ha, ha. Are you jealous because I found a dead body without you?" I teased. Aurora and I had found a sand-covered corpse while we were together on a golf course.

"Ah, memories," she said with a grin. "If you weren't sniffing out a dead body, why were you at her house?"

"Like I said, she owed us money. Poor Skye took the order. She is beside herself, feeling guilty about not getting a deposit."

Aurora was quiet for a minute. This was unusual. She typically talks a mile a minute. I waited. She said, "I don't like to speak ill of the dead. But I'd heard stories about Alicia. She was always looking for a way to make money or cheat somebody out of it. I played golf with her once. Only once."

"Sounds like there's a story behind that."

"It was a ladies' outing, and eight of us played. We put in money for each hole. At the end, the low scorer would get all the money. I won," and Aurora shot me a rueful smile. She's a killer shark when it comes to golfing. Her name is enshrined on the wall at the Old Head Golf Course in Ireland because she won a tournament there. The fact she'd won this local golf outing was a forgone conclusion. She continued, "All together, I should have collected two hundred bucks. The custom is to pay up when we go for drinks or food. We put away our golf bags and went to the club for lunch. After the first round of drinks, Alicia excused herself to use the bathroom and never came back. It's not the money, Cara. You know I don't care about that. They say golf is a gentleman's game, a game of honor. She proved she has none."

"What was her goal? What are a few bucks to a wealthy widow?"

Aurora gave me a smirk. "Haven't you heard that old saying about the difference between a rich man and a poor one? A poor one will walk a mile to save a dollar and a rich man will walk five miles."

She made a good point.

"Alicia would never, ever have enough money. Prescott left her his house and a small fortune, but she blew through it. Bill and Prescott used to be friends, back when Prescott was married to Mary, the first wife I told you about. Bill says Prescott was upfront with Alicia about his estate before they tied the knot. On his death, the bulk of his money would go to charities, but he set aside plenty for Alicia to live on. A gracious plenty. That wasn't enough for Alicia. After their wedding, she found photos of

Mary, wearing jewelry, her family diamonds. Alicia asked Prescott where the set was and when she could have it? But Mary's collection had gone to an auction house after she passed. In accordance with her wishes, the proceeds were split among various charities. That infuriated Alicia to no end. Bill says she never got over it. In fact, a lot of the club members quit socializing with Prescott and Alicia because once she'd had a few drinks under her belt, she'd start complaining about how unfair it was that she didn't have a diamond as big as the other wives had."

"Is that true? Does everyone have big rocks?" I had never been to a fancy country club function. I wanted to know if Alicia had a good reason to feel slighted.

Aurora waggled her hand back and forth, letting the sunlight glint off her own 13-carat solitaire. "Some have nice pieces, and some don't. It's not a contest. Sure, if you have a small diamond, you might feel a twinge of envy, but is a stone really that important? Is it worth carping at your husband nonstop? Alicia thought it was."

"But skinning local merchants? Isn't that low-life? Okay, all together, she pocketed $1600 between Rocky's bill and mine. Is that worth a reputation?"

"It is to her. Let me give you an example of how she operated. She bought that Bentley convertible of hers, brand new. When it came to getting the first service, which was free, she took it into the dealership. After she picked it up, she drove the convertible home and swore to the manager that one of the mechanics must have smoked in her car. She wanted a lump sum of money in damages or a new car. She raised such a stink that he finally gave in and wrote her a check for several thousand dollars. Cara, I know the service manager. That's where Bill gets his car serviced. None of the workers there smoke. Period. She either made that up or waved a lit cigarette inside her car."

Aurora swung her legs around so they rested on the floor. "The point is, Alicia collected a couple hundred here and a thousand there, and on and on. She's a grifter. When you consider her bad behavior, it's a wonder she wasn't killed a long time ago."

I wanted to know more. I baited Aurora. "Was Prescott like that?"

"Heavens no," said Aurora. "I didn't know him for long, but he was a classy guy. In fact, Bill told me that Prescott was appalled when he discovered his new wife's shenanigans. It must have been like being married to a kleptomaniac, a sick person who keeps stealing and can't help themselves. Prescott gave Alicia an allowance. When he heard about her tricks, he increased the amount, but it was never enough for her. Besides, her deal was the con. She loved taking money from other people. Even though she lived very well and she had everything a woman could want. Poor old Prescott. After being married to a plain woman, he must have thought he was the luckiest guy in the world to have snagged Alicia. But it turned into one of those fairytales where the beautiful princess is wearing a disguise to conceal a creature that is really ugly and disgusting."

"That's awful," I said. I remembered that particular fairytale. I had always found it sad. Bailey heard the distress in my voice. He jumped into my lap, stood on his hind feet, and stared into my eyes. I rubbed his ears.

"Why didn't Prescott divorce Alicia?" I asked.

"He was an Irish Catholic. One of a dying breed, if you'll excuse the pun. Prescott went to his grave believing in faithfulness and keeping his vows and all of that. Sad state of affairs, actually. He wanted to love her. Honest he did."

I walked outside with Aurora. Carrying the bag with her mail, she gave me a hug. "Do you want me to find out more about Alicia Morrison?" she asked.

"Could you? It might be helpful," I said. "Anything you learn would be helpful."

Friday all day, I restocked shelves as Fourth of July merchandise flew out of the store. Fortunately, I'd purchased supplies we could easily upcycle into fun holiday items. We added red, white, and blue stripes to candles. We stenciled "Uncle Sam Wants You" on trays covered with patriotic-themed paper and a thick layer of Mod Podge. Skye made banners out of recycled jeans, featuring the words "Happy 4th!" Bippy had mastered the art of the lacey crocheted top, perfect for wearing as a beach coverup or over a simple tank top for a more modest look. Even MJ had come up with an idea. Using plastic juice bottles, the large quart size, MJ fashioned Uncle Sam lanterns. These were an ingenious example of recycling at its best. With Skye's help, MJ painted on faces. Adding a glittery top hat to the long neck of the bottle, and a quilt batting beard, MJ lit up Sam by dropping a small balloon light into the container. It was so much fun.

What I love about my store is the never-ending flow of creativity. One idea begets another, and on it goes. In the beginning, MJ would never have tried anything remotely crafty, but she's slowly dipped a toe into our handmade waters. Skye has always been interested in making stuff. The first day we met she was wearing her handmade jewelry. But back then, Skye had a huge fear of being laughed at. Also, she didn't have a market for her work, so making things was enjoyable, but it seemed like a waste of time. My store provides encouragement and a financial reward for her efforts. Honora has always been a crafter, but living with EveLynn used to make the situation difficult. EveLynn has to have everything just so. When Honora's workspace gets messy, EveLynn throws a wonky, as the Brits say. Here in the back of the store, Honora is free to do as she pleases. Bippy is a talented needleworker. She loves to crochet, but her work languished without a purpose until I proposed selling her wares.

A few minutes before noon, MJ approached me with a sour look on her face.

"What's up?" I asked.

"Rafe texted me. He had something come up. He can't meet with us."

That was right! We'd planned to eat at Lola's Seafood.

"It's okay," I told her. "We're busy, so maybe this is for the best."

MJ crossed her arms over her chest. "That's exactly why I didn't marry him."

I nearly choked, but I should have known better. MJ is the most frequently engaged woman I've ever known. Or was I extrapolating? Did I misunderstand? I asked, "Did he ask you to marry him?"

"At least a dozen times. But he was forever canceling our dates because he had big cases come up. So irritating!" And she stomped off.

CHAPTER 16

Saturday, the next to last day of June, dawned hot with a weak breeze. The drive to my store seemed to take forever because the narrow roads were clogged with bicyclists. I have nothing against bikes. Scratch that. To be honest, I never used to hate bike riders, but living on the island, I've come to see them as a menace. Despite the many signs forbidding them to ride three abreast, they still do. This makes them impossible to pass. In defiance of the sign telling them to walk their bikes over the bridge, they ride their bicycles. This is dangerous because those skinny racing tires could easily catch in the grates of the drawbridge and pitch the riders headfirst into the path of a car. Don't even get me started about the curve on the south end of the island. It's impossible to see around that bend, and yet, bicycle riders insist on bunching up. Nearly every year, an elderly resident hits and kills a bike rider because the driver didn't see the cyclist until too late.

On my way to work, I ground my teeth in a combination of annoyance and frustration as I waited for the cyclists to move to one side or turn or stop so I could pass safely. Keeping my speed even, I crept along behind them. I keep reminding myself that the riders also have a right to be on the road. As for being late, that was my own fault. I should have left home earlier.

At a stoplight, I drove around the bikers carefully.

One wearing lime-green spandex gave me the finger.

That put me in a foul mood. When I finally made it to The Treasure Chest, I was feeling pressured. Running behind drives me nuts.

My mood worsened when I walked through the store on my way to unlock the front door. Plaster silt had collected in piles all around the store. Skye had texted late last night to say that Lou's attempts to install security cameras had failed. He'd only succeeded in drilling holes in several spots. If she'd known he left a mess, she would have had a cow, a full-grown heifer. Luckily, we had no early customers. I was able to use a microfiber cloth to clear the dusty surfaces.

Honora came in ten minutes late. I assumed that she too had to weave her way around bikers. The weekends are prime time for group rides. Maybe having no customers this morning was a good thing.

The store didn't stay empty for long. Soon we were busy as folks shopped in preparation for their Independence Day celebrations. By noon, we were nearly out of the patriotic-themed soft goods created by EveLynn. Through gritted teeth I called the young woman, bracing myself for a tense interaction. She answered with a curt, "Yes?" The greeting alone was enough to make me yearn to end the call. Instead, I asked if she might be able to make more placemats, cloth napkins, table runners, and other accessories in time for us to sell on July 2 and 3. I carefully avoided asking her to "whip" them up. I'd learned the hard way that she resented any suggestion that her efforts were not labor intensive.

"Yes."

"Yes, you can make them, or yes, you can make them in time for me to sell?"

"Yes to both."

"When could I expect them?" I had to be incredibly specific with EveLynn. If I left anything to chance, the result was invariably unpleasant.

"Will I get a bonus?"

I stifled a groan. Recently, one of her interior designer customers had told EveLynn she was owed a bonus for finishing a rush job. Since then, EveLynn asked me about a bonus whenever I requested unscheduled work.

A thought came to mind. Instead of naming a sum, I should ask EveLynn what she might expect from me.

"A dozen blueberry scones," she said in a perfectly flat voice.

"All right. A dozen blueberry scones it is," I said, feeling I'd gotten off lightly.

"Tell Mom to look in her trunk. She'll find more table sets and other pieces. I put them in a box with your name on it."

Why that little minx! She'd played me. I opened my mouth to protest, but EveLynn beat me to the punch. "Send the scones home with her tonight," she said before ending the call.

I immediately grabbed Honora's keys from the hook where she hangs them, walked outside to her car, and collected the box marked CARA.

I was inventorying the items when Honora stuck her head into the back room. "He's here. It's Skye's ex-husband! I recognized him from a photo. But we're safe. I pushed the new panic button. The police will be here any minute."

Honora looked so proud of herself that it broke my heart to tell her the buttons didn't work. "Um, Lou didn't get them connected. He tried, but he wasn't successful."

"What!?"

Rather than belabor the point, I dialed 911 and asked for immediate assistance. "A stalker is here in my store."

"Sorry, ma'am. We can't do anything unless he threatens you. Has he threatened you personally?"

"No," I said slowly. He had threatened Skye and her son but not me.

"Call us if he does," said the dispatcher before she hung up.

This was a nightmare.

"Honora? Did you remember to bring me a hatpin?"

She shook her head. "I forgot to grab one for you. Here, take mine."

"Phone Skye and Bippy and warn them."

"Skye had a doctor appointment, but Bippy is up there with Nick."

"Okay, call her, please. I don't want Bippy coming downstairs with the baby. Call Skye and warn her so she doesn't walk in on Bucky. Hide in the bathroom and lock the door if you hear a scuffle." Tucking the hatpin between my fingers, I straightened my shoulders and walked out to meet the infamous Bucky.

Only one person stood on our salesfloor. Bucky was thin to the point of looking undernourished. The tattoo of a lightning bolt zigzagged from the corner of one eye to his cheekbone. His light blue eyes were flat and devoid of warmth. As I approached, he shoved his hands into the pockets of his jeans and smirked. His white tee shirt was stretched tightly across his chest, displaying an admirable set of pec muscles. There was a sense of coiled energy, like Luna before she pounces on a lizard. Yet he also had a bizarre sexiness, a cocky attitude that beckoned to the woman in me. In short, I could see why women fell for him.

"Ah-ha," he growled. "The one and only Cara Mia Delgatto. How's it hanging, pretty lady?"

Be strong, I told myself. You need to project an attitude of strength or he'll run over you.

"You must be Bucky. Why are you here?"

Picking up a porcelain platter that had been custom made for us and painted with seashells, he looked at me. His was an expression of pure calculation. He was planning something, but what? My job was to keep him from going upstairs. I could deal with Bucky, but if Bippy was alone, could she? I had to protect her and Nick. I shifted the hatpin in my hand, tucking the glass head between my fingers to expose the long pin. Another time, I'd used a similar hatpin to stop a would-be assailant. I could do it again, if necessary. In fact, if things got ugly, I would put Bucky's eye out. All of the rage I've ever felt roared into action. Adrenaline flooded my body. Fight or flight? *No way.* I would fight and I would win.

Bucky opened his mouth, but I rushed to say, "Get out, Bucky. Turn around and leave. We don't want you here."

He dropped the platter. The crash was ear-splitting. The plate shattered into a handful of pieces. One ricocheted off my bare calf, piercing the skin. That shard landed on the floor two feet away, leaving a trail of blood. I did not look down. I kept my eyes on Bucky. He was counting on me folding like a cheap card table. I refused. If he trashed the store, that was good news. I would ban him, and I would tell the police that he'd threatened me personally. Was it true? Not strictly. Bucky hadn't said as much, but he acted menacing, and that was enough for me. And now he'd drawn blood. I was thankful for the cut. It would serve me well.

A red light strobed the walls of the store. Stripes of garish color moved from spot to spot. A crimson glow reflected off of Bucky's tee shirt.

"Bucky? I think that's your cue. Exit, stage right. If you run fast enough, you might get away. Believe me, I will press charges." My voice was steady. I didn't even glance down at the cut. I was Wonder Woman. I was impervious. I was not about to buckle under Bucky's malicious glare.

"Yeah. Matter of fact, I got a business appointment on the other side of town," he said. "Mind if I use your back door?"

"Not if you hurry," I said and I led the way.

His escape was nearly comical. As I stared after him, his white tee could be seen bouncing up and down. Bucky ran through the alleys of downtown Stuart, Florida. I hoped he would never come back.

I knocked on the bathroom door, and Honora came out. Police radios crackled outside while she swabbed my cut with iodine, an old-fashioned remedy I could cheerfully have done without. Bippy had heard the crash from the safety of her apartment. She phoned Honora, who told her the coast was clear. Nick had slept through everything, but Bippy hurried downstairs to hear about the drama with Bucky. The Stuart police took my statement.

All in all, I'd been lucky to get hurt. The injury convinced the officers that Bucky was a threat to me, Honora, and my store. Skye hurried in from her doctor's appointment and immediately came to where we were gathered. I told her what had happened. Her face turned white. "It's over and done with," I told her. "I've had worse cuts while prepping food. Bucky landed himself in a kettle of hot water."

Skye sank down into a chair, covered her face with her hands and cried softly.

CHAPTER 17

The next day, the dogs and I sat on my deck and listened to the sound of the ocean. Since the store didn't open until noon and two other people were scheduled to work, this was a rare treat. I should stockpile my energy for the upcoming last-minute sales in advance of Independence Day, but I find it hard to sit in one place for long. Bailey encouraged me to stay put because he jumped into my lap and snuggled there comfortably. Gerard curled up at my feet. The blue-green waves rushed toward us in an endless cycle of kinetic energy. As I watched, the white foam caps expanded and broke apart. I closed my eyes and repeated my favorite mantra: *And all will be well, and all will be well, and all will be well.* Slowly, I began to believe that. Somehow things would work out. But how? Would Bucky get thrown back in jail? Would I ever get the paintings back? Would Chief McHenry find Mrs. Morrison's killer?

Honora texted that she had news about the housecleaner. I phoned her to learn more.

"She's the woman I told you about. Her name is Connie, and

she loves animals. She can start on Monday at eight, but you'll have to provide the cleaning products you'd like her to use," Honora explained. "I knew Connie's grandmother, Esmeralda. She raised Connie. The girl was devastated when Esmeralda died. Such a blow! Esmeralda had been ill for a long time, which left Connie with a lot of medical bills. I was so glad when she confirmed that she could come and help you. I feel like I did her grandmother a good turn."

Honora told me the cleaner's hourly rate, which was reasonable. One part of me wanted to beg off more expenditures, as the loss of the Highwaymen paintings was cutting into my revenue. Another part reasoned that without the burden of cleaning house, I could put more energy into the store. That would free me up to create additional income.

Honora offered to swap shifts with me, arriving early on Monday so I could come in after lunch. That way I could meet my new cleaning lady, show her my place, and introduce her to my fur babies. It made sense because we'd be busier after noon than before lunch.

"Honora, you're a treasure. What would I do without you?"

"Cara, I feel the same about you. Did you see we have two customers on the wait list for my classes? MJ told me we should video my class. I think that's a splendid idea. How about it? What do you think?"

"I think that's brilliant. Who can do the recording?"

"I thought I'd see if Bippy could do it. If we record it twice, a good editor can use either day to get the best final product."

Mentally, I calculated how much we could make on the kits for the stall. The profit on the class would be considerable. Selling the video session online would be even better. Once set up, it would join other classes we taught virtually. We could also sell kits that students could buy rather than rounding up their own materials. This was definitely good stuff. I was pleased with Honora's initiative.

Honora covered the phone and talked to somebody else. She came back to me. "Cara? You've been working too hard. Bippy says she'll help us handle things on Monday. You don't need to even come in!"

I started to argue, but Honora put her foot down. I ended the call and felt better than I had in a long, long time. Even if we never sold another Highwaymen painting, my business would survive. The online classes would help me make my nut, my base expenses. During Covid, we'd switched to online sales. After we reopened for walk-in business, I'd turned my attention away from online sales. That had been a mistake. Online sales allowed us to sell every minute of every day in every country in the world. I should have focused on growing our online presence rather than concentrating on our retail location. Honora's classes have always been popular, but so far, they'd centered around the winter holidays. A Fourth of July Fireworks Stall would make a timely addition to our product offering.

"Good news," I told the dogs as I stretched out again and closed my eyes. I must have dozed off because the ringing of the phone startled me. The morning had drifted by. My watch told me it was nearly one.

"Cara? Chief McHenry here. Say, I'm down at Mrs. Morrison's house. An estate agent is here, inventorying Mrs. Morrison's belongings in preparation to auction them off. The agent found something odd. Something you might be able to explain. Are you busy? Can you drive over?"

In front of Mrs. Morrison's house, there were two Jupiter Island police vehicles and a gold Lexus SUV. I surmised that the law enforcement officers had gathered to review whatever it was that the estate agent had found. This show of force seemed a bit excessive to me, given how long they'd had to process the crime scene, but what did I know?

Nada.

Before leaving my place, I'd pulled on a skort, a combination skirt and shorts, plus a knit polo shirt in shades of blue. My skin felt slightly sticky because I'd slathered on sunblock. I did my best to ignore the way my fleshy bits stuck to each other. I should have dusted my body with baby powder. Oh, well. I had obeyed the chief's command to come running. I doubted he would complain or even notice that my skin felt tacky.

The chief stepped out to greet me as I locked my car door. "You can't handle anything," he warned me. "In fact, I'm going to ask you to slip on these booties and keep what you see to yourself. Can you do that?"

"Yes." Curiouser and curiouser, I thought.

After I pulled on the fabric shoes, the chief opened the front door and waved me inside. Someone had used a lot of bleach on the place plus a pine-scented cleanser. This gave the air a one-two punch. The caustic smell nearly knocked me over. I've never cleaned up that much blood, but I bet it's a doozy to erase.

"This way," the chief said as he motioned me forward. In the room where I'd found Mrs. Morrison's body, a small scrum of men had gathered. One was clearly the real estate agent, given that he was wearing a suit and tie. Two uniformed state policemen stood to one side, rigid like sentries. Two other men in white Tyvek moved around with a sense of purpose.

"You can go now." The chief waved to a man wearing a charcoal-striped suit. The civilian had a bronzer glow to his skin, and a haircut that screamed, "I am hip."

"But—" started the agent.

"Go," said the chief. "Please."

A uniformed cop walked the agent out. The other men gathered around one piece of furniture. Their attention focused on an upended armchair with its wooden feet sticking in the air. They looked like the naked legs of a woman when her skirt flies up. One man in a Tyvek coverall snapped photos of the armchair while another took samples. What he was testing, I couldn't tell. But I do know a little about furniture, since we sell it at the store. Usually, the area underneath an upholstered chair would be covered in muslin as a sort of dust cover, but this was bare, exposing its wood struts.

"Go on over there, Cara," the chief urged me, pointing at the chair.

I moved swiftly, compelled by the anticipation that I was privy to something novel. I stopped a foot away and examined the chair bottom. The skirt had fallen away to reveal a wire grid that reminded me of a rack for cooling cookies. The metal rim had been stapled to the armchair's wooden frame. In this odd position, the grid functioned like a shelf, supporting a flat rectangle wrapped in plain newsprint. As a hiding place, this spot was ingenious. When in its normal upright position, the chair's upholstered skirt brushed the floor, hiding this secret compartment. A person would need to tear the furniture apart, quite literally, to discover this alteration.

"Ready?" asked Our Main Man in Tyvek.

The chief and the Other Tyvek Man, who'd been snapping photos, nodded. Our Main Man in Tyvek withdrew the wrapped package before looking to the chief for further instructions.

"Do it," said the chief, in a commanding voice.

The tech tore away the newsprint to reveal a four-sided frame of unfinished wood, the back of a canvas. With great care, the tech flipped the piece over to reveal familiar colors and imagery. My mouth dropped open. For the second time since I'd moved to Florida, I'd witnessed the unveiling of hidden Highwaymen art. This was a whole lot better than stumbling over corpses!

"Looks like a Highwaymen painting," I said. "All of the details are right, but we need to get MJ to examine this. She knows everything—"

"No," said the chief. "I don't want anyone to know what we've found. Not yet."

"But I don't know enough about evaluating original oils! I can't look at a painting and tell if it's authentic. MJ can."

"That's fine." The chief patted the air. The movement brought a whiff of his musky cologne. "I'm not asking you to verify anything. Not right now."

"If it is authentic, why would it be here? Stored like that? That's not safe. That's a valuable piece of art, if it's really a High-waymen piece."

"How valuable?" The chief gave me a quizzical look.

"We recently sold a painting about that size by Newton for $4500. See what I mean? You can't be casual with art like that. I keep—kept—all of our inventory in a climate-controlled safe. Someone would have to be careless or an idiot to stuff one under a chair."

As if in response, Our Main Man in Tyvek carefully set the exposed canvas on the wooden chair legs. The two uniformed cops edged closer to get a better look at the landscape. One asked, "Chief? Should we upend the sofa?"

"Might as well."

Like the chair, the couch held a secret. Four more wire grids were stapled under the wooden frame. My heart lurched. Was it possible? Could this be a newly discovered cache of old High-waymen paintings or ... could these be the forgeries? Had we found the source? Had it been Alicia Morrison?

After Chief McHenry's nod, the cop closest to the sofa reached into the space formed by the grids. He withdrew a papered parcel. When the wrapping was pulled away, we stared at another upside-down frame, one more Highwaymen painting. Systematically, the chief and his men examined every piece of upholstered furniture. They found five paintings in all.

"This doesn't make sense," I whispered. The chief's face had become increasingly gloomy. I couldn't be sure if these were forged paintings or not. If only I had MJ's ability to look at a picture and instantly recognize the painter!

"What do you know about this?" The chief turned to me. His soft gray eyes were cold as granite. His accusatory tone was made even more threatening by his stiff posture.

My head spun as I realized he was accusing me. But accusing me of what? Conspiring with Mrs. Morrison? I'd never even met the woman. Hiding forged paintings? How could I have had access to her furniture? My mouth went so dry that my teeth stuck to my lips. I tried to answer him, but it took a lot of effort.

"What do you mean?" I managed.

"We got a tip earlier this morning when the real estate agent arrived for a showing . A cleaner had knocked over a chair. The agent went to set it upright, and he thought things looked suspicious. My mind went immediately to you, Cara."

"What?" The eyes of the law enforcement officials burned into my skin. My heart threatened to jump out of my chest. My feet told me to run. My body told me I needed an escape route. Under the circumstances, making a fast exit was impossible. All I could do was breathe deeply in an effort to restore my equilibrium.

"I'm not sure why you stored your haul under this furniture," said the chief evenly, "or why you involved Mrs. Morrison. Here's what I am sure of: These paintings give you an incentive for murder. It doesn't look good for you, Cara."

"Except I didn't know they were here! You won't find my fingerprints on any of those canvases. How would I benefit from this? There's a good chance these are forgeries, and fakes actually do my business a lot of harm. We recently lost our entire inventory because Irving Feldman learned about a fake, and he thought it was our doing." The words were out before I could stop myself. My father always cautioned me about talking to the police. Here I'd gone and given the chief a carload of information that made me look bad.

Feeling trapped, I repeated myself. "These don't benefit me! And I didn't hurt Mrs. Morrison. I didn't even know the woman." Heat was working its way up my neck. My heart raced. My vision narrowed. The cut on my calf stung. The room seemed to swim out of focus.

"Ah, but these paintings do benefit you. You can sell the fakes and pocket all of the money rather than sharing it with Mr. Feldman."

"But who would patronize my business once the word gets out that I'm selling forgeries?"

Chief McHenry raised an eyebrow. "If we hadn't stumbled on these, who would know you were selling forgeries? Are these fakes? I can't tell."

My temper spiked to a vigorous boil. "That is exactly why I suggested that you let me bring MJ Austin here. She can discern the difference. I can't. If I was guilty, would I have suggested bringing in an expert? Not very likely!"

"So you say. Don't leave the area," the chief warned me. "You might want to talk to your lawyer."

I pinched the bridge of my nose rather than let tears stream down my face. "Got it," I said, turning on my heel to leave. The floppy fabric booties rubbed my ankles all the way out of the house.

In my car, it took two tries to get the key in the ignition. I forced myself to pull away from the curb slowly when I ached to floor the gas pedal. My teeth chattered as I inched down the street, trying to decide what I should do next.

MJ and Skye were scheduled to work, Honora would join them, and the store would be closing at five. I texted my crew to say that I'd decided to take the rest of the day off. I deserved a break. To me that meant I should purchase an entire bag of Reese's Peanut Butter cups and eat them all, because it doesn't count as "time off" if you don't have chocolate. A bottle of Ménage à Trois California Red Blend from California might help, too. CVS had both. The wine was on sale, so I bought two bottles. As I pulled out of the CVS parking lot, I noticed the time was eleven. Rather than skip lunch, I went directly to Taco Bell and ordered a Mexican pizza. My dietary choices reminded me of my pal, Kiki. I phoned her on my way back to the island, but I only got her voice mail. Kiki understood the value of therapeutic eating. She would have gotten several bottles of Diet Dr Pepper to wash everything down. But I would make do with the wine.

Back at home, my fur babies greeted me happily. I dug into the Mexican pizza and chased it with one bottle of wine. Feeling better, I decided to open the other bottle. That's when I decided to drink myself into oblivion.

I'd never really cried about Dan's death. I'd been fighting with Poppy the day the message came from Gavin, Dan's stepson. My grandfather believed that Covid was a myth, a cosmic joke. He insisted he was too tough to die. In a last-ditch effort to drive home the seriousness of this infection, I drove Poppy to the hospital. He carped and complained and cursed at me the whole trip. With my jaw set tight, I steered into the hospital parking lot. There sat the refrigerated van they were using as an overflow morgue. The huge vehicle spoke volumes, offering a more credible message than I'd been able to deliver. We spent the trip back to my grandfather's house in a troubled silence. But after our excursion, Poppy did go and get his shot. I'm sure it saved his life.

As I poured from the second bottle, I thought about the day I'd heard Dan was dead. I'd been driving down Federal Highway after taking Luna to the vet for a check-up. My phone had dinged to advise me of an incoming text, but I wasn't able to read the message until I got back to my house. Gavin's phone had sent me a message, but I couldn't believe the words on my screen. Surely, Sonya had put her son up to a vicious prank. Rather than accept the truth, I ignored the text. Dan had not died. Not Dan. No way. After a troubled evening, I took a hot shower and went to bed late.

The next morning, a new text popped up. My son had talked to Gavin. Tommy, sweet young man that he is, wanted to know, "Are you all right, Mom?"

Tommy was in St. Louis with his father, Dominick. When Covid struck, Tommy's school closed down to offer lessons remotely. He'd driven up to Missouri at his father's request. They'd converted my ex-husband's restaurant into a carry-out business, limiting the number of staff members and keeping contact with the public to a minimum. The plan worked better than anyone had suspected it would.

"Tommy? Are you sure about this? You know how Sonya operates. This is exactly the sort of stunt she would pull. Maybe she's tricked Gavin. Dan can't possibly be dead."

A long silence ensued. Finally, Tommy said, "Mom, when I called him, Gavin was crying. He was there at his mother's condo when the military detail came to Sonya's door. That's how they inform the next-of-kin, you know. The service shows great honor to the dead."

Phone in hand, I collapsed into the nearest chair. My heart was ripped from my chest. My vision went blurry. I wanted to hit someone, something, anything, to quell my mounting frustration. Dan was gone? Impossible! "No, no, no. He promised me he would be okay."

"Mom," said Tommy, "do you want me to come to Florida? To be with you?"

No way did I want my son to take a chance on catching Covid while using public transportation. The thought of Tommy in a crowded plane was enough to bring me to my senses. Nor did I want him to make the long drive from St. Louis to Hobe Sound.

"Absolutely not. I'm stunned, that's all. I'll be okay. I, um, need time."

For the next seven days, I walked the beach all day, from sun up to sun down, with the sand squishing between my toes. I kept thinking I'd see Dan. I certainly looked for him. I believed he would come loping toward me with that long-legged stride of his. He would throw his arms around me. He would kiss me, and he'd tell me it had been a mistake.

Only it wasn't.

A month after Dan died, Jack crossed the Rainbow Bridge. My poor little rescue Chihuahua, the one who'd been tossed out of a moving truck, had finally been too worn out to go on. He took his last breath while in my arms.

I gathered my losses in my heart, but I wouldn't let myself cry. That would be an act of surrender. As long as I didn't receive an official notification, Dan wasn't dead. I tricked myself into believing that someone in the service would get in touch with me, although that was absolutely preposterous. Like a drowning man clutches at a straw, I needed something to hold onto, and that was the trick I played on myself. The constant thought that Dan would come back eventually.

Dan wasn't dead until someone in uniform told me.

Dan wasn't dead.

Jack wasn't gone.

Jack didn't die in my arms.

And a new mantra: The chief didn't suspect me of being a cheat, a thief, and a murderer.

Everything was going to be okay.

Honest.

CHAPTER 18

After feeding the animals, I had a couple of glasses of wine and finished the second bottle. Then I phoned MJ to tell her what the chief had discovered under Mrs. Morrison's furniture. MJ was ominously quiet as I shared my news. After I finished, she said, "What a moron the chief is. Of course, you didn't hide paintings under Mrs. Morrison's furniture. You know better than that."

I concentrated on not slurring my words. "He thinks I'm the person behind the forgeries. That I found a painter and came up with the way to distribute the artwork, selling fakes instead of originals. He thinks I was in cahoots with Mrs. Morrison."

"Huh. That's highly unlikely. This was a pretty sophisticated scheme. Not your style at all, Cara. I suspect this has been going on since before Covid shut things down. Besides, like you told the chief, selling fakes would undercut your profit. Not to mention that this stupid stunt caused Irving to take back his mother's collection! There's no reason for you to fake the paintings. Of course, you didn't arrange to have forgeries made! Why would you? And when would you have found the time? And how did you sell them?" She wasn't her usual linear thinking self. This mess had rattled MJ, too.

"All good questions, and I don't have an answer," I said. "Do me a favor? Tell Skye about this. Honora, too, if you get the chance. I'm not up to sharing the story one more time. I have some serious drinking to do."

"You go, girl."

———

In the back of my pantry was another bottle of wine, an expensive one that Dan had purchased. I opened it and poured myself a glass. By the time I got to the bottom of the bottle, I was having trouble walking across the room. Sometime during my drunken haze, the phone rang. I must have answered it and slurred my words because a short time later, there was a pounding at my door. I didn't want to open it. I didn't need company; I needed Dan. I decided to ignore the noise, and I was very nearly successful except that Hercules lived up to his name and put his shoulder against the wood. My door gave way under Herk's attentions. I didn't even hear him come in.

He gathered me to him and stroked my hair. "Shhhh," he said.

I hiccupped, "Dan."

"I know, I know," he said.

I told him about the paintings. How we'd found them under the furniture. How someone had phoned the chief.

"You didn't talk to the cops, did you?" Herk managed to keep his voice absolutely flat, but I knew he was struggling to not sound appalled.

"Yeah, some, see, I thought the chief was my friend, but he wasn't!" That coincided with a wail of grief.

"It's okay, all right, we'll get it sorted." Herk's words ran into each other.

Either I fell asleep or I passed out. I woke up in my own bed. My quilt would have been tucked under my chin, but Gerard is a covers hog. Bailey rested at my feet. The sun was rising, peeping through the blinds. The light hurt my eyes. As it turned out, I hadn't downed three whole bottles of wine. Only a little more than one and a half. I'd been too messed up emotionally to pay attention to the levels in the bottles. Thank goodness.

"You might want this," said Herk, appearing out of nowhere and offering me a glass of water and a pair of Advil pills. "Your friend Honora called. I explained you were under the weather."

I swallowed the pain meds gratefully and sank back down into the covers. Herk perched on the edge of the bed. "Cara? I called a friend who is a criminal attorney. I think you need to talk with him. He can be here in two hours."

"Can't. Cleaning lady is coming."

"Yup, okay. You spoke to Chief McHenry yesterday, and he didn't caution you, did he?"

"No."

"Okay," Herk used his hands to scrub his face. "One more time, kiddo. Did he caution you? Recite the Miranda warning?"

"No." That much I knew. I was positive I hadn't heard the standard spiel advising me of my rights.

"Then the lawyer can wait until after the Fourth of July. Go back to sleep. I'll let the cleaning lady in."

The effects of the wine had mainly worn off by the time Herk answered a knock at the front door. I didn't bother to get out of bed, but the dogs jumped down to greet the intruder. I have no illusions. Neither animal would protect me unless licking someone to death counts as punishment. I heard Herk greet someone, a person who sounded female.

"Bailey!" she said, calling out to the dog after telling Herk,

"*Hola.*" That's the limit of my Spanish, although it was immediately clear that Herk knew the language well. He and my new housekeeper chattered like a pair of parrots, using words I didn't understand. I closed my eyes and prayed that the pounding in my head would stop. The pain was enough to make me moan in misery.

Eventually, the Advil kicked in and I drifted into slumber. The sounds of the vacuum cleaner occasionally rumbled through my dreams. By my calculations, Connie worked for three hours. During her cleaning spree, I'd been able to burn off the rest of the booze. Even though I didn't bother to get out of bed and greet her, I could hear her talking with Herk outside my bedroom door.

"Not to worry. I will come back for cash, please. Miss Honora trusts Ms. Delgatto. It's okay."

I didn't hear a car leave. That was odd. Had Connie walked to my house? Not that it mattered. I closed my eyes.

This was the first time in my life that I'd had enough booze to incapacitate myself. Ever. Shame buried inside of me, and my throat swelled with emotion. And to think that I'd been soused in front of one of Dan's friends! How humiliating! I pulled the covers over my head and resolved to never get out of bed. How could I face Herk? What must he think of me?

I didn't have long to find out. After a rap on my bedroom door, he entered with a cold bottle of Gatorade. "Drink this. It'll help rehydrate you."

I turned my back on him. "I'm so embarrassed. Please go away."

"Not on your life. I owe it to Dan to see you through this. I'm guessing you've been hanging onto this misery for a while. Am I right? See, I've watched soldiers go through this. It's like you push it down until it bubbles up and erupts like a volcano."

Although the pillow muffled my voice, I said, "I never cried after I got word about Dan. It didn't come to me directly. Since I wasn't his wife or his next of kin, I only got a text from his stepson, and I didn't believe it. After I heard about Dan, I lost one of my dogs, a little rescue Chihuahua, and by then, I couldn't cry. My feelings were what kept me strong. They were all I had. They felt like a steel rod inside, holding me up, but hurting me all the same. Does that sound ridiculous?"

"Nope. All of us cope differently. When our world goes to pieces, we pick up what's left and try to patch life back together. We use tears and booze and food and sometimes sex to make sense of the mess. We try to make the new pieces of our lives match up. Some of us never do move on."

His big hand patted my shoulder, the one not completely covered by my duvet. The gesture was awkward, as if he was worried that he might hurt me. "Come on now, kiddo. Drink this Gatorade before it gets warm. It's nasty stuff, but your body needs the hydration."

I did as Herk told me. As my head cleared, it dawned on me that I was in a vulnerable position. I hardly knew this man. He was in my bedroom. I was not totally sober.

Alarm bells went off. I drew away from Herk.

Herk must have recognized my fears. He cleared his throat. "This seems like a good time to tell you that you don't have to be scared of me. I won't come on to you. I bat for the other team, if you know what I mean."

Yes, I did. I said, "I don't care." But I did. I cared because his admission meant I was safe.

"Yeah," he said, sounding resigned. "I didn't think you would be upset. Dan was cool with it, too. I figured that being upfront would make it easier. No dancing around. No worrying about my motive."

"Your motive?" I asked. The Gatorade was working magic.

My cells seemed to take on the liquid like a dry sponge soaks up water.

"I'm not hanging around because I'm hoping to put the moves on you," he said.

"That's good to know, because right now, I've sworn off men. I can't risk having my heart broken one more time."

"I hear you," he said.

CHAPTER 19

After coaxing me into drinking another Gatorade and plying me with more Advil, Herk left to go to work. Turns out, he was a big fan of sticky notes. He used a yellow one to tell me he'd fed all of my pets and let the dogs out. A sticky note on the refrigerator informed me there were four more bottles of Gatorade inside. A pink sticky note explained that the only cash he'd carried was a one-hundred-dollar bill, and therefore, I owed Connie for her cleaning.

An orange sticky note gave me the name and phone number of a criminal lawyer in Miami who'd been primed for my call. In tiny precise writing, Herk added, "He served with Dan."

How odd and yet comforting it was to have Dan protecting me from the grave. I tucked that particular sticky note into my wallet. Until I needed legal advice, the note could wait.

Honora texted me to say she hoped I was having a restful day. She reported that she'd added another craft session to accommodate the waitlist for her Fourth of July Fireworks Stall class. Mentally, I calculated the profits and realized, not for the first time, how lucky I was to have employees who took it upon themselves to drum up business.

Poppy needed a reminder that he'd agreed to dress as Uncle Sam. As the years roll on, my grandfather has become a little forgetful, and I didn't want a rude surprise tomorrow. A quick text to him brought an answer: *I ain't forgot. Make sure that fancy costume fits me.*

I picked up his Uncle Sam costume and hemmed the pants. The cuffs had been pinned up. Since I had the time, I chose to alter these the right way. Instead of adding a tuck between the sleeves and the cuffs, I totally ripped off the cuffs, shortened the sleeves, and handstitched the cuffs back where they belonged. The task provided me with intense satisfaction, the joy of a job well done.

About three, I sat down with a sheet of paper rescued from my recycling bin. I decided to organize my thoughts and work on the conundrum of the Highwaymen paintings. How had the whole scheme worked? A mind-map would give me the freedom to explore ideas. I asked myself several questions, made various notes along spokes and inside circles, and didn't come to any big conclusions, except for one important fact: Alicia couldn't have been working alone.

To deliver paintings, she had to have an accomplice. Point One: Her white Bentley Continental GT Coupe didn't have enough cargo space to hold one of the larger paintings. Point Two: She needed a forger. Nothing I'd heard attributed artistic talent to the woman. Somebody with talent had copied the landscapes.

After scribbling down Point Two, I gave myself a big mental dope slap. Of course, Mrs. Morrison needed a painter who could forge the pictures. That was the whole basis of her scam. Where would she find one? How would she search for one? She would need a person who kept his or her mouth shut, a person who couldn't or wouldn't sell the landscapes without her help. Otherwise, the forger would be able to circumvent Mrs.

Morrison and collect the money, cutting her out as the middleman.

I set the mind-map on my dining table and walked outside. Sitting on the Adirondack chairs, I tried to imagine someone who could forge paintings. The artist would need talent, of course, and supplies. How could I track down talent? Since that's an intangible asset, tracing it would be difficult. How could I search for supplies? Those were tangible. I wondered how many local shops sold large canvasses and oil paints?

A lightbulb went off.

Katrina and Eddie would know. They not only painted murals, they also did decorative paintings on furniture. I could talk to them tomorrow.

In the meantime, I hit upon Point Three: Alicia needed a sales funnel to bring in potential buyers. She couldn't advertise, and yet she had to let people know about her side hustle. These had to be people with the money to buy Highwaymen paintings. Aurora had promised to collect information for me about Alicia. Maybe she could fill in this missing piece. I gave her a call.

The next day, the ill effects of my binge were mainly gone. The shadow of a headache reminded me how stupid I'd been. Even after the booze wore off, my body protested. The Gatorade and Advil had quelled my hangover, but I was still dehydrated. I knew I'd be using the bathroom all day because I planned to down more bottles of the sports drink. I could also tell that my binge had used up all of my vitamin B. I felt cranky. My irritation mounted as my bladder became full on the way back from picking up Poppy at his house. He refused to put on his Uncle Sam uniform until he got to The Treasure Chest. His stubbornness annoyed me. I knew he'd hog the bathroom and take his sweet time getting into his gear. As soon as we got to The Treasure Chest, I bolted out of the car to use the john.

I came out of the restroom with wet hands, flapping them in the air instead of drying them on paper towels. I figured Poppy would be right behind me. However, Poppy took his sweet time getting himself ready for his star turn. Over one arm he carried his Uncle Sam costume, which I'd carefully slipped inside a plastic dry-cleaning bag. Under his breath, he muttered complaints. Why did my grandfather insist on being difficult? Tommy's voice answered in my head: *Because that is how Poppy rolls.*

Yes, and it was probably what had kept Poppy going during the war.

Once he was properly attired in his red-and-white striped pants and blue shirt, I managed to remind Grumpy Gus that he'd also committed to having a Fourth of July barbecue at my house with me. I forewarned my grandfather that we would not be alone. "A new friend of mine, a guy named Herk will be joining us," I said, keeping my eyes on the front of the store. A line was forming outside the entrance. The day had dawned sunny and clear, so my guests could wait on the sidewalk comfortably. As usual, I'd set an alarm on my watch rather than trust myself to open up on time.

"Suit yourself," said my grandfather, "I'll be there on the Fourth, but what kind of name is Herk?"

"I'm not sure. It's short for Hercules. You can ask him. Also, he's a veteran, a friend of Dan's, so you'll have plenty in common."

"Hercules," muttered Poppy darkly. "What sort of mother names her child Hercules?"

I wouldn't speculate on that.

Honora arrived early to set up for her classes, even though

they didn't start until ten a.m. I thanked her for hooking me up with Connie.

Honora folded her hands over her belt like one of those friars in the movies. "Such a good person. Esmeralda's death sent Connie into a tailspin. They only had each other, and Connie's grandmother had given up everything to get here."

I opened my mouth to ask for details, but Honora spotted Poppy. In his costume, my grandfather looked every inch the dandy. Honora actually blushed with pleasure. Like a moth drawn to a flame, she fluttered around Poppy. Her attention charmed him into a better mood. "Hang on," she told him. "I have something for you to give to passersby."

Grabbing a navy-blue tote bag, she pulled out small plastic baggies filled with red, white, and blue M&Ms.

"Where did you buy those?" I asked. "I didn't know you could get specific colors."

"You certainly can. I ordered them months ago. I figured that Poppy needed something to pass out to prospective guests."

I marveled at Honora's great marketing instincts. I only prayed that I'd be as "with it" as she was at her age.

Since it was early in the day and not too hot, I decided to go outside and take a good look at my new mural. Katrina and Eddie had not arrived yet. That gave me the chance to take my time looking at their progress. In the center of the wall, a majestic poinciana tree spread its branches, replete with red-orange blossoms, over a serene landscape. Several Snowy White Egrets searched for tidbits to eat, their coloring standing out against the lush Florida grasses. It appeared to me that the artists were working on palm trees in the distance. It was obvious why they needed their tall ladder. I looked at my watch, wondering when they would show up. As if she'd gotten a cosmic message, Katrina sent me a text message: *Worried about*

people walking under our ladder. Could be dangerous! Will finish up
on July 5, if that's okay.

Her decision made perfect sense, but it precluded me from
asking her about an art supplies dealer. I considered calling her
back but decided against it. Customers were lining up outside of
the shop, a sure sign the day would be busy. The best I could
muster was a thumbs-up emoji as a reply to Katrina.

The rest of the day flew by. EveLynn had restocked her soft
goods yet again. Skye had woven small sticks and twine into
rectangles that she painted red, white, and blue. These were
transformed into hip American flags in all sizes. Our guests
snatched them up like a pelican does fish in the ocean. MJ had
sourced antique postcards and other images with vintage Uncle
Sam portraits on them. These she'd shared with Sid, our
computer guru, who turned them into digital files for scrapbooks and journals. With my permission and money from the
store, MJ purchased a Cricut, a computer-controlled cutting
machine. Using it, she'd made vinyl silhouettes of Uncle Sam
and ironed them onto red, white, and blue tie-dyed tee shirts.
She'd also enlisted an artist to paint patriotic symbols on small
window screens. These could be wedged in an open window to
catch a breeze.

Not to be outdone, Bippy had crocheted a half a dozen
amigurumi Uncle Sam dolls. Three of these sold within the first
half hour that our doors were open.

I'd come up with a unique way to use the hardback covers of
out-of-date history books. After removing the pages inside, I
covered the outsides with Mod Podge and added ribbon
closures. This made them perfect for protecting a digital reader,
such as a Kindle. The larger covers were turned into purses by
adding a gusset on the sides. Then I sewed on handles and a top
closure.

It is always gratifying to hear people "oooh" and "aaaahhh"

over our handiwork. By five, all of us had been run off our feet. An exhausted Poppy dragged out a folding chair and sat on the sidewalk next to my front door, fanning himself with his top hat. Honora rang up the final purchase by her fireworks stall students. Skye had been buzzing like a honeybee from customer to customer. She groaned as she pulled over a stool to take a load off.

"Heard any more from Bucky?" I asked Skye.

"No, but Lou and some of his cop friends have been keeping an eye on him. You do plan to press charges, right? From what they've seen, he's replaced Mrs. Morrison with another gal pal, yet another woman several times his age. A sugar mama." She made a sound of disgust. "Honestly. He's always looking for the easy life."

MJ came over, pulling up another stool. We were all tired. In fact, I was too tired to find a seat. Instead, I leaned against the wall. "Skye, is it possible that Bucky killed Mrs. Morrison?" I told her and MJ about the chief's discovery of a hidden stash of paintings. I'd decided I didn't care whether Chief McHenry wanted me to tell them or not. This concerned our livelihood. "These were large canvases. I'm not sure they would have fit in Mrs. Morrison's Bentley."

"You're thinking Bucky did the deliveries?" Skye asked.

"That would make sense," said MJ. "You'd need a van. You'd want to crate the paintings to make sure they weren't jostled. By the way, Cara, I've continued calling the customers who didn't buy from me. Two were out of state. That would definitely require crating the art and transporting it. Those were large canvases I sold."

"What I really need is a line on the artist. The artist would be able to confirm what happened, from beginning to end. Frankly, I'm not nearly as worried about who killed Mrs. Morrison as I am about tracking the provenance of the forged artwork. Her murderer doesn't have a beef with me."

"But the chief leaned on you," said Skye. "That's a sign of trouble. This man has turned against you. That has to be dealt with, Cara. You live all alone on that island. Until Chief McHenry is convinced you didn't hurt Mrs. Morrison, you're at risk."

She had a point, but I hated to think about it. Her baby was being targeted for kidnapping. I could fend for myself, but Baby Nick couldn't. But I felt too exhausted to get into this. Instead of arguing and belaboring the point, I agreed with Skye. "If I can figure out who forged the paintings, I can trace the artwork back to Mrs. Morrison and follow that thread back to the killer. What other reason can there be for someone conking her over the head?"

"One reason could be that she got sick and tired of Bucky. I bet he was mooching off of her, and she turned down one of his endless requests for money," said Skye. "His dad has cut him off, or so I've heard. A job servicing swimming pools wouldn't produce the sort of income Bucky aspires to. Not even close. He took that job for access to women with a certain lifestyle. That's who he is."

"I'd hoped to ask Eddie and Katrina where they buy their art supplies. I figured I could ask the art store vendors about customers who bought a lot of canvases, but Eddie and Katrina begged off today. Actually, they did the right thing. I don't need to add an insurance claim to list of problems. That tall ladder could be a hazard to pedestrians."

Honora tottered toward us with a cup of hot tea in one hand. Skye got up and grabbed a wicker chair for our friend. I must have looked at the cushy seat with longing because Skye dragged one over for me, too. "You need an art supply store?" Honora asked. She'd only heard the tail end of our conversation.

"Yes, I'd hoped by asking around, I could figure out who was buying a lot of canvases," I repeated myself.

"Hmm. That's one way of tracing things, but it might be unnecessary. I think I know who your painter is," said Honora.

"What?" All three of us—MJ, Skye, and me—stared at Honora.

Before she answered, Poppy sang out from the back, "I'm leaving. One of my VFW buddies is picking me up."

We all shouted, "Goodbye!"

Honora said, "As you know, I volunteer at the Jupiter Community Center. I work at the front counter."

No, I didn't know that. How on earth did she manage to keep so many balls in the air?

"They recently displayed artwork by students taking oil painting classes. One in particular caught my eye." She looked for a spot to rest her teacup. Skye took the drink from her. That freed Honora's hands to flip through her phone. At a certain point, she paused and enlarged a photo. "Here," she said, passing the phone to me.

Thank goodness I was sitting in a wicker chair with arms. Otherwise, I would have been picking myself up off of the floor. The picture on Honora's phone was the image of a Highwaymen painting, a technicolor. "Technicolor" was the name given to paintings with brilliant reds, oranges, and yellows, duplicating our phenomenal Floridian sunrises. Honora had wisely zoomed in on the information card posted beside the landscape. It read: *In the style of the Highwaymen paintings.* The artist was Julio Entrada.

I returned Honora's phone and whipped out mine while my friends vied to see the image for themselves. I dialed the Jupiter Community Center, but they were closed for the holiday.

Honora gave me a look filled with pity. "I already tried that, Cara. The teacher left town during the Independence Day break, and no one working at the center will share her phone number. Rest assured, I'll do my best to wiggle it out of someone next week."

"But what are the chances that this person is our forger?" asked Skye, staring at Honora's phone. "Anyone could copy the Highwaymen style."

"But not just anyone could do this good of a job." MJ took Honora's phone out of Skye's hands. "I'd bet a month's salary this is our creep. Now that he can no longer sell his work to Mrs. Morrison, he's turning to the open market to find buyers. See? There's a price on the work. Three hundred bucks. That's fairly standard around here for a canvas by an unknown artist."

As I'd requested, MJ had told Skye about my encounter with the Jupiter Island Department of Public Safety, and how they've found paintings under Alicia Morrison's furniture. Thank goodness I didn't have to go over that painful story again.

Skye frowned. "Why put up a sign and say this work is 'in the style of the Highwaymen painters,' rather than try to pass it off as an authentic Highwaymen piece of art?"

"Because without the accompanying letter that I wrote and signed to authenticate the piece, the landscape has no market value," said MJ. "It's my reputation that was being copied. Somehow Mrs. Morrison got her mitts on one of my authentication letters. She reproduced it, changing the dates, description, and the landscape dimensions. When paired with a painting that's this close to a Highwaymen original, she could command the big bucks."

"What are you thinking about the paintings found under her furniture?" I asked.

"I'm assuming she had the forger paint iconic scenes in a variety of sizes," said MJ. "That way she could always compete with me. When she found someone looking for a Highwaymen painting, she'd qualify them, find out what they were shopping for. Size, color, subject matter. I bet she even sent the buyer to our website. Once they knew exactly what they wanted, she would tell them she had a line on a painting that, coincidentally, was a perfect match for what they had in mind."

Skye wasn't interested in how Mrs. Morrison's business worked, but she was concerned about me. Turning my way, she said, "How did the police treat you, Cara? Any sense of whether they considered you a person of interest?"

"Yes," I said. "I certainly felt like they considered me a prime suspect. Even though I was shocked when they found the paintings hidden in the upholstery. Chief McHenry was quick to point out that the artwork gave me a motive for killing Mrs. Morrison. According to the chief, I was running my own forgery business, cutting out Irving, and taking all the money for myself."

Honora gave me a sad smile. "Hang in there, Cara. Better days are coming."

"I certainly hope so."

CHAPTER 20

"Why on earth are you in such a bad mood, Cara?" my grandfather said as he settled into the passenger seat the next morning. Despite the hassle he'd given me yesterday, I'd handed him his costume and tried again to have him fully dressed as Uncle Sam before we hit the road. Since he'd co-operated, I owed him one. Reluctantly, I told him about the paintings that had been found at Alicia Morrison's house.

"We got time for coffee?" Poppy asked.

Actually, we did. I pulled through a Dunkin Donuts drive-up. When the server saw Poppy's outrageous attire, she insisted on giving us free donuts as well as our drinks. Rather than get crumbs and coffee on my clothes while driving, I parked us in an empty space

"Alicia Morrison, eh? That woman has been trouble since poor Prescott Morrison meet her. He was caught up in her web. She was like one of them big garden spiders, a Joro spider, the ones that weave them huge webs. We talked about them, remember?"

Yes, we had. At first, these giant arachnids scared me to

death. Female Joro spiders have bodies almost three inches long, and their circular webs can span three feet. They like to spin their nets near light sources like the security lamp on my porch. When I first moved to Florida, I regularly freaked out when I walked into the sticky threads that seemed to go on and on. But that was nothing compared to when I encountered the female architect of the web. Their size compares to the fishing spiders we had in Missouri, but their black and yellow stripes make them as colorful as a bumblebee. I complained about the garden spiders to my grandfather. Poppy patiently lectured me on how beneficial these creatures are, since they feed on the mosquito and no-see-um population. Only then did I view them as an asset.

I still avoid walking my property at night, and I am especially careful when I walk close to any lights. "Why was Mrs. Morrison like a Joro spider?"

"That's the best way to describe her. See, I knew Prescott because we were members of the same VFW. I used to tease him about slumming it when he came to a meeting. He was a little high-class for the joint, but only because he married up. That job of his, teaching college, was exactly what he needed after his wife Mary died. The man was totally broken up. She was not much to look at, but she came from money, and they adored each other. He loved teaching at Miami Dade College, seeing as how he was pretty much retired from his business. It put a spring in his step to be talking to young folks. About a year after he got that part-time teaching gig, he met Alicia and from then on, it was Katy bar the door. That woman had him wrapped around her little finger in nothing flat. Pitiful. Just plain pitiful."

"The second wife was good-looking?" I struggled to remember the face of the corpse I'd seen. Funny how adrenaline impacts your ability to think. Closing my eyes, I brought up the dead body. Dark brown hair, dark brown eyes, and red lips. Yes, she might have been a stunner. Hard to tell in retrospect.

"She was a Cuban cutie and lovely to look at. A real head-turner."

"I'm confused. Her name was Alicia. That doesn't sound Hispanic."

"It ain't. Her true first name was Adoncia, only when she and Prescott married, she changed her first name to match her new last one, kinda. She became Alicia because she thought it sounded more 'American.' She came over in 1960, and she said she never wanted to look back, although she actually did go and visit when Obama lifted restrictions. I know about that because the local paper made a big deal out of the exiles returning to Havana."

After tossing away our trash, I pulled into traffic and headed toward The Treasure Chest. As I drove, Poppy whistled show tunes. He made the trip enjoyable.

We sold out of all Independence Day merchandise at noon. I kept the store open and offered guests raincheck coupons. I would have happily closed early, but Honora's Fourth of July Fireworks Stall class was scheduled until four p.m. That meant I needed to stick around while the last of her students finished their projects. As she'd predicted, the attendees were eager to buy supplies to make more miniatures.

"Don't forget," I told Poppy as I drove him home. "We're having a barbecue tomorrow."

Before I left his driveway, I read a new text on my phone. Connie had written: *Can I come tomorrow and get the cash for the cleaning?*

I'd forgotten all about her. How embarrassing! I answered: *Yes, of course! I'll be home.*

My trip to Seaspray took forever. The streets were clogged with bicyclists. Their neon jerseys gleamed in the sun. Here and there were relief stations, card tables where volunteers distributed cold water and Gatorade. Vans with the logos of bike stores muscled the shoulder of the roads. These vehicles offered to fix flat tires and make adjustments. Wherever helpers were parked, bicyclists spilled over and onto the pavement. A few ignored the oncoming traffic altogether, refusing to give way to the cars. I slowed to a crawl when I realized one or two had encroached on my driving lane. Today, the bicyclists aroused envy in me. I was tired of working. I was tired of following rules and getting harassed by the law enforcement community. Nothing had gone right for me this summer. Pete Slatkin's dressing down still rankled, and to my mind, he owed me an apology. I wasn't responsible for Mrs. Morrison's death, and yet, I was paying a stiff price for calling 911. Should I have turned around and left her body there, cooling and dribbling blood? Maybe. But then I would have had to ignore Bailey. And what about Eddie? Were the cops bugging him like they were hassling me? Then there was Skye. I hadn't heard a peep about the authorities bothering her! Had they exonerated her so quickly? Or was it because her husband was a cop. Or had they backed off because Nick had been threatened. Then there was Bucky. My leg was healing, but I still felt jumpy. Had he continued to stalk my store? Was he dangerous?

At a stoplight, I called Skye. She sounded surprised to hear from me since we'd been working together such a short time ago. I gathered my courage to ask, "What's happening with you and the police? Are you still a suspect?"

"No, thank goodness. Like I told you, I didn't touch anything. They couldn't find my fingerprints or any other evidence. One of Mrs. Morrison's neighbor's CCTV captured me leaving the premises and showed Mrs. Morrison talking to Bucky after I left."

"Thank goodness. Hey, I'm sorry that I haven't been more

concerned about you. It must seem awfully selfish hearing my worries about the paintings, considering that you're still dealing with Bucky." The light turned green, and I moved ahead cautiously.

"Not to worry. They've slapped Bucky with all sorts of charges. I think he's out on bail, but he was warned not to contact me. Lou is still trying to install security cameras and panic buttons." She laughed, and the sound was an instant mood lifter. "Lou doesn't like to follow directions. He thinks that's cheating."

"I'm perfectly content to let him do anything he wants, especially if it makes you and Nick safer. They're cracking down on Bucky?"

"Yes, but I told you about his father's connections. And yes, he has another girlfriend. A wealthy older woman. I feel sorry for her, actually. Bucky mailed me a letter. In it, he promised to never bother me again if I would meet with him one more time. I tore it up and threw it away. Then he sent a message through his lawyer."

"What?"

"Yes, Bucky has a sleezy attorney on retainer. The lawyer sent me a letter with Bucky's request to meet with me. Can you believe that? What gall! The letter came on the law firm's letterhead along with a greeting card. Get this! It had lovebirds on the front. Inside Bucky pledged his undying love. He told me I was a drug that he couldn't get out of his system. Bucky swore on a stack of Bibles that all he needed was one more chance to talk to me, and then, he'd leave me and my baby alone."

"Do you believe that?"

"Not on your life."

I said, "Good girl."

That night I dreamed of bike riders. My cell phone rang at the break of dawn. That could only be one caller, Aurora Hamilton. Because Aurora gets up with the birds, she expects the rest of us to move our fat bottoms out of bed, too. My voice was croaky when I said, "Hello?"

"Good morning, sunshine." Like her namesake, Aurora is always a bright light on the horizon. I adore her, but I'm a slow riser. Fortunately, she knows my habits.

"What time is it?" I asked.

"Almost seven. Don't tell me I woke you up!"

I groaned. "Okay, I won't tell you that you woke me up. Let's pretend you didn't. Is there a particular reason that we're on the phone this early?"

"I couldn't wait to tell you what I heard at the club last night."

"The club" is shorthand for the swanky country club where Aurora and Bill are members. I have no idea what the dues are, but I know they're out of my league. The country club is the hub of the Hamiltons' social life.

"You were at the club last night?" I knew there would be a Fourth of July celebration, complete with fireworks this evening, but why would they have an event the night before? That didn't make sense.

"It was my friend Elizabeth's birthday. Her 70th," explained Aurora. "You remember me talking about Elizabeth and Sterling? Bill's dear friends from two wives back?"

Aurora is a fourth wife, and she handles her situation with the sort of panache a United Nations representative would die for. Nothing fazes Aurora. She often says, "I knew what I was getting into, and it didn't matter, because I fell in love."

"Right. Elizabeth and Sherlock." My mental fog was clearing.

"Elizabeth and Sterling," she corrected me. "As you can guess, the bubbly was flowing. Everybody got a little tipsy. I asked Elizabeth what she knew about Alicia Morrison. Once upon a time, the two of them were friends. Of course, Elizabeth knew that Alicia had been murdered. She told me the most amazing story. Seems that Alicia was furious when she learned that Mary's gems were going to be sold at an auction house and she—Alicia—couldn't stop the sale. The proceeds went to charity."

I nodded, even though Aurora couldn't see my response. Honora had told me that Alicia was ticked off when Prescott didn't deck her out with his late wife's jewels.

"But Prescott Morrison had money!" I protested. "Couldn't he buy his second wife a set of baubles?"

"That's the problem. Before he met Alicia, Prescott set up a trust. The bulk of his fortune was already promised to charity. Alicia knew about it before they married, but she was convinced Prescott could break the trust to make her happy. He said he couldn't and wouldn't. In Alicia's mind, that meant Prescott didn't love her as much as he'd loved Mary. Every social event became a reminder that Alicia was a second wife. As you know, that doesn't matter to some of us."

Aurora had been totally candid with me from the get-go. She didn't care who knew she was Bill's fourth wife. Sure, his long-time friends gave her a rough time. At first, they refused to speak to her. They would actually talk past her when they met her in person. When the cold shoulder approach didn't dim Aurora's bright lights, they sneered at her, making comments and asides just out of Bill's hearing. Aurora feigned deafness. That really burned their cookies. They had assumed, given the proper "cold shoulder" treatment that Aurora would pack up and walk off into the sunset. Yes, it was a cliché, but clichés have sticking power because they're rooted in truth.

Bill's friends never did come around. At least, not all of them. Some eventually realized that Aurora was good for him as well as being a delightful woman in her own right. Others continued to make catty comments or ignore Aurora. Aurora systematically dropped them. By adopting the stance *nil illegitimi carborundum,* Aurora held her head high and sailed through life with a smile on her face.

"Alicia harbored resentment about Prescott's dead wife's jewelry for how long?" I asked.

"Forty years."

I closed my eyes. What if I'd had forty years with Dan? That would have been wonderful. Could I have put up with Sonya? You bet. Would jewelry have mattered to me? Not even a little bit.

"You have to understand," said Aurora in a gentle voice. "Alicia lived through the revolution in Cuba. While she was in school, she was indoctrinated with Castro's teachings. He attended an elite Catholic school as a boy. He knew that compulsory education was the way to transform Cuban citizens into faithful Fidelistas, followers of Fidel Castro. He actually said, 'Revolution and education are the same thing.' Alicia never got over the fear of being a refugee. Never."

Now I had insight into the woman's motives for being money-grubbing, but what difference did that make?

"You've heard of hungry kids who hide food? Elizabeth told me last night that Alicia was similarly fixated on money. That's why she always skimmed a little cream off the top. There's a point here, Cara. Are you still with me?"

I guess I'd been quiet too long. "Yes, I'm following."

"Prescott was bedridden the last days of his life. You know he made it to 94?"

No, I hadn't known that.

"He did. When he was failing, Alicia went through his old photos in preparation for the funeral service. She found photos of Mary decked out in her jewels. Pictures Alicia hadn't seen.

She went a little bonkers. She decided to one-up a dead woman."

I moved my legs under the covers and disturbed Luna. She gave me a scathing look before hopping off the bed. Bailey took that as his cue to come and lick my face. I added, "How do you triumph over a woman who's six feet underground? What a crazy idea!"

"By acquiring bigger and better gems. Alicia went through Prescott's things and found the auction catalog in his papers. Looking at the color photos of Mary's gems changed her mind. She decided she didn't want Mary's cast-offs after all. Instead, she wanted a set that was better than Mary's had been."

"Let me guess. She flew to New York and had a jeweler make her a couple of pieces while Prescott was too sick to object."

"Not even close," said Aurora. Her voice suppressed a chuckle. "Here's the part that Elizabeth whispered to me last night. Alicia Morrison had that master faker in Palm Beach make her a full parure."

"A full what? A master who?"

"There's a master jeweler in Palm Beach who specializes in fakes. He made Alicia a complete set of matching jewelry to her specifications. A necklace, earrings, brooch, ring, and bracelet. She even had a tiara made. She said they were copies of her own family jewels. Ones she'd been forced to leave behind in Cuba."

"I don't get it. Why have a fake set made? How would that satisfy her envy for Mary Morrison's things?"

"Because Alicia's fakes were more glamorous than what Mary had."

"But they were still fakes! And people knew they weren't real." I was shaking my head in confusion.

"Only Elizabeth knew. Nobody else could tell the difference. Hold on," Aurora continued. "Here's the best part. You know that a lot of families in Cuba were forced to hide their good stuff when they fled the country? Some gave the treasures to friends to keep for them, but a lot of them actually buried jewelry in their backyards. Alicia told folks that her parents had had money, once upon a time, and she'd grown up looking at her mother's diamonds. But that her mother had buried her nice things in the back yard."

"What?" I couldn't imagine planting fine jewelry in the dirt.

"Think about it. You know you have to leave Cuba because you're an elite. Castro is going to toss you in jail. You manage to get airline tickets to Miami, saying you're going for a family vacation. If you bring your precious jewels, the authorities will know you're planning to relocate permanently. Instead, you wear the bare minimum, a wedding band and simple earrings. You pack an overnight bag. You climb on the plane, smiling to yourself because last night under a full moon, you dug a hole and buried your fine parure in the soil. You bank on the fact that Fidel won't be in power forever."

I didn't get it, and Aurora knew I didn't. She put it another way. "All of the Cubans who fled their country thought, and continue to think, that they're living here in exile, not permanently. They plan to return to their country someday and retrieve their belongings."

That did make sense. Granted, it was hard to believe. Putting valuables in the soil? Yuck. Come to think of it, one of my mother's friends from Georgia had told her a similar story. When the Yankees were coming, the residents of Savannah buried their fine silver on their property. Same principle, different locale.

"And then?"

"While Prescott was gasping his last, Alicia got the chance to visit Havana. She wore her fake jewels to the airport. The State Department specifically warns US Citizens not to wear flashy jewelry when going to Cuba, but Alicia did. Here's the trick. She told the flight attendants that her diamonds were fake. In fact, she went so far as to show one of them the certificate the Palm Beach guy gave her, proving she had paste gems. When she arrived in Havana, she stayed in a nice bed and breakfast. Alicia showed the proprietor the paperwork for her jewels and asked to have the fakes locked away for safekeeping."

"Why lock them away?"

"Alicia told the b-and-b owners that she was worried about being the victim of a violent robbery. She said she was afraid that a thief might think her jewels were real. Rather than wear her nice pieces as she toured Cuba, she thought it was best to have them locked up in the b-and-b's safe."

"Got it," I said, even though I couldn't see where this was going. Sounded to me like one of Aurora's longwinded and pointless stories, a trait I loved in her. She had such fun relating these winding narratives that I reveled in her storytelling.

Aurora giggled. "The fakes were under lock and key, while Alicia was out and about in Havana, right? She told Elizabeth that in the dead of the night, she went back to her old family home. She dug up her mother's real parure. Literally. She bragged about it later to Elizabeth. She claimed she retrieved all of her mother's jewelry, treasures her family had buried! At the end of her vacation, Alicia swapped out the fakes for the real gems. That's how she brought the good stuff with her back into the country. She used the jeweler's certificate for the fakes to get the real parure through customs."

"Let me see if I'm following this. Alicia must have had a photo of the original jewels?"

"That's right. Who knows how she got it? Maybe she'd kept a picture of her mother's things. She'd always claimed to have come from money, although I never believed it. Her parents had both passed away years ago. They never got out of Cuba. Does it matter where she got the photo of the jewelry? Alicia had one, and she'd hung onto it. The Palm Beach jeweler used that picture to make the fake parure. The real stuff matched the paste pieces exactly."

"Huh," I said. "That's one heck of a story. Now that she's dead, what will happen to Alicia's parure?"

"Are you sitting down?"

"Actually, I'm lying in my bed, pinned to the sheets by Gerard, Bailey, and Luna. Why?"

Aurora made a scoffing sound. "I don't want to be responsible for you falling on the floor when I tell you the best part. See, on our way home, I told Bill what Elizabeth had told me. He explained that Prescott had the last laugh. Okay, Bill isn't an attorney, but here's what he suspects will happen. Alicia had the fake jewels made and brought the real ones back before Prescott died. That means the parure was joint property. Prescott set up the estate papers. Alicia simply signed off on them. The will included a clause that everything outside of the trust would be owned in joint custody in entirety. They had no living relatives, so he specified that any worldly goods left after both of their deaths would be auctioned off. The proceeds will go to charity."

"That means..." I paused. "That the new gems, the ones Alicia brought back from Cuba because she was steamed about Mary's collection, are going to be auctioned off? And the money will go to charity?"

"That's right. None of the Morrisons can wear that jewelry anymore!"

CHAPTER 21

I lounged around in my bed for another hour. Over and over, I replayed the story about Alicia Morrison and her family jewels. What an odd twist that the gems would be auctioned off. Had the crime scene unit found the parure onsite? Was it possible that Mrs. Morrison's death had been a robbery gone wrong? If so, was the killer somebody from the country club? Someone who knew the story, maybe overheard it? Maybe even a worker? How far had the story about Alicia Morrison's quest for a parure traveled? Surely the tale had been repeated beyond the walls of the club. It was too juicy to keep secret.

I needed to talk to Chief McHenry, but as I opened my contact list to the Jupiter Island Department of Public Safety, I paused. Today was Independence Day. The beach would be overflowing with people. The island law enforcement officers would have their hands full, literally. And I was expecting Herk and Poppy for a cookout. Dealing with the local cops could wait. The house was clean, thanks to Connie. I turned around in circles, trying to get a grip on what I needed to do and in what order. The animals stared at me with questions in their eyes. Why was I chasing my own tail?

The truth was that I still felt bone-weary. I'd been riding an emotional rollercoaster. Today was a well-deserved holiday, and since cooking always soothes my soul, I would indulge my passion. Setting the table was a good first step, and such an easy one that I knew it would get my mojo going.

An hour later, a white damask cloth covered the long table. The plates and flatware gleamed. White napkins rested under the forks. I chopped an English cucumber to make a water-melon, cucumber, and cherry tomato salad. After that, I assembled a platter of nibbles to hold us over until our mains were ready. But what should I add to the salmon?

French fries? Baked potatoes? I couldn't bring myself to look at another spud. Over the past month, I'd eaten my fill of chips with sandwiches from Pumpernickel's Deli. I stared into my pantry. An orange box of Uncle Ben's Wild Rice caught my eye. That would make a nice complement to salmon steaks. If I made the rice in the rice cooker, I could ignore it. Any food that doesn't require babysitting is a bonus when you're feeding a group. We needed one more vegetable, and I chose broccoli cooked on a sheet pan, tossed with lemon juice and olive oil before being sprinkled with parmesan cheese.

The meal would be well-rounded and healthy.

We were missing a yummy dessert. For that, I dragged out my ice cream maker and a package of frozen mango chunks. In short order, I had a soupy mixture going. I dumped it in the cold ice cream tub. There it churned and churned, working its way to creamy perfection.

Poppy sent me a text. *Hankering for corn on the cob. Will bring if you'll cook.*

I wrote back: *Sounds good.*

Bailey whined.

"Outside?" I asked the small pooch. When I walked to the sliding door, I saw what had caused the dog's whimper. Dark, fat-belly clouds poised like a row of toads on the horizon. A distant crack of thunder sent Bailey shivering. No doubt about it, we were not going to be cooking on the grill. Not today. Reaching under my kitchen counter, I dragged out a deep pot, perfect for boiling corn on the cob.

By noon, neither of my guests had shown up. I wondered if I might be eating alone. The dogs cuddled next to me, both shivering as the storm whipped up. My feet were propped on my coffee table, a bad habit, but one I can live with. Rather than sit still, I grabbed a composition notebook and a pen to make a list. One: Make sure I can keep Bailey. Two: See if Eddie has been cleared of Alicia Morrison's murder. Three: Get status of security systems that Lou is going to install. Do I need to hire someone? Four: Follow up on the video editing of Honora's class on Fourth of July Fireworks Stall. Five: Call the Jupiter Community Center and get in touch with Julio Entrada. Is he the forger? Six: Tell Chief McHenry about Julio Entrada. Could the artist be the killer? Seven: Tell Chief about Alicia Morrison's jewelry. Where is it? Could her death be a robbery gone wrong?

The doorbell rang.

Herk stood on the porch. In one hand was a bouquet of flowers, wrapped in green and white Publix cellophane. I let Herk in, thanked him for the blossoms, and went to grab a vase. I set out the platter of sliced cheeses, cornichons, crackers, and grapes. My kitchen is immediately to the right of the front hallway, and it opens into the living/dining area. A waist-high counter juts from the wall. I set the starters on that counter. Herk pulled up a stool and perched on it while I passed him a paper plate and napkin.

"Beer or wine?" I turned to the refrigerator. "I also have hard cider."

"Cider, please." Herk wore a dressy black tee shirt covered by a nice gray jacket. His jeans were dark blue.

I handed him a can and went about arranging the flowers in the vase.

"My grandfather Dick Potter will be here any minute," I said.

"Dick Potter? The dude who used to own the Gas E Bait?" Herk asked as he balanced himself on a bar stool. He took a swig of hard cider.

"That's the guy," I said. My timing was impeccable as Poppy's red Ford F-150 pulled up next to Herk's yellow truck. Parked beside each other, they made a colorful pair. My grandfather climbed out and walked to the house on stiff legs. I continued to fill Herk in with the details. "I call my grandfather Poppy, as do most people. You can, too. That's him in the flesh. Have you met?"

"At the VFW. Many times. He's a grand old man."

"He is at that."

Poppy came onto my porch, his cowboy boots scuffling as he lugged a large plastic grocery bag. A splash of rain pockmarked his white cotton shirt. Any minute now, it would be coming down hard. "Carwash rain" was what I call our Floridian downpours. The pale yellow corn silks poked out of the sack that Poppy was holding. I let my grandfather in and kissed his scruffy cheek. After relieving Poppy of the corn, I introduced him to Herk. The two men immediately recognized each other. They shook hands, but Poppy's attention was immediately distracted by Bailey.

"Look at this. What a cutie. Your fur babies are multiplying, Cara. Who is this little rascal?"

I introduced Bailey to Poppy. The dog sniffed his alligator skin cowboy boots with intense interest. My grandfather immediately took to the fluffy pup.

"Let me get the water boiling for the corn," I said. "The ears will only take seven minutes. I can pop them into the water while the salmon cooks. Do you want well-done or a little pink on the inside?" I turned on the stove burner, adjusted the placement of the pot of water and gave my guests my full attention.

Outside, the rain hurtled down. I took the watermelon salad out of the refrigerator. Poppy offered to toss it.

The doorbell rang. "Who could that be?" I wondered. I hadn't heard a car. My heart lurched. Against all odds, my mind went to Dan. Was it possible? No, it wasn't. I moved to the front of the house. The visitor crowded under the protective overhang of my roof. It had to be Connie the Cleaner. The poor woman was soaked to the skin when I let her in and introduced myself. Looking for a car, I asked, "Where'd you park?"

"I rode my bike. It wasn't raining when I set out." She had the squat build of a person accustomed to hard exercise.

"Let me get you a towel." Connie dripped water on my Saltillo tiles. Although she was older than I, she dressed like a teenager. Her face was lined, and her hair streaked with silver. She followed me to my linen closet. Her black high-top Converse shoes squeaked with every step. Once she had a fluffy towel in hand, she applied it vigorously, wiping down her clothes. I could see they were well worn.

I excused myself to grab the cash from my bedroom.

My guests spoke loudly. I counted the bills and listened in. Of course, Connie knew Herk. She mumbled, *"Hola."* Poppy gave her a polite hello.

In deference to my limited counterspace, Poppy stood with his back to my dining table and facing into the kitchen as he tossed the salad.

I came back with the bills in hand.

Herk addressed Connie in Spanish. Their conversation seemed jerky and disjointed. Poppy stopped mixing the salad. A stray bit of cucumber landed on my table. He picked it up and threw it back into the wooden bowl. The salad gave off the perfume of summer. Poppy squinted at Connie, "You're Mexican?"

"Guatemalan," Connie said, tucking the cash into the front pocket of her pants. I walked around her, past Herk, and toward the stove. Steam rose from my big pot. The water was starting to boil.

"But you must have spent time in Cuba," said Herk. He took a chair next to my table. His new spot gave the rest of us more room to maneuver. After checking the progress of the hot water, I poured olive oil into a cast iron skillet. This was the secret to a crispy crust on the salmon.

While I seasoned the pink steaks, I wondered why Herk made that comment about Connie being from Cuba. What was the point?

The lush fragrance of olive oil filled the air.

Connie's face hardened and her voice became brittle. "I am from Guatemala," she insisted as she stroked Bailey's head with one hand. Her other hand moved to her back pocket. Her khaki pants were wet enough to make them cling tightly. "Bailey," she said, "you are a good boy."

Herk stared at woman. His face creased with confusion. "You say you're Guatemalan, but you speak Cubano like a native? That's amazing. Cubano can be hard to master."

A thought hit me. The shocking implication slammed me against the nearby kitchen counter. "Connie? How did you know Bailey's name?"

"What?" Connie's eyes darted from me to Herk to Poppy and again to me.

"When I was holed up in my room on Monday, Herk let you in to clean. You'd never been here before, but you immediately called Bailey by name. How did you know the dog's name?" Realization made my stomach flip. Before thinking it through, I blurted, "Did you work for Alicia Morrison?"

With practiced ease, Connie whipped a knife from her back pocket. The blade flicked out like a serpent's tongue. As I gasped, she threw an arm around Poppy's neck. The knife edge pressed against his skin, creating a thin red line. He sat still there on the chair.

"Don't anybody move," she said. A ribbon of blood oozed from the cut she'd made to my grandfather. "I need keys. You are both driving a truck? Good. Put your keys on the counter where I can reach them."

Herk fished around in a jeans pocket. He held up the keyring like a prize. Poppy reached into the pocket of his pants and fought to yank out his keys.

Blood trickled down Poppy's throat even as he tried to get his keys. Thanks to decades in the sun, his skin is loose, and that proved a blessing. Connie hadn't held the flesh taut enough to cut him deeply. Even so, the smell of fear filled the kitchen and mingled with the fishy scent of raw salmon steaks. My stomach roiled. Would Herk's keys be enough for Connie? Would they provide sufficient enticement for her to leave? Or would she wait for Poppy's keys, too?

Poppy's pristine white shirt was dotted with drops of blood. Would Connie walk away from this situation? I didn't know and couldn't guess. If my hunch was right, she'd already committed one murder. Why should she stop now? As if reading my thoughts, she inched toward my foyer but she didn't turn loose of Poppy. She forced him to get up and move with her, like a human shield. I backed closer to my stovetop. Locking onto Poppy's eyes, I sent him a signal. I could only pray that he understood. He blinked twice. Good enough for me.

"You are coming along, old man." Connie moved the knife. A second line of blood appeared on Poppy's throat. "We're going for a ride. A very long ride."

He gurgled. Was it a word? I stared at him hard. He was sending me a signal. He nodded, ever so slightly.

I picked up the pot of hot water and hurled it at Connie's feet.

"Second degree burns," said Herk. We were walking away from the hospital where the ambulances had taken Connie Acosta and my grandfather. "She'll be all right, eventually. Hard to believe that Poppy was barely touched by the hot water. Those cowboy boots protected him pretty well."

I'd been counting on that. "Still, I'm glad they're going to keep him overnight. With his diabetes, an infection could be life-threatening. Who knows how dirty Connie's knife was?"

"How'd you put it all together?" Herk gave me a tiny fist-bump to the shoulder.

"Bit by bit. It took me too long, actually. See, when I walked up the driveway at Mrs. Morrison's house, the garage door was open. An old bicycle rested against a wall. It couldn't have belonged to Alicia Morrison. She would have bought something new. A little later, as I waited by the body, I heard the squeak of rubber soles on the floor. Fast forward to Honora's explanation that Connie was free to clean my house because her former employer died. The dead employer had to be Alicia Morrison. On top of that, Connie called Bailey by name! How else could she recognize him? His name isn't on his collar. Mrs. Morrison was Cuban, and so was Connie. There had to be a connection. Here's the real question: Why? Why did Connie bash Alicia Morrison over the head? Did Mrs. Morrison complain about the work Connie had done for her? Short her pay?"

While Herk and I stood next to his truck and talked, the automatic doors of the hospital rolled open. Out walked Poppy.

His neck was swathed in white bandages that reminded me of a turtleneck. "Can you give me a ride?" he yelled.

"Poppy! You're supposed to stay there! Your GP wants you to be under observation."

Poppy made a desultory wave. "Huh. Ain't nothing wrong with me. If'n you insist, I'll spend the night at your place, missy. I might need help wrapping these bandages. They'll probably fall down some while I sleep."

"He is impossible." I shook my head.

Herk grinned. "Being hard-headed seems to run in your family."

———

I was happy to have Poppy stay with me. The fact I'd burned a human being with hot water didn't sit right. Once my adrenaline left me, the blues set in, and guilt came along for the ride. I'd read about burn victims and their misery. It was the stuff of nightmares. How could I have done something like that?

Poppy looked at me over a bowl of chicken noodle soup. I keep a quart of it in my freezer at all times. This seemed like an appropriate night for heating the healthy broth. He asked, "What's on your mind? You look like somebody kicked your dog."

"Am I that transparent?" I shrugged. "I feel absolutely awful about splashing that woman with hot water."

"You regretting the fact you saved my life?"

"Don't be ridiculous. I would always choose you over someone else. You know I would. But burns are serious business. The fact I've condemned Connie to so much pain sticks in my craw."

"What other choices did you have?" He waggled hairy eyebrows at me. "Eh? She was already carving me like I was a

Thanksgiving turkey. You do know I lost a lot of blood, don't you?"

No, actually I didn't. That was slightly comforting news, in light of what I'd done to Connie. Even so, none of this made sense. I said, "I'm still having trouble with the facts. Why on earth would Connie have killed Mrs. Morrison, and why do it with a bust of Stalin? What does that have to do with being Cuban? Or does it?"

"See, here, young 'un. That-there island of Cuba has had more than its share of turmoil. I remember when Fulgencio Batista was in power. He was a good-looking man, heroic even. Now his was a profile that would have made a good statue. But Batista played favorites with certain segments of the population. With the backing of our country, he promoted his cronies. Cubans got sick of it. They didn't cotton to us being the power behind the throne, if you get my drift. Along came Castro aided by Che Guevara. Together, they overthrew Batista. Basically they slammed the door on America. They was fed up with our interference. But that left Cuba without the resources provided by the United States. Nature abhors a vacuum, and the Soviets recognized an opportunity. They offered Castro military aid, which he was happy to have. In return, he nationalized everything owned by US citizens. The Cubans went from being betrayed by us to being best friends of the Soviets. That's a long way around the barn, but it's the best I can do to explain why some Cubans—and it wasn't that many—looked up to Stalin. Especially during the Cold War. After all, Joe Stalin was the man who transformed Russia into a global power. It was Russia's desire to be a super power that encouraged them to offer aid to a little, bitty island on the other side of the globe."

Stalin. Back to Stalin. On a lark, I opened my phone, googled his name, and hit "images." Busts of the military leader in plaster, gold, and bronze flooded my screen. "Holy cow, Batman," I said. My phone showed a vast number of ways one might choose to decorate using an image of the Soviet leader. This shocked me. When I heard the name Stalin, I thought of the people he'd murdered.

"You're saying that Cubans overthrew Batista because they wanted to replace him with Castro? That doesn't make sense. Not to me."

Poppy gave me a narrow-eyed glare as he rested his spoon next to his empty bowl. "A lot of folks supported Fidel Castro back then, not knowing he would turn out worse than his predecessor. See, missy, that's how it starts. Leaders get attention by making promises. People buy in. Leaders get the power they crave. Things don't go as expected, not for the little guy. But the leader and his circle of pals are having a fine time. They don't want to give up life at the top."

"How do we know? How can we tell when things are going wrong? The Cubans thought they'd traded up when it came to leadership, right? But they hadn't. And then it was too late to do anything."

He hooted with laughter. "Ain't that the biggest question of them all? Who do you trust? It's a question you ask yourself every day of your life in all sorts of situations. You pull up to a four-way stop. Do you trust that the other cars will stop? Maybe, maybe not. You gotta stay vigilant. Keep your eyes open. Question everything. No, missy. The Cubans thought Castro would make their lives better. Definitely fairer. They hoped he would open the markets and improve trade. Stamp out corruption. Quit relying on patronage to fill key positions. In the end, Fidel was every bit as bad as Batista. Or worse."

That was an unsettling view of history.

"Do you suppose Connie hit Mrs. Morrison because of the Highwaymen paintings? Was Connie the forger? Or did Connie help set up the buys? Connie didn't run with a moneyed crowd.

Not when her primary mode of transport was a broken-down Schwinn bike."

"If Connie was a forger, that-there girl was the neatest forger I ever did see," said my grandfather as he played with a Saltine cracker.

"What do you mean?"

"Ain't you noticed that folks who do a lot of painting tend to wear their work? It's durn near impossible to be around paint without getting it in your hair or under your nails. I didn't see any spots on Connie. Did you?"

"Nope." He was right. I'd seen Eddie's forearms peppered with paint.

"Then why did Connie get angry enough to kill Alicia Morrison?" I picked up my empty bowl, set it inside Poppy's, and headed for my kitchen.

"That's a real good question," said Poppy. "Maybe we'll never know the answer. The cops ain't tasked with the why of it. Only with the who and how. Usually, it's the lawyers who take all them pieces and weave them together to make a pitiful picture."

Poppy was right. I didn't want to wait until a trial for an answer, but the justice system was incapable of moving along quickly. Furthermore, nobody owed me an explanation, although an apology from Chief McHenry would have been nice.

CHAPTER 22

I'd planned to have an inventory clearance sale on July 5. When I got to the store, I nearly laughed out loud. I found exactly two overtly patriotic-themed items on our shelves. I'd been aware we'd sold a lot, but I wasn't sure how much stuff we'd moved. The naked shelves were a nice surprise. We'd done a good job!

I wanted to tell everyone about Poppy's near brush with death. However, Chief McHenry phoned. "Could you keep everything under wraps for eight hours?" he asked.

"Why?"

"We're getting a statement from Connie Acosta. I'd like to have everything buttoned down before we go public."

I gritted my teeth. "My staff is not the same as the public."

"I know, I know, but you get my drift. Just give me a couple more hours, please?"

I hung up, wanting to strangle the man.

A robust pot of Death Wish coffee was ready for my crew when they came into work. Honora brought a loaf of banana bread to share. I hit the button to start the kettle of water for her tea. Quickly, I explained that we needed to restock shelves. "If possible, we should get this done before we're open. The salesfloor looks like a field stripped bare after an attack by locusts. Good job, everyone!"

After we fixed mugs of our favorite hot beverages, we headed for the salesfloor.

"How was your weekend?" asked Skye as she gave me a careful sideways hug so we didn't spill our drinks.

I returned the embrace, noticing she'd lost weight. Those were pounds she couldn't afford to shed. I said, "I don't think we'll have to worry anymore about being accused of Alicia Morrison's murder. More on that later."

"That's the best news I've had in weeks," Skye said, but her voice sounded strained.

"Is everything okay with Nick?" I asked.

"Yes," she said with a slight hesitation, "and Lou thinks he's figured out what he was doing wrong with the security system. He's promised me that he will get everything up and running tonight after work."

"Any more from Bucky?"

"He's sending me messages via my iPad. I forgot to change the number on that device. Bucky still claims that all he wants is the chance to see me one more time so he knows it's really over. I'm not responding. Sooner or later, Bucky has to give up. Let's talk more after we resupply the shelves," Skye said.

I carried boxes of merchandise onto the salesfloor. While rearranging the last of EveLynn's soft goods, I was interrupted by Honora. "Cara? EveLynn wants to know what you're short on so she can start sewing," said my friend as she waved her cell phone in my direction.

"To give her an accurate answer, I need to check the sales tape," I said. "Obviously, we've sold nearly everything she sent, but I can only give her an estimate."

"She'll want to know what sold best last year," Honora

warned me. "Why don't you work on the numbers while we finish with the shelves? MJ, Skye, and I can take it from here."

Back in my office, I ran the register tape. We'd exceeded my projections and made a profit during the doldrums of summer. Yet to be calculated would be the earnings from Honora's classes, as we'd charged those separately in order to keep track of her students. I opened my computer and scrolled through Excel spreadsheets, looking for the soft goods we'd sold last year.

Eddie stuck his head into my office. "Hiya, Cara. Hope you had a good Fourth of July. Wanted you to know that Katrina and I are here, finishing up. We'll be using the big ladder, so we'll string up a pink caution tape to warn people. You might want to come and look at our work. If you see anything you'd like changed, we can do that now."

"Sounds good." I sent a silent prayer of thanks because I could write him a check for his work on the mural without having to worry. "I'm in the middle of doing a bit of accounting. Be right out."

But I didn't go outside as quickly as I'd hoped. The numbers completely consumed me. That happens. I'll get fully focused and lose all track of time. Especially when I'm running figures. You could call it my super power. And I had to send EveLynn the information she needed. It took more time than I thought it would.

Honora poked her head in my door. "Cara! I forgot to tell you. My classes were wonderful, and I've been getting emails and texts about them nonstop. Wait until you read all of the positive feedback! My students want to know when I can teach another session. Can we schedule it today? I want to strike while the iron is hot."

MJ joined Honora. Before speaking, MJ raised an eyebrow,

asking Honora a silent question. Honora shook her head. "I didn't tell Cara. Not yet."

"Tell me what?"

"Honora phoned me at home on the third. She couldn't get you so she told me about that art student at the Jupiter Community Center."

I vaguely remembered Herk saying that Honora had phoned. My ears perked up. "We were hoping to call his instructor today. If he's the forger—"

"I'm way ahead of you. He is the forger." MJ's jaw tensed. "I know he's the one."

Seeing how the conversation was going, Honora turned away.

"How can you tell?" I asked MJ.

"A handwriting analyst looks at the way people form their letters. For example, do they begin from the bottom and stroke to the top? Or from the top down? Do they open their curved letters into a circle? Or are they oval and narrow? In principle, that's how I look at paintings. It's harder because I couldn't get close to the piece in Jupiter. I had to view it through a glass case in the community center's lobby. But based on what I saw, we've found the forger."

I didn't say anything. Instead, I tried to work this through in my mind. "Alicia Morrison must have asked this guy to complete a variety of paintings in various sizes."

"Focusing on iconic Highwaymen scenes," added MJ.

"Once he gave them to Mrs. Morrison, she stored her inventory under her furniture."

"What?" Honora stuck her head back into the doorway. Her mouth dropped open. "Someone stored Highwaymen paintings under furniture?"

"Nobody told you?" I asked as the older woman sank down into one of the chairs in front of my desk.

"No, I must have missed it," Honora said as she wrinkled her face in dismay.

"I tried to tell you, Honora, but you were busy signing up a student for your class," said Skye, taking a spot in my crowded doorway. "I guess I should have kept after you."

"Not to worry," said Honora. "You did your best, Skye. But I want to make sure I've understood what you all are saying. The forger is definitely the young man who is now exhibiting his work at the Jupiter Community Center? He copied Highwaymen art for Mrs. Morrison. She stored the paintings in her home, under her furniture? You still don't know how she connected with potential buyers, do you?"

"I strongly suspect she told members of the country club that she'd purchased a collection of Highwaymen pieces. Probably borrowed Essie Feldman's story. A prominent collector died and all of her art became available. Mrs. Morrison would say she snatched up the paintings at a discount, knowing they would accrue value. She might have shown people our website and explained how her offerings were similar. Maybe Mrs. Morrison offered a birddog fee to anyone who introduced her to a potential buyer," I said. I hadn't devoted a lot of time to this puzzle, and the ideas came to me all at once. Everything that Aurora had told me coalesced into a plausible scenario. Of course, Alicia Morrison would use her country club membership as a way to solicit buyers for her bootlegged landscapes. Where else could she find people with the money, the taste, and the financial acuity to buy up emerging art? Hadn't she proven, by copying her mother's jewelry, that she was savvy to the value of a good fake? Indeed, she had.

"But how did she steal sales from MJ?" asked Honora. Her eyes were like small blue marbles as she attempted to understand this complex scheme.

"I think it was pretty simple," said MJ. "Mrs. Morrison would tell a potential buyer to review our website. Maybe even tell the buyer to talk with me first. I would waste my time educating the prospect about Highwaymen art, and my explanation would establish the value of the pieces. A lot of the time, buyers ask me if they can take a photo of the art they're considering. They need to visualize how it will look in their home. I always say yes, because I want them to be happy with their purchase. In this case, the potential buyer would share the picture of our art with Mrs. Morrison. She would match it to art she owned or she would offer to track down something similar. In this case, tracking art down would mean asking the forger to copy a piece. Always, she would discount my price, making it look like we were price gouging."

Skye leaned against the door jamb, looking relaxed. Knowing that Bucky was probably behind bars had taken a weight off her.

"Alicia Morrison's plan worked perfectly until Irving crossed paths with one of her buyers at his athletic club. That particular buyer decided that MJ and Irving had connived to rip him off," I added. "By supplying a faked certificate of provenance signed by MJ, Mrs. Morrison not only authenticated the fake landscape, she also reinforced the idea we knew we were overcharging buyers."

My phone dinged to remind me it was time to open the store. Fortunately, my crew had done a marvelous job of filling the shelves with merchandise.

Immediately after I hung out the welcome sign, I had a visitor.

Chief McHenry strode in with his head on a swivel. He took in our various offerings, working his way to where I was standing near the back. Slowly, his expression changed from speculative to approving.

"Cara!" he said as if he was shocked to find me here. "The

officer on duty yesterday told me about your 911 call. How's your grandfather doing?"

I wasn't about to make nice with Chief McHenry. He was not my favorite person. I confined my comment to one word: "Fine."

The chief rested his hands on his Sam Brown belt, adopting a manly pose. "Good to hear. Miss Acosta has admitted she hit Mrs. Morrison with that statue."

Bust, I mentally corrected him. *Alicia Morrison was conked in the skull with a bust.*

But I said nothing.

"I figured you deserved to hear the whole backstory. Is there a place we could sit down?" He craned his neck, as if he could spot a lounge in the midst of my little store.

Despite strong feelings of resistance, I led him to my office. Skye and MJ would cover the sales floor. I did not offer him coffee. I wasn't about to let the chief off the hook easily.

He took one of the plastic bucket seats across from my desk. Pointedly, his eyes focused on my coffee mug. I ignored the hint.

"Well now." The chief started and crossed his legs so one ankle rested on his knee. "This whole shebang goes back to Cuba. Miss Acosta came from a wealthy family. Her mother's people owned sugar fields. Her dad was a doctor. There was only one child, a girl, named Consuela. Connie for short. Getting out of Cuba was almost impossible for professionals like Dr. Acosta. When their chance came, only Connie and her mother were allowed to leave. They could only take the clothes on their backs and small suitcases, because their story was that this was a short trip, supposedly to see a sick relative in Miami. That relative was Esmeralda, Connie's grandmother.

"Two nights before they were to leave, Dr. Acosta was arrested and thrown in jail. That was common, as Castro targeted the elite. The Acostas had known this was a possibility, and they were prepared for it. Their plan was for Mrs. Acosta to return to Havana after making sure that Connie was safe in the US. Because Mrs. Acosta couldn't take along her valuables, she dug a hole in their yard and buried all her fine jewelry, including an expensive set with a necklace, a bracelet, a ring, and I don't know what else."

Mentally, I supplied the word *parure*. The set had been a parure.

"Unbeknownst to Mrs. Acosta, someone had seen her digging in the dirt. That person was Teresa Castellanos, the live-in maid. Teresa was considered part of the Acosta family. She loved helping Mrs. Acosta dress up for parties and balls. She would come home to her own daughter and brag about the fabulous jewelry that Mrs. Acosta wore. Teresa had a soft spot for little Connie Acosta. As it happened, she lavished so much attention on Connie that her own daughter became jealous."

I interjected, "Let me guess, Teresa's daughter became Alicia Morrison?"

"That's right. Teresa's daughter was Adoncia Castellanos, but we knew her as Alicia Morrison." The chief paused. "Could I have a cup of coffee? This recitation is making me dry."

I wanted to say, "Tough luck," but I didn't.

After he had a cup of black coffee, he went on. "Dr. Acosta died in prison. Although Mrs. Acosta planned to come back to Cuba, she never did. She passed away shortly after her husband died. For years, Adoncia pestered her mother about the disposition of the Acostas' valuables. Teresa Castellanos remained silent. She knew that Connie was safely living with her grandmother somewhere in Florida. Believing that Cuba would always stay isolated, Teresa made peace with the fact that Connie would never come back. On her deathbed, she told Adoncia what she'd seen on the night that Mrs. Acosta buried her treasures in the dirt."

"Adoncia was determined to have a better life," said the

chief. "She lied about her age, telling the aid workers she was five years younger than she was. That got her a seat on a Freedom Flight, one of the handful of trips that airlines made from Cuba to the US. The Freedom Flights were paid for by an aid group in the US. This same philanthropic organization worked to build new lives for Cuban citizens who were part of the diaspora. Do you know what a diaspora is?"

I stifled the urge to roll my eyes. What was this, a pop quiz? Chief McHenry had a lot of nerve. He must have caught the change in my expression because he mumbled, "Sorry about that. Look. I messed up, Cara. I should have trusted you. Can we move on?"

I reminded myself that for a man like the chief to apologize was a very big deal, indeed. "I'll try to put it behind me" was the best I could do.

"Adoncia enrolled in Miami Dade College where she met the grieving widower, Prescott Morrison. When they married, she changed her name to Alicia. She must have thought she had it made, hooking a rich older man, but she'd grown up hearing stories about Mrs. Acosta's jewelry, and she coveted a set of her own. In fact, she thought it was her due. When she learned that every piece of Mary Morrison's collection would be sold for charity, she went nuts."

"I know what happened next. Adoncia/Alicia Castellanos Morrison went back to Cuba, dug up the Acosta family gems and pretended they were good fakes in order to bring them into this country." I sat back and tried not to smirk.

The chief looked astonished. He hadn't counted on me knowing the backstory. He lifted his coffee mug, which I suspected was empty, and pretended to take a drink.

He cleared his throat and said, "Alicia Morrison didn't count on the fact that Connie Acosta knew her mother had hidden her diamonds before leaving Cuba. Mrs. Morrison also wasn't aware that Esmeralda had moved to Hobe Sound with her grand-daughter, Connie Acosta. You know that monthly glossy publication? It comes free in the mail? The one all the society people are featured in? Well, guess who popped up on the cover wearing the Acosta family diamonds?"

"Alicia Castellanos Morrison," I said.

"You betcha, and Esmeralda recognized her. She also recognized the fancy necklace and other stuff. That must have been one heck of a shock. Shortly thereafter, Esmeralda died. Losing her grandmother was the final straw for Connie Acosta. She felt like she'd lost everything."

I knew that feeling, but I didn't comment.

"Connie actually blames Alicia Morrison for Esmeralda's death. Says that picture broke her grandmother's heart. And then Connie decided she wanted revenge. She took jobs cleaning houses here on the Island. Eventually, she was hired by Alicia Morrison, who couldn't keep good help because she was such a pill. But Connie was a smart one. She planned to bide her time until Mrs. Morrison removed her gems out from the wall safe."

"Did you find the jewelry?"

"It's still locked away." He hooted a laugh. "You're never going to believe this. On that particular morning, Connie was there at the house cleaning, even though it was a Sunday. Mrs. Morrison had been out by the pool, drinking champagne with her pool guy. After the pool boy left, Mrs. Morrison tuned the TV to a Spanish language station. The reporter was discussing improved relations between the US and Cuba. Mrs. Morrison made some sort of smart-aleck crack about how anyone who moved back to Havana was stupid. She'd been there, seen the place, and it was a dump. Connie had grown up on her grandmother's stories, full of love for her country. And Connie was still grieving Esmeralda's death. Mrs. Morrison's remarks hit a raw nerve, and Connie snapped. She picked up that statue and hit her in the head. You know the rest."

"And what about the paintings?" I asked, leaning back in my big office chair. I wasn't done with the chief. Not yet. "You accused me of having them forged."

"Not really accused. That's awfully harsh, Cara. I wondered what you knew." He wore a pained expression, as if I'd done him wrong.

"Am I in the clear?" I didn't back down.

"Connie told us about another Cuban refugee, an artist, who was working for Mrs. Morrison to copy paintings. We still have to locate him. He lives in Jupiter. We'll find the man."

Great, I thought.

"Do I have your permission to share this information with Irving Feldman?" I asked.

"I already did. He should give you a call any minute now," said the chief, looking rather pleased with himself.

"How about sharing this with my crew?"

"I don't see why not." He unfolded himself and got to his feet. "I'm not sure if we can recoup the money Mrs. Morrison owed you. I've mentioned it to her attorney. I told him about you and Rocky. He'll contact you."

I had already concluded that I would have to write the debt off as a loss. I had one more question for the chief. "What about Bailey? Mrs. Morrison's dog?"

After the chief left my office, I went ahead and wrote the check for Eddie and Katrina. As I walked through the store, I gestured to my crew. "Time to view the mural!" MJ, Skye, and Honora hurried after me.

MJ separated herself from the others and took me by the

elbow to momentarily stop my progress. She whispered in my ear, "Pete knows he owes you an apology. I suggested he give you a gift certificate for vet services."

"That's better than an apology," I said. "Thank you."

The mural was glorious, and not quite done. The colors brought the dull brick wall to life. Those who avoid harsh Floridian summers never see the poinciana trees in full bloom. These are breath-taking, and the painters had captured every bit of their glory. I marveled at the talents of Eddie and Katrina. My crew was equally enthusiastic. The idea of this landscape had been inspired, and I was certain it would attract new visitors to my store. As we stared at the mural, cars drew to a stop and forgot to move forward when the light changed. The vehicles behind them tapped their horns.

"We'll have to get used to honking," I said, as I handed Katrina a check for the balance of the job. She stepped neatly around the drop cloth, protecting the sidewalk.

Honora added, "There'll be a lot of that!"

I noticed a patch of brick wall showing, just to the right of distant palm trees. I pointed it out.

"I'm working on that, Cara," said Eddie, moving the gallon can of blue paint closer to the ladder. "It'll be done in a jiffy."

CHAPTER 23

After taping a "Closed for Staff Meeting" sign to my front door, I assembled my crew in my office to give them the good news about Alicia Morrison's murderer. They were unaware that Connie had attacked my grandfather, and this seemed like a natural time to share. As I relayed the story, their eyes went from shocked to horrified. Honora, in particular, was stunned. She rocked forward in a plastic chair and covered her face with her hands. "Oh, Cara! And I suggested that she clean for you!"

"Guess what? She did a great job with my house. Honest, she did. Now I need another housekeeper. Preferably one who won't try to kill my few remaining family members. I still feel bad about tossing scalding water on her feet. Good thing she was wearing a pair of Converse high tops."

MJ had taken the other chair, leaving Skye to lean against the doorframe. MJ said, "Worrying about whether you hurt a murderer? That's incredibly childish."

"No, she's not," said Skye with a huff. "Cara's empathetic and kind."

"Matter of opinion," said MJ.

"Anyway," I broke in while making a "time out" signal with my hands, "the situation with Alicia Morrison is a problem we can cross off our list. Also, Bailey is mine. The chief offered to take him to the animal shelter but I put a stop to that."

Skye's phone buzzed. Excusing herself, she slipped out of my office.

"Thank goodness!" Honora clutched at her heart. "That Havanese seems like a very sweet puppy, Cara. I know you miss your little Chihuahua."

"I wonder what Irving will say about all of this." MJ frowned. "He certainly owes you an apology."

"He owes you one, too," I said. "The chief told me that he had spoken to Irving, and Irving had promised to call me. Any minute, according to the chief."

MJ got to her feet and offered Honora a hand up. When both ladies were standing, MJ shot me a look of disgust. "Irving Feldman calling to say he's sorry? Don't hold your breath, Cara. You might end up passed out on the floor."

I agreed. "I think I'll call Herk. He has Irving's phone number. If anyone can encourage Irving to make that call, it'll be Herk."

Honora left the office. MJ turned to go but I stopped her. "Wait a sec, MJ. What do you think will happen to the fake Highwaymen paintings?"

She shrugged. "Chief McHenry probably locked up the ones he found at the Morrison residence. They could be used as evidence. Do you really care? As long as they aren't floating around, muddying up our waters, does it matter?"

I rocked back in my desk chair. "I don't know. Let me think about it."

"You might also ponder how to get Chief McHenry to issue a press release clearing us, once he has his loose ends tied up. Better yet, I'll write one and ask him for permission to send it out. How does that sound?" MJ brightened with the prospect of announcing she was back in the business of selling expensive art.

"Great," I said. Life was looking up.

There was a thump, followed by a weak cry.

MJ and I frowned at each other. She asked, "Did you hear that? Sounded like it came from the outside of the building. Don't tell me that Eddie or Katrina fell off that tall ladder!"

MJ raced toward the front door. I hurried out the back. What I saw took my breath away.

Bucky wrapped his belt around his right hand. His left hand gripped a metal rung directly above his head. At the end of the leather strap dangled Skye. Her toes brushed the sidewalk. Her legs scissored in the air, trying to find solid ground. Her fingers scrabbled at her throat, fighting to loosen the belt.

MJ screamed, "Let her go!"

Bucky pulled up on the belt, hauling Skye several feet off the ground.

"Shut up or I'll drop her. She'll get hurt, bad," said Bucky. It wasn't a long drop but her body would definitely bump its way down the slanted metal steps. That would make for a painful and awkward journey. But whatever bumps and bruises she collected would be so much better than choking to death. With the belt wrapped around Bucky's hand was it possible he could snap her neck? I didn't think so. I had to hope he couldn't.

I approached the ladder from the back of the building. Everyone else was on the other side, having come out the front door. The rest of my crew huddled together. Honora gripped MJ's arm, while MJ stared at Bucky defiantly. Eddie stood slack-jawed and stunned while pressing Katrina close to his chest. She couldn't stand watching this tragedy unfold. I didn't want to see it either.

I had to do something. Even though I'd only been with Dan for a short time, he'd often talked to me in general terms about his work in Special Ops. "Panic kills," he'd said. "They drum that into us over and over. When you panic, you don't think through your options. Only when you approach a problem with a clear head can you be successful."

What would Dan do about this? First, he would assess the situation.

Katrina and Eddie must have been taking turns at the top of the ladder, painting the blue Floridian sky when all of this went wrong. That would explain the dropped paintbrush and its splattered halo of baby blue. On my side of the ladder was that gallon bucket of paint. A faint fragrance of ammonia wafted up from it. The can looked nearly full. Its lid was resting, wet side up, on the drop cloth. I stared down into the thick blue liquid. How peaceful it seemed despite what was happening.

"Put her down, Bucky!" MJ screamed. A group of tourists who'd been waiting for the crosswalk sign to change stood on the far side of the street, watching the drama unfold.

Honora's eyes were wide as Frisbees. She was white with fear. Only Bucky felt in control.

Good, I thought. I can use that to my advantage. Bucky's back was facing me. He had no idea I was behind him. He had climbed enough rungs that he was higher than my head. I couldn't reach up and tug him down. He seemed glued to that spot, six feet up, as he kept yelling, "I only wanted to talk! But she wouldn't even do that! This is all her fault!"

"You're such a creep!" screamed MJ. "Why would anyone talk to you?"

"Let her go!" yelled Honora in a quivering voice. Across the street, a customer leaving Pumpernickel's saw what was happening. He turned and ducked back into the deli. I prayed he was going for help, but could I depend on it? Was Bucky going to murder Skye before our very eyes? Her face was crimson, her eyes bulging, and her fingers merely stabbed at the belt.

Skye is lightweight, but she's still a full-grown woman. Holding her up had to tax Bucky's strength. He was tiring, and he struggled to keep his balance. He wobbled a bit, letting the belt slacken, and in response, Skye kicked out, flailing and failing, trying to find enough oxygen to breathe. The sudden movement gave her foot a chance to search for, and find, a rung. She was able to push herself up a few inches. That change of direction knocked him further off balance. He tightened his grip on the step above him. This proved a disadvantage because he was stretched out. He had less control over Skye. His left arm must have been spasming with the effort to keep her prisoner.

Now was the time to act. I grabbed the can of bright blue paint. Relying on the assistance of centrifugal force, I swung my arm in a wide circle until I'd made a complete arc.

I aimed the can toward Bucky's head and let her rip.

EPILOGUE

I closed the store for a long, long weekend. I didn't care about sales. All of us needed a break. Skye was still in the hospital, recovering from a bruised larynx and multiple other bumps and scrapes. We took turns visiting her. I pointed out that she truly lived up to her name, Skye Blue, because she was covered in the sky-blue latex paint when they loaded her into the ambulance.

My aim had been off. I'd hoped to hit Bucky in the head. I've never been a good pitcher. Instead, the can slammed into his back. The shock was enough for him to turn loose of his belt. I rushed to break Skye's fall, and no one cared that Bucky hit the sidewalk hard. He broke his left arm and tore his meniscus. As we soothed Skye and tried to comfort her, Bucky writhed with pain.

"Tough luck," I said to the moaning figure.

The next day, Irving called me on my cell phone to "apologize" for any "misunderstandings." I bit back the urge to scream at him. Did he have any idea how much pain and suffering we'd been through?

"Cara?" he prodded me. "I said I'd like to bring the paintings back to your store."

Did he expect me to gush with gratitude? Nope. *Not today, buster.*

I said, "We'd love to have them, but there will be a restocking fee because of the hassle. Also, we need to adjust MJ's commission rate higher, and you need to give me a budget for advertising. We've lost a lot of consumer confidence thanks to your decision."

That weasel tried to balk. "But I had good reason—"

"No. You signed a contract. You violated that contract. You impugned our reputation. That's not easy to repair."

"All right, all right," he groused.

Early the next day, I took both dogs for a walk. This was a strange experience. Gerard sniffed high, and Bailey sniffed low. When Gerard lifted a leg to pee on a bush, Bailey scooted under the big dog and got a golden shower for his efforts. I couldn't help but laugh.

I had Bailey in the outdoor dog wash when a white sedan pulled up, followed by a yellow truck.

The man who climbed out of the white car was wearing a military uniform. He introduced himself as having served with Dan. The visitor said, "He asked me to deliver a letter to you, if anything happened."

I took it. I couldn't open it. My hands shook too hard. Bailey was still covered with dog shampoo. After the military guy left, Herk climbed out of his truck. "I'll finish up with Bailey," he said after a quick survey of the situation. I was happy to let my friend take care of my dog.

Sinking down onto the first step of my deck, I tore open the envelope and read:

Dearest Cara—

I'm sorry that we fought before I left. I should have known better. You had my best interests at heart. I'm writing this from the hospital, praying that I get better. But in case I don't, I need you to know you're the best thing that ever happened to me. The biggest mistake I've ever made was not marrying you right away, Covid or no Covid. Even if it had just been the two of us and a small wedding. Because you're the woman of my heart, and no matter what, you'll always be a part of me.

Love, Dan

~The End~

ACKNOWLEDGEMENTS

I'd like to thank all of the wonderful beta readers for their thoughtful input in making this book better. They are in no particular order, Wendy Green, Rebecca Flowr, Frank Wright, Debra Holland, and Amy Gill.

Your time and input is appreciated.

~ Joanna

MISSED OTHER BOOKS IN THE SERIES?

Follow the **Cara Mia Delgatto Mystery Series,** a traditional cozy mystery series with witty heroines, and former flames reconnecting, set in Florida's beautiful Treasure Coast – https://amzn.to/30z9urN

Looking for other great reads? Joanna has a series just for you!

Kiki Lowenstein Mystery Series, the lovable female amateur sleuth, with an emphasis on paper and needle crafts, in a Midwest (St. Louis, Missouri) setting...you'll love. The first book, Paper, Scissors, Death, was a finalist for the Agatha Award. – https://bit.ly/3P2QWdC

The Jane Eyre Chronicles, Charlotte Bronte's Classic Strong- Willed Heroine Lives On. – https://amzn.to/3r3Ybmd

The Confidential Files of John H. Watson, a new series featuring Sherlock Holmes and John Watson.
– https://amzn.to/3bDnSWo

The Friday Night Mystery Club, Book #1 set in Decatur, Illinois in 1986. A nasty divorce leaves Cragan Collins with a mountain of bills and her grandmother to support.
– https://bit.ly/3D9EaDk

A REVIEW IS LIKE APPLAUSE TO AN AUTHOR!

Did you know there are more than 12 million books on Amazon? They are adding books at an astonishing 7,500 a day.

Your review will help other readers find Joanna's work. Even a quick rating or brief remark will make a huge difference.

Thank you in advance!

Sincerely, Joanna

You may leave a review here: (https://bit.ly/4a1Qdlq)

FIND A MISTAKE?

Don't tell Amazon...tell us! And if it's a bona fide mistake, we'll send you an Amazon Gift Card. We're passionate about providing a great reading experience. But even three proofreaders can miss things, so let us know! Email Stacey at <u>Stacey@ JoannaSlan.com</u> and tell her what you've found.

ABOUT THE AUTHOR...

JOANNA CAMPBELL SLAN

Joanna is a *New York Times* and a *USA Today* bestselling author who has written more than 70 books, including both fiction and non-fiction works. She was one of the early Chicken Soup for the Soul authors, and her stories appear in five of those *New York Times* bestselling books.

Her first non-fiction book, ***Using Stories and Humor: Grab Your Audience*** (Simon & Schuster/Pearson), was endorsed by Toastmasters International, and lauded by Benjamin Netanyahu's speechwriter. She's the author of five mystery series. Her first novel—***Paper, Scissors, Death: Book #1 in the Kiki Lowenstein Mystery Series***—was shortlisted for the Agatha Award. Her first historical mystery—***Death of a Schoolgirl: Book #1 in the Jane Eyre Chronicles***—won the Daphne du Maurier Award of Excellence. Her contemporary series set in Florida continues this year with ***Paint Can Kill: Book #9 in the Cara Mia Delgatto Mystery Series.*** Her fantasy thriller series starts with ***Sherlock Holmes and the Giant Sumatran Rat.*** Her newest series set in 1980s, ***The Friday Night Mystery Club,*** features five housemates, single women, struggling to make their way in a man's world.

When she isn't banging away at the keyboard, Joanna keeps busy walking her Havanese puppy Jax and the family cat, Miss Maple. An award-winning miniaturist, Joanna builds dollhouses, dolls, and furniture from scratch. She's also an accredited teacher of Zentangle®. Her husband, David, owns Steinway Piano Gallery-DC and seven other Steinway piano showrooms.

Contact Joanna at JCSlan@JoannaSlan.com.
Follow her on social media by going here
https://www.linktr.ee/JCSlan

Made in United States
Orlando, FL
02 March 2025